BASTARD BROTHERS OF CARNAGE

OUTCAST

BLAKE BLESSING

Blake Blessing

Outcast

Cover: Vicious Desires Design

Editing: Heather Long

Editing: Villain Era Book Services

❀ Created with Vellum

This is dedicated to all my Matías girlies and Kickstarter baddies. Without your love and support, Matías would never have gotten his happy ending. <3

FOREWORD

Welcome to the Blake Blessing house of madness!

Outcast is listed as the 6th book in the Bastard Brothers of Carnage series, and in many ways, writing this book felt like closing a chapter on a world that's lived in my head for years. It is the last and final book, though I hate to say anything is final...

I encourage you to start with Addict as you will have a good amount of series spoilers in this book.

HOWEVER- This is also a standalone for a specific and I daresay, beloved, side character from the BBoC series. You CAN enjoy this book on its own.

You will get some see some of our favorite characters from the BBoC series, and you'll be introduced to some new faces. You never know when they'll pop up somewhere else! ;)

While this is set in the same world as BBoC, this book is decidedly less dark. You will still have dark themes, and a side of strange and unusual torture.

Because we had to give Matias his HEA, right?!

I'll leave you here and see you on the other side!
Enjoy!

PROLOGUE
MATÍAS

4 years ago

My heart pounded in anticipation.

From both the soft curvy body pressed between me and the wall, and the near discovery of Tomas stumbling across us. The man was an idiot, but he was dangerous because he'd sing like a canary to my father to get more power.

My father, Vicente. Head of the Institution, otherwise, known as the Castillo cartel.

"What the hell are you doing here?" I growled against Rita's ear. Tonight was another festival, one of many that Father held in his city.

Rita shouldn't be here. The Dirty Dogs weren't enemies, but they weren't exactly welcome when Vicente wasn't given explicit details about why they were here and when they'd leave.

Or what was in it for him.

She laughed, the sound full and throaty as her nails dug into my chest before she slid her hands up around the back of my neck. Never mind that some ass might wander down the alley and see us. We were barely out of the light and every fucking person here would recognize me.

I was the spitting image of Vicente, unfortunately.

"Don't be such a fucking coward." Her dark brown eyes twinkled as she leaned up on her tiptoes, pressing her succulent lips against mine. Anger in my gut whipped alongside desire.

She was delicious.

Ever since I'd met her, she'd had a fire about her that was wild and thrilling. The woman was every man's temptation with curly, black hair and miles of curves. To top it off, she wrapped up her sex appeal in bright red gloss that was just as addictive as she was.

I licked my lips, tasting that sweet, cherry flavor as I grabbed her hips and pressed her deeper into the wall.

"That was Tomas who just passed us. You know who that is?"

In the dark light of night, I could just make out her eyes rolling. "No, nor do I give a damn."

"You should. He's a weasel who'd do anything to climb the ladder. And finding the gang princess under the heir to the Institution would be like candy to a pedophile. He doesn't want it, but he'd use it to get exactly what *he* wants." My words were low and forceful. I wanted her to understand exactly how dangerous this was.

Except, she huffed. Like I was an idiot.

"You worry too much."

"You don't worry enough!" I fired back.

Pausing, she studied me in the shadows. Her thumbs made soft sweeps against the column of my neck as her lips drooped and I shivered in the cool, night air.

"Then let's get out of here, Matías. Let's go strip on the

beach or tear it up in one of my clubs. That way you can breathe and lose that giant stick up your ass."

I chuckled, shaking my head as I pulled her away from the rough concrete wall. Graffiti art shimmered in the few places the light touched as we headed deeper into the alley and away from the main celebration.

There was no winning with her. She was a spoiled brat at the best of times, but damn did I love her.

Sliding my fingers down her arm, I caught her hand in mine. She started swinging our joined hands like we were a bunch of stupid teenagers.

We were. We were being stupid. Her for coming here in the first place, and me for entertaining her when anyone could see us.

But no matter how dangerous this was, I couldn't turn her away. I wouldn't.

"Beach or club?"

"What?" I glanced at her before scanning the alley ahead and behind us.

"Where are we going from here? Because you're not dropping me off or sending me on my merry fucking way." She snorted and started swerving her hips in a dancing motion. "The night's young and I'm tougher than you are. I'd win in a fight."

I didn't even answer that as I quirked a brow toward her.

"Let's go to the club." That was the safest option. Javier's men were ruthless when it came to protecting their territory. And they'd go apeshit to protect their princess.

I could also actually relax and enjoy myself there. Any other men from the Institution would be shot on sight.

She tossed an unimpressed look over her shoulder. "You're starting to make me feel like a dirty secret."

Shaking my head, I tugged her back against my side.

"You're not a dirty secret. You're a precious one. Of our two fathers, yours is sane and mine is not. I like your pretty head right where it is. I'd rather not see it on a stake because he's throwing a tantrum."

A shiver worked its way up my spine as she stopped walking.

Glancing up, she narrowed her eyes. "You think Vicente would do that? Murder the daughter of a dangerous organization that wouldn't hesitate to rain fire on his ass?"

I rolled my lips. "I think my father is insane and his ego is the most important thing to him. He's unpredictable and that's why we have to be careful."

Rita sighed, absolutely put out, but in the next breath, she was already moving on from the serious moment. "Fine. My car is two blocks over."

I twirled her around before bringing her back into me, lightening the mood. The last thing I wanted to do was let my father be a dark cloud over the few stolen hours with Rita.

Call me a fool, but it was these moments that made all the others bearable.

Being the only legitimate son of a psychopath was a lonely place to be. I'd learned that time and time again, any time I'd attempted to make any sort of connection with anyone.

Even my own brothers.

~

I PARKED Rita's car on the sidewalk in front of the club entrance. A few bystanders jumped out of the way and flipped us off.

"You crazy-ass motherfucker," one man called as I stepped out of the car. He didn't recognize me.

Why would he? I was in Dirty Dog territory, and for the most part, gangs were beneath Vicente unless he could use them for his gain or entertainment. Javier, Rita, and maybe a few of his trusted men, were the only ones ever invited to Institution events.

Ignoring them, I walked around the car to open Rita's door. But the men had already shut up. Rita had her hand in mine, stepping one stiletto out at a time. When I glanced over my shoulder, a handful of lower-level Dirty Dogs had surrounded the men.

They got the idea and stumbled down the street.

"You're always causing issues," Esteban grinned, dimples popping out. Crossing his arms, his eyes were glued to Rita as we joined the small group at the door entrance.

"They caused their own issues by not recognizing my car. It's not like it's a sedan." She wrinkled her nose as she glanced back. Her black and red homemade Lamborghini Veneno sparkled under the streetlights.

It was a beautiful car that the Dirty Dogs had sourced, chopped, and rebuilt just for her. And it was so recognizable, no one dared to touch it.

Her car might not have been the only one like it on the continent, but it was damn sure the only one with metallic stilettos hanging from the mirror with a stuffed animal, snarling, dog head.

She pulled me inside and the crowd shifted out of her way like water.

Unlike Vicente's clubs with popular American club tracks, this one, like most of the Dirty Dogs' places, played the local music. The rolling beats and drums made specifically for latin dances. And the Dirty Dog establishments catered to them all.

You wanted to dance bachata? No problem. Salsa or samba? They played music for it. The Dirty Dogs' clubs were about having a good time and they looked good doing it.

Rita raised one hand in the air, swaying to the music as she led us toward the stage. That's where she loved to be. In the spotlight.

Where I should want to be too. But we were so different, separated by miles of life experiences, it was a wonder she even wanted me.

A drunk kid, probably around twenty, tried to slide up against her, reaching for her ass, but she caught his throat, digging her sharp, blood-red nails into his skin right before she tossed him away. All without missing a beat.

It was ruthless. She was a different creature than anything I'd ever grown up with and I wanted to fuck her so hard anytime she exercised a tiny bit of personality.

Because Rita did not give one fuck.

A staff girl carried a tray of shots over her head, and Rita pulled her hand away to grab two. Turning, she handed me one as she rolled her glass against her smirking lips. I tossed it back, keeping my gaze locked with hers.

She followed, and immediately, the liquor set off a round of tingles through my body. They burned like ice cold needles in the best way.

Grabbing my shirt, she yanked me against her. "Are you better now?" Rita asked against my neck as she started rotating her hips against mine.

I was a shit dancer, but I gripped her hips and did my fucking best to match her rhythm. This made her happy. For one goddamned second, I was enough to make someone else happy.

Just me. And my actions. Nothing else.

That was the second most intoxicating thing about being with Rita. The first was how alive she made me feel. The third was how she seemed to want me above everyone else.

Wasn't that the trifecta of doom?

Someone comes along and makes you feel important, wanted, and alive.

Then boom, you were catapulted to your death because you got lazy.

If it wasn't for my years-long relationship with Javier, the leader of the Dirty Dogs, I'd be sure my father sent her to test me. But she was no more in his pocket than my half-brother, Andre, was.

She trailed kisses along my neck, and giggled as she did. There would be a red-smeared line for everyone to see and that was exactly what Rita wanted.

The Dirty Dog princess was possessive. She got off on any mark she was able to leave on me. I wouldn't put it past her to try and maim me permanently one day.

I couldn't even care.

"I love the way you smell," she whispered in my ear as we danced.

"Like sweat and bad decisions?" I called over the music.

She laughed like I'd made a joke. I was dead serious.

"No. Like mine."

That...did something to me.

Lowering my head, I barely brushed my lips against hers when my phone buzzed in my pocket.

Freezing, I held my breath. What were the chances that was my father on his festival night?

High.

That was how my life went. As much as I wanted Rita in the center, it revolved around my father and his whims.

I pulled back and slipped my phone from my pocket.

Valentina: Daddy is having a bit too much fun. If you want to save a few lives, you should probably join him.

Closing my eyes, I forced myself to exhale.

"What's wrong?" Rita gave me a shake.

"I have to get back to the mansion," I shouted over the music.

"Why?" she snapped.

I shook my head. It didn't matter. She wouldn't understand. "Can you take me back?"

"This is bullshit." She pushed me away from her. "When are you going to stop treating me like some gutter whore you're too ashamed to take home to Daddy?" She spewed her words like venom.

"It's not like that, and you know it." I tried to pull her against me, but she stepped out of my reach.

"You need to grow a pair, Matías. All you're doing is letting your father walk all over you. You're going to run the Institution one day. Act like it."

I laughed at her retreating back as she headed toward the front of the club. She'd take me back, because she wouldn't make me call one of my men here to get me. But she had no idea what she was talking about.

Tomorrow, she'd text me like tonight never ended the way it did.

The drive back was silent. She stewed in her hurt feelings, and there wasn't a thing I could think of to say to erase all the obstacles between us.

Pulling up to the edge of town, she idled the car.

"Are you going to tell him about us?" She laid her hands

on her thighs and glared out the windshield. This girl and her skewed perception of our world.

Javier was a good father, he loved her. Truly loved her, and he taught her about his businesses, but sometimes, he gave her a false sense of the world.

It broke me to shatter it.

I sighed. "I can't."

"I don't fucking understand you!" she yelled. Her head whipped my way, and the red light from her dash reflected in her eyes and highlighted the angles of her face. Rita was gorgeous, hard stop, but when fire reflected in her eyes, she was a force to be reckoned with...and worshiped.

Her mouth set into an angry line and she glowered with so much resentment, I almost shrunk back in my seat.

But I was taught better than that. So I didn't show any reaction at all.

That made her furious.

"I'm Javier's daughter. I'm as much gang royalty as you are. Why the hell do you think he'd care if we're fucking?"

The Institution wasn't a gang, but I kept that to myself.

Her words stung. We were doing more than fucking. But I wouldn't admit that.

She wouldn't either. Not when I didn't make it safe for her to do so.

"Just get the fuck out of my car. You fucking asshole. Just leave." She pointed at my door, and as much as I hated to leave her this way, I got out.

I couldn't chance her idling here and someone seeing her. The disappointment leaking from her cut at my back. I'd never fucking felt so tired or defeated. What the hell was I doing with her anyway?

This was too dangerous for her, and if she got hurt, it would rip me to shreds.

~

THE WALK to Father's mansion was quick, and I had a light sweat coating my skin as I passed through the front doors.

Whatever shit he was up to, he was doing it quietly. The sounds of the festival completely mute inside the sound-proofed walls.

Moving through the rooms, I cleared each one and my heart beat harder and harder.

Where the fuck was he? There were no dead bodies, no rape. Nothing to show he was going off the rails.

Then I made it to the Gallery.

He sat in his chair on the platform at the far end of the room, leaning back like a king as he sipped amber liquor from a crystal glass.

His favorite concubine, Pilar, and a new favorite, danced naked in front of him. They didn't speak and there was no music. They just writhed together in a sensual dance that was meant to entice.

Vicente Castillo liked the finer things in life, and as much debauchery as he craved, sometimes he only wanted to see the beauty. The art.

Or the subjugation.

His gaze flicked my way but his expression never changed.

"Pilar, that's enough for the night."

She immediately pulled away from the younger girl and walked toward him, dropping a soft kiss on the apple of his cheek. Then both women excused themselves.

I was more grateful in that moment than I ever had been that he wasn't like some of his men who preferred young girls. As jittery as I felt, I'd have thrown up in the corner.

"Where have you been tonight?" His words were even. Bland.

It set every alarm off in my head.

"Enjoying the festival." I clasped my hands behind my back so he didn't see them shaking.

"The Institution is a grand legacy, don't you think?" He held the crystal glass up so that the light refracted off the liquid inside.

My mouth went dry but I ignored it. My hands had always been the tell. Father had made sure the rest was beaten out of me. Metaphorically. He reserved the actual whippings for his other son. A less important, illegitimate one.

Yet everyone knew exactly who his offspring were.

"Absolutely."

One corner of his mouth twitched. "I've spent my life building it exactly the way I wanted it to be. A difficult and bloody road. One I enjoyed very much." He grinned.

I dipped my head. It was as much of an acknowledgement as he wanted.

"And I will thank you not to sully it with weak, low-class blood."

He *knew*. Somehow, he knew about what I'd been doing. About Rita.

"I don't know what you're talking about."

"Of course, you do. Don't take me for an idiot. I've been receiving reports for quite some time that you've been fucking Javier's daughter." He shrugged. "I've let you have your fun, now it's time to toss her away...Or I will dispose of her *my* way."

Black edged the outside of my vision as I tried my best not to swallow. I didn't want to give him any indication she mattered. Just in case this was a bluff.

"Fucking is my right." I didn't deny Rita in that sense. That would be too obvious. But I could downplay what she meant to me. "That's what you've always taught me."

His grin turned into a smile, but his eyes grew colder. "As long as you're not trying to tear down what I've worked so hard to build. When you marry, it will be to someone I approve of. Who doesn't have a family that has the means to take some of my power from me. There will be no alliances, no truces. No marriages for the better good of society." His top lip peeled back in disgust.

"Who said anything about marriage?" I jerked my head back in surprise. Rita and I had never even hinted at the subject. I wouldn't dare because of what it could mean for her.

But why had *he* jumped to that conclusion?

"Glad we're on the same page, son. If there are no feelings, then it's best to move on. You've enjoyed her sweet pussy, so you fuck your way to the next piece. I do have an entire Gallery you've never used." He waved his hand at the empty glass panels on the wall where women usually danced for his guests.

What the hell did I say to that? I wasn't like the men he associated with. I didn't rape women because I was stronger, more powerful. Just the thought had bile rising in my throat.

"Unless you really do care for her?" He raised his brows.

"No," I answered too fast and satisfaction slithered through his eyes.

"I don't mind a gang war. It's been too quiet around here lately," he said as he leaned forward.

Reaching for the mask I'd worn all my life, I smiled. "I don't mind a little excitement. All you have to do is say the word."

He laughed and slapped his knee. "I knew there was a

reason you're my heir. Outside of the obvious ones. Go back and enjoy the festivities. Valentina was pouting when I kicked her out earlier. You could find her and make her feel better."

Not fucking likely.

I bowed my head and walked toward the entrance. When I was almost to the door he called my name.

"Matías..."

I turned to face him.

"If you're lying to me, the girl will die. I'll send her to Randall first, just to make sure you learn your lesson." Then he grinned wide. "Not that you care about such things."

One side of my mouth lifted even as my stomach rolled. "I'm my father's son."

"That you are, my boy. That you are."

I walked out of there with one thought.

I would not be the reason Rita was sent to the chambers. She would not die because of me.

1

MATÍAS

Present Day

The seagulls cawed overhead, circling the edge of the cliff.

Fuck, there was a bird there caught in a fishing line about halfway down the wall.

"Oh my God. Someone has to get that bird," one of the tourists on my tour whispered to her tandem buddy.

My kayak rocked as I shielded my eyes and glanced up. The seagull flapped its free wing tirelessly before giving up and falling back against the rock face, only to start trying to escape all over again.

It was trapped in a way that it would only get free if someone saved it.

That person couldn't be me. Not right then. I was in the middle of a kayak tour.

The seagull hung a good thirty feet above us, calling out in distress. The easiest way to free it would be to cut the string from the top.

"Don't worry," I smiled at the tourist. "When our tour is over, I'll go cut the string if someone doesn't get to it first."

"You will?" An older woman with ridiculously oversized sunglasses and a sun hat frowned at me. She didn't believe a word that came out of my mouth. I didn't blame her. Why would you trust a kayak guide in a tourist destination? She didn't know me from shit.

"I will." I nodded. Other kayaks from my group were making their way to my meeting spot out of the way of the boats that traveled by.

There were two ways to reach the inside of the Benagil caves. By kayak or by boat. Paddle boards were also an option but I classified those in the same category as kayaks. You still had to paddle yourself there.

The tourists started whispering and pointing to the bird. A boat passed by and when they saw my group pointing, they glanced up and started pointing and shouting too.

Rio, the driver of the boat, glanced at me and shook his head.

Yeah, we were on the same page. We needed to get these people out of here or the tours would be ruined.

Sticking two fingers in my mouth, I gave a sharp whistle. "Let's go! The path is clear!" I pointed to the cave.

The southern coast of sunny Portugal was made of beautiful beaches, high cliffs, and a network of caves you could paddle into or through.

This place was gloriously disconnected from the rest of the world.

They had WIFI, but the Portuguese people were different. Their values were different. And the tourists were mostly elderly people and young families from Europe. Sometimes the States.

And I needed this.

This anonymity after fucking off from the life I'd had before.

Blowing out a breath, I paddled through the cave, leading the way. Blue light reflected off the water and around the limestone from a hole at the top.

This place was stunning. Exactly what I needed to recharge and figure out my next step, and there were enough English speaking tourists that I easily got a job.

We made it to the Benagil cave, and I gave my spiel on how the cave was formed, how it would change over the next couple hundred years, and pointed out the fossils in the rocks. As much as it pained me, I even made a few expected dad jokes. Then I moved off to the side while the group spent fifteen minutes exploring in the cave.

"Hey, my man." Henry jogged over. He was the one American working for the tour company and he was insufferable. So different from the local people.

I gave him a half-smile, then glanced back at my group, making sure none of them were wandering places they shouldn't be. Or not trying to piss in the water because there were no bathrooms here.

Not that I cared about that, but sizable boats constantly floated in and out for their tours. I couldn't have anyone in my tours getting struck because of their stupidity, and kayak tours were the only ones who could get out and step foot on the sand.

"There's going to be a party at Cav's house tonight." Henry stepped closer and lowered his voice.

"Cool," I murmured. If I showed the right amount of disinterest, Henry usually left me alone for a few days after. He had what I believed the Americans called *pick me* energy.

He wanted to be the cool guy that everyone liked and wanted to be around. He was a solid ten years younger than me and more shallow than the water on the beach at low-tide.

Stepping even closer, he shrugged his shoulders and got a wild glint in his eyes. "You'll want to come to this party. It's going to have some crazy shit, man."

"Not interested." I never went to parties. I never hung out with the guides past grabbing a beer after a shift, and that was with a very select few.

The only person I really spoke to was an elderly Portuguese neighbor who was cranky as fuck and teaching me Portuguese. As a Spanish speaker, I thought Portuguese would be an easy language to learn, but it was more difficult than I'd anticipated.

Portuguese people sounded like Russian people speaking Spanish, but using words I'd never heard before. And the few run-ins I'd had with Brazilian Portuguese? Those were different words too. Everyone used different fucking words.

"Come on. It's not often that there's any good stuff to take." Henry dropped his head back like I was too slow to pick up what he was putting down.

Somehow, this Cav guy was going to have drugs at his party. Which scared absolutely no one because unless you were the dealer, drugs were decriminalized in Portugal.

"Why the fuck would I want anything to do with that?" I let my true feelings slip through for a second before I reschooled my features to that of a pleasant, tour guide.

Drugs had almost ruined my brother, Lafe. It wasn't his choice to get wrapped up in them. It had been forced on him by our father, so who could blame him for tasting the goods just to deal with his shit life?

My past was scarred by many things, and some were too much to ever want to revisit.

I counted drugs among them.

That, and I'd never make myself vulnerable around any of these *pendejos.*

Henry blinked, then smiled like I hadn't snapped at him. "It's nothing that's going to kill you. Just make the night a little more enjoyable. Cav's hooked up with some people who are supplying the party. They want to network."

They wanted to find local footmen to push their product.

I pulled a face in disgust. Was this what low-life crime was like outside of the Institution? Or fuck, even inside it but street level?

As the only legitimate son of Vicente Castillo, everything I'd seen of the top officials of the Institution were more like rabid businessmen with vicious ambitions and cut-throat moves. Very formal and self-important. I had to be one of them for so long...

We were nothing like this watered down version of kids trying to get drugs distributed.

"I'm not going to deal drugs." I cut my eyes at him. He couldn't see them behind the mirrored sunglasses but he must have felt the heat because he straightened up.

"Hey, hey, hey." He raised his hands. "Not so loud."

I almost rolled my eyes, but I hadn't changed that much since leaving South America.

"Listen, I just thought since, you know..." He glanced around.

"Thought what?" Don't ask me why I was humoring him.

"I've seen you with your shirt off. That's a gunshot wound. I know what those look like. I've seen enough movies. And you're from somewhere in South America, which you've still never told me where." Henry raised his brows like he was chastising me. "I figured you'd be into this kind of stuff. No." His eyes widened. "I didn't mean that because of where you're from. I just mean that you have this cool accent, and with the scar, I thought you'd have to had seen some stuff, that's all. Like Scarface or something."

My mild expression slowly melted off and my lips pulled down.

All that kept flashing through my head were those final minutes before I received the gunshot wound.

Trying to help my half-brothers stay alive. Trying to prove myself to them so they'd finally accept me as family. But it had all been a useless effort.

The four of them were so tightly bonded, that even after they did accept me, and I truly believed they did in their own way, it wasn't what I thought it would be. They had too many memories tying them together, and too many old perceptions of who they had always thought I was to ever let me fully in.

It hadn't stopped me from trying for *her*, though.

I stood by the half-wall at the edge of the cliff, staring out at the ocean. The night sky was clear and the stars were bright. El Chato was a fantastic restaurant to get good food, and meet with people off radar. I'd used it a time or two to meet Javier.

This time wasn't nearly as pleasant. I swallowed down the sour taste in my mouth as I waited. Valentina, my snake of a sister, texted that she was out here. Yet, she wasn't.

If she didn't show up soon, I'd give up on her. There were a thousand different ways to get the information I wanted. I'd simply have to take the time to flush all of them out.

Someone, somewhere in the organization knew where Grace Black was.

Heels tapped quietly on the stone and I turned around. The woman coming around the side of the building was perfection according to society's accepted beauty standards. She was also the female version of me. Between Andre, Valentina, and myself, Vicente's genes had run strong.

And her eyes were sharp and frigid. Just like Vicente's. I'd always known she was a psychopath, like him, and the eyes gave it away.

"I didn't think you were coming." I raised a brow.

"You have something you want to ask, and I have something I need." She waved her hand as she stopped a few feet from me. Her anger was palpable. It was a wonder the guard creeping up behind her didn't shy away from fear of being burned.

"What happened to Amorette's sister?" I dove right into the meat of why I wanted to see her.

One side of her lips curled up as she glanced at me out of the corner of her eyes. "Trying to slide between that whore's legs? It's not enough that she's fucking every illegitimate child Vicente had?"

Had...because Valentina had him killed. I'd never guessed I'd be living in a world where my sister was a bigger threat than my father.

"Don't start with that fucking shit." I glared at her. I'd entertained the idea of Amorette for a span of ten seconds. But it didn't take long to figure out it was what she represented that drew me in. It wasn't actually her.

That tiny woman was the spoke in the wheel of my brothers, and it seemed like an easy way to join them.

Still, just because I didn't want her didn't mean I didn't care for her. She was the sister I wished I'd been given. Not this viper in front of me.

And when she was taken by my father's people, so was her identical twin sister. Only we couldn't find any proof of where she was or where she'd been. Even though our hierarchy had been shaken up since Vicente's death, I still had sway, and I could help in ways my brothers couldn't.

I wanted to find Grace for Amorette, and my brothers.

"You know it's true. And it's disgusting. We're better than taking sloppy-seconds. Or thirds, or fourths, or in your case, fifths." She wrinkled her nose.

"If you say another word like that, I'll fuck you up." It didn't matter to me that she was a woman. In our world, that meant nothing.

I didn't hold the same values, and this bitch? She'd deserve it and I couldn't find it in myself to believe otherwise.

She smirked and faced me. "You wouldn't dare. Anyway, I might have the information you want. But there's something I want in return."

The hairs on the back of my neck stood up. She was every inch as manipulative as Vicente. Whatever she wanted would not be good for me. Hell, she'd already had too much fun whipping me in the basement.

All for giggles.

"What do you want?" I asked, but I already knew this was pointless. I might as well walk away now, except my feet stayed glued to the stone. Information was power.

"Turns out there are some holdouts who feel a woman shouldn't lead." She shrugged. "I could kill them. Or you could come to my side and show support."

Valentina didn't care either way, that was clear. But what she did want was the quickest path to ultimate power. For whatever reason, she thought that was getting me to her side.

"There's no fucking way that I would ever do that, you psycho bitch. But you do know where Grace is. If you tell me, I'll make sure your death is quick. No torturing like our brothers want to do."

"Your brothers maybe, not mine."

"Tell me where she is." I pulled myself up to my tallest height and did my fucking best to intimidate her.

"Come to my side," she returned.

"Hell will swallow us first," I growled, losing my patience.

Multiple sets of footsteps were coming our way. Fuck, my brothers found me. With Valentina. They were going to think I was a traitor.

All because of this cunt.

"Tell me where Grace Degas Black is."

Valentina turned to look at her guard. "Plan B."

"You fucking cunt! What is your game? What's your goal? To kill us all? It's never going to happen."

"Matt?...Matt?" Henry's face wavered back into view. "You okay, man?"

The world rocked as I fought to hold my balance. I was close to passing out. "Yeah," I gasped, working hard to find my breath.

"What's wrong? You look like you saw a ghost."

Not a ghost. Only the shock and betrayal on my family's faces before I was shot and kicked over a cliff. That they could think I was conspiring against them had hurt more than the bullet-shaped hole ripping through my body.

2

RITA

Three Days Earlier

I stared at the name plaque on the door.

Margarita Aguilar- Co-Founder
Black Point School for Girls

An elite school helping those less fortunate on the outside. On the inside? A place to teach girls how to handle themselves and how to make a career out of it.

Twisting the knob, I pushed it open and stepped inside. The hallway was empty. Why the hell wouldn't it be at 10:30 in the morning? All the girls were in classes and learning how to kickass.

Me? I needed my beauty sleep. I couldn't properly kick ass unless I had a solid eight hours. It just wasn't happening. Then I needed an extra hour to get myself ready for the public.

I wasn't high maintenance though. I knew some bitches who needed three.

And I still looked better. It was these good genes I got from my dear old *Papá*.

The light coming from the floor to ceiling windows nearly blinded me as I dumped my designer bag on the table. Every inch of the office was sleek, but sexy. I'd paid massive bucks for a woman to decorate it to my tastes.

It was nothing like I'd ever been part of before.

Growing up a Dirty Dog, I was used to dingy warehouses, seedy clubs, and oil-stained auto shops. When my girl, Amorette, and I first built this place, I'd been out of sorts.

I didn't belong. And I sure as hell didn't wear pencil skirts and button-downs like she did. From the very first second the doors opened and we made our offices here, she was right at home, floating around with her five-two self, glaring at people down the end of her nose like she knew she was smarter than them and didn't give a fuck.

She didn't look at me that way. We had a special bond, one I forced because girl besties were hard to come by in gang life. The only girls in the Dirty Dogs were *the girls* who serviced the clubs and hangouts, or old ladies and daughters who weren't allowed at the compound.

I plopped my round ass in the chair as a knock came at the door. Then it cracked and Amorette poked her head in.

"Morning," she said with a sly smile on her face. No matter how hard she tried to get me to come in at eight, it wasn't going to happen.

"What's up, bestie." I grinned, and she returned it. As much as I needed a girlfriend, she had needed one more. And that Blanca bitch wasn't the ride or die kind. She was the stab you in the back if it suited her kind, and Amorette couldn't convince me otherwise.

"We've had another issue with Molly. She's starting fights in the dorms." Amorette smoothed some of her black hair off of her face as she sat down in the seat across from me.

Even after giving birth only a few months earlier, she barely took up half of it.

It was like a high metabolism was her super power. I was only mildly jealous. I loved my curves and I loved good food and an even better cocktail.

"So?" I asked as I curled my nails over the ends of the chair-arms. Carefully. I'd had them done the night before and they were filed so sharp, they might puncture the expensive leather Andre picked out.

Now that was something I never saw coming. Being connected to the brothers of the man I–

Fuck that. Fuck that so hard with a jolly red dildo.

I would not think about that lying coward. If I did, I'd cry, and I was too much of a badass to cry.

"You don't see the issue?" Amorette quirked a brow.

"We're training assassins. Spies. Bodyguards. We're teaching these girls how to kill with their pinkies and be unapologetic about it. Starting fights is a byproduct of that goal." I leaned forward, resting my elbows on the desk.

I was proud of these little *chicas* too. They were cute as shit, just like Amorette, until you turned your back on them.

"Rita," she sighed. "We want them to have control. If they go around fighting everyone, it will get them killed. That's not what I'm working toward. Maybe she needs to be sent back home."

My throat closed up. We would not be sending Molly home. The very worst feeling in the world was to be cast away from something that was important to you. If we did that, who knew what Molly would do or grow up to be.

The one thing I was certain of, Molly would make decisions she'd regret. They'd probably come back to bite her in the ass.

"Why are you smiling?" Amorette asked slowly, her brows furrowing in confusion.

"Shit, I am smiling." I touched the corner of my mouth with my index finger, careful not to smudge the red gloss. It was transfer proof, but the temperatures outside were enough to melt asphalt. I wasn't taking any chances.

"Yes, in a sad sort of way. I'm asking why."

"Don't be such a smartass." I wish I had something to toss at her, but all I had was a crystal paperweight and a stapler on my desk. Items I never used but the interior decorator said every desk needed. "Look. Let's give Molly a chance. The last thing we want is to be the beginning of her villain origin story."

We had too many real examples for that. Amorette more so than me.

Outside of typical gang drama and the shit with the Institution before Vicente and Valentina met their end, I had a great life growing up. Loving parents until my *mamá* passed. A club that would die for me, and the training to take care of myself.

Then I was cast away. It fucked with my head and my perspective about everything.

"You remember when I tried to force Parker to fuck me?" Parker as in one of her many men. While she was with him. It hadn't been that serious. I'd backed down fast, but I'd been committed to the cause for about ten minutes.

Amorette barked out a laugh. "That's a memory I tried to bury. Why are we friends?"

I grinned and shifted in my chair. "Because I'm awesome with killer style, and I'll cut a bitch for you." Then I remembered Molly. "I lost my head like that because I'd been kicked aside. That asshole we're not naming made me feel like scum. Like I was lower than a cockroach. Cornering you guys seemed like a good idea to get some of my power back. All I'm saying is, let's not be so quick to cast Molly aside."

"Rita." She raised her eyes, impressed. "That sounds eerily close to a moral compass."

I scoffed. "Please. I'm still the self-serving princess you know and love, but I can relate to Molly." I glanced at my watch. "Let's go check on her. I don't have any meetings this morning anyway. Maybe if we chat with her, she'll calm down."

"Okay," Amorette answered too quickly.

"Hmm." I didn't stand up.

"What?"

"Why do I feel like this is a trick?" I squinted at her, but she just smiled.

"No trick. I love when you take charge. It looks good on you."

I rolled my eyes. "You're just living your best life and projecting." We laughed and left my office.

The school was in the next building and the dorms behind that. With the associations both Amorette and I had, we thought it was best if the girls weren't constantly in the same building as us.

We had a pretty good handle on our shit, but one never knew when it would blow up in our faces.

"How's my precious little pearl?" I asked as I held the door open to the outside.

"Oh you know, slobbering all over the place." She slid sunglasses on her face that she'd grabbed on our way out. I put mine on too. The sun was vicious and we would not be wrinkling before our time.

"And the daddies?" I smirked. That was one fucked up arrangement, but it worked for her, so who was I to judge.

Honestly, having four, raging-hot alphaholes fawn all over you and your child was a dream. Just not mine.

"Twirled around Cossette's little finger. Especially Lafe and Parker. And Andre." She huffed out a laugh as we passed through the wrought iron gate to the school. I'd added this. It just completed the image I had in my head of those stuck up places I'd seen in the movies. "Actually Grey might be the worst."

"So nothing has changed and they're all deliriously happy."

High-pitched yells from the practice field floated around the corner of Little Love Hall.

It was ridiculous and cutesy for an all girls' school. I rebelled at first, but caved. Who gave a shit what the buildings were named?

Amorette slowed and tipped her face my way. "They are happy. Especially since we received the call."

I pressed my lips together. "We're not talking about that."

"We have to talk about it sometime. You still never told me–"

"We're not talking about any of that." I sped up, opening my stride until her tiny legs couldn't keep up. So Matías was actually alive. And he'd spent his time away from us hunting down *her* sister.

Who fucking cared?

It was at best another nail in the coffin of reasons he wasn't right for me. I couldn't trap the breeze in my hand anymore than I could force Matías to love me.

He broke my heart and scattered the pieces across the street without any remorse.

Knowing that he cared for Amorette enough to find her sister, sliced into the tender muscles of my heart more than I wanted to admit. How did I come back from that?

If Amorette wasn't so fucking likable in a prickly, driven way, I'd have hated her guts.

What was it about her that had men falling all over themselves when I couldn't hold on to the one man I wanted. Had only *ever* wanted?

Whispers of drunken memories tried to take over but I ignored them. I'd done so many things I'd regretted since Matías tossed me aside. The very best thing for me to do was pretend I hadn't done them.

Girls ranging from twelve up to sixteen trained in hand to hand combat on the field. Olga, a German battle ax with Russian family roots, yelled commands and prowled around the pairs, tossing out corrections and the rare praise.

I didn't see the little blonde head I was looking for, so I kept going.

A few of the girls noticed me and smiled. I tried to return it, but it seemed more like a grimace. They didn't see *that*, taking their attention quickly back to their opponent before they were knocked in the head.

Olga gave me a chin dip, and then looked behind me.

That little chihuahua was closing in. I needed to pick up the pace.

I entered the side door of Little Love Hall and headed straight for the administrative offices.

"She deserved it!"

Ah, there was Molly. I didn't know every single girl, but Molly had already been in trouble a number of times. First, stealing rolls from the cafeteria. But who cared about that? When I found out, I yelled at the cooks to give them more food. Then she cheated on a written test. Amorette had handled that issue, but I spoke to Molly later.

Life is hard. Take all the help you can get and use every single fucking resource you can. But don't get caught. That's how we stayed alive and thrived.

"Molly," I said as I stepped into the office.

Ms. Garcia, the house mother, stopped her rant and Molly glanced up. "Ms. Aguilar!"

She ran straight to me and wrapped her arms around my waist.

Damn. This kind of stuff got to me every time. It was like shocking myself with experiences I never knew I wanted. No one in the Dirty Dogs would even dare to touch me like this. Not the Dirty Dogs' precious princess.

"Ms. Aguilar, Molly is being reprimanded for fighting. I already notified Ms. Black." Ms. Garcia spoke with a heavy accent. She was as local as we could find, and for the most part did a good job, but like Amorette, sometimes she got lost in the rules.

"I need a word with Molly. Amorette is behind me. You can discuss it with her." It would give me a few extra minutes without the bestie bringing up things that made me stabby.

"Of course." She twisted her lips to the side. Most likely she was confused on why she'd need to talk to Amorette again. As long as she did it, it didn't matter what she said.

I touched Molly's shoulder and she backed away. Pointing to the conference room behind her, she took the hint and led the way. There was a large rectangular window next to the door that was perfect for me to stop Amorette in her tracks if she tried to come in.

Molly didn't sit at the table. I didn't ask her to. Amorette was insanely intense on not forcing the girls to do little things like that. She wanted them to have as much control as possible unless they were in a class setting.

I, however, took a seat facing the window.

"Ms. Aguilar. I started the fight, but those other girls are nasty! You should hear the things they said to me!"

Molly was one of the girls who had been saved from the Gallery. Well, not the actual Gallery, but the girls who were being trained for it.

I was so fucking glad Amorette and her men had shut that operation down. The Dirty Dogs weren't innocent. *Papá* had dabbled in the skins business himself, but now all the girls were locals and paid for their services. That I could stomach.

What happened to the girls at the hands of the men running the Gallery...

That also made me stabby.

Molly was only twelve, taken from the streets in Texas. Blonde hair, big blue eyes, and mean as a snake. She had her own set of rules and she really didn't like it when the other girls broke them.

"What did I tell you?" I asked. If she wanted to tell me what happened, I'd listen, but there was a bigger lesson here.

"Keep my nails filed so they're sharp as hell."

I pressed my lips together to stop my laugh. "That's important, but not what I meant."

She squinted one eye. "Don't let no bitch keep me down."

"Nope." I beamed. I'd really imparted some wisdom on her. I'd have to have Amorette add these nuggets to the manual she'd written. The code for the girls.

"Don't get caught."

"Right. Use all the resources at your disposal, but *don't* get caught. You wanted to punish these girls?"

Amorette stormed into the office, her face red and her blue eyes blazing. Ms. Garcia engaged her, but she stepped toward the conference room.

I raised a finger and she stopped, glaring at me.

See? The window was perfect.

"They said nasty things. You can't do that and expect people to like you." Molly fumed, balling her hands up by her thighs.

"Fair. But fighting got you caught. What's the lesson?"

She glanced up at the ceiling, sticking the tip of her pink tongue out. Eventually she returned her attention to me. "Punish them a different way?"

"Right. Show them a little karma, but not in a way that will come back on you. I learned that the hard way. You're lucky I did, so I can help you avoid the same mistakes."

She stared at me for a beat, then two, seeming to think my suggestion over. I thought we were getting somewhere until her next words.

"But it's satisfying to land my fists into their faces."

I let myself laugh this time. "Fair, but they're in training too, and pretty faces are just as much a weapon as sharp nails. You can't damage school weapons."

Molly slumped and grumbled under her breath.

Amorette held up a hand as she answered her phone. Immediately the blood drained from her face. Before she said anything, she barreled toward the door, swinging it open with so much force, the handle probably dented the wall.

"It's Javier! He's in the hospital!"

Papá. I jumped up. That couldn't be. He was invincible. Larger than life.

"What happened?" I patted my waist and hips like I was going to find my phone, but I'd left it in my office.

Amorette gulped. "Heart attack."

3

ESTEBAN

I took a long swig from the cold beer and pulled the cloth from the back of my jeans to wipe my face.

"This shit is out of control. Who came up with this idea?" Leo spit on the concrete, and I swore it sizzled. The heat was definitely doing the devil's work today.

Sliding my thumb over the condensation on the bottle, I sighed. I wasn't at the bottom of the chain anymore. It had taken me a couple years, but now I was solidly in the middle. Due, my best friend, and I both were. He started right before me, and since then, we were inseparable. Except for when I was chasing Rita, taking it upon myself to be her bodyguard.

That was probably why Due and I had been promoted to officers. I'd kept Rita from doing something that would have gotten her killed the year before. Due had backed me up all the way.

Javier appreciated it, but damn, none of it mattered. Not when I had to sit out behind this shithole and supervise the "new" business.

The sound of metal cutting into metal came out of the

bays and another wave of heat rolled over me. Fuck, we needed to add air conditioning. We'd already had two guys pass out from the heat in the last two days.

"Javier," I answered in a bland tone. That shut him up for about two seconds.

Leo was a newb. Brand new as of last month and he hadn't grown up here like most of the other guys. Damen recruited him from his hometown somewhere south of here. So his self-preservation was still a little weak.

Don't get me wrong, I could bullshit with the best of them and make a joke out of anything. People loved me. But I knew when not to question my highers. Javier was the highest there was. This was his club and he was like a father to me.

"Okay, but seriously? We were doing just fine in the drugs business. That's what Damen said."

Now he was throwing his friend under the bus. I shook my head.

"When Dirty Dogs had the girls, the gang lived like Kings." Leo licked his lips. "Now we have to pay for that shit." He scoffed.

The Dirty Dogs was a gang through and through. We were rough, dirty, and wild. We more than dabbled in crime. Around here, in this melting pot of Latino cultures, being a Dirty Dog was the highest honor.

But that didn't mean we hadn't changed over the years. The last year especially had been the largest overhaul I'd seen. All because of Rita and how she had Javier wrapped around her cute manicured pinky.

Or so the guys gossiped.

I never participated in that shit, and I shut it down when I could. Partly since it wasn't true. Mostly because I'd tie up any man who went after Javier or Rita, then toss them in the ocean with a nice weight around their waist.

Unlike most of the other Dirty Dogs, I hated blood. I didn't want to dirty my hands with it. I preferred to take care of business where they died a slow death and I didn't have to see it. Just knowing it sucked for them at the end was enough for me.

"Things have changed. We're not trafficking anymore. We're also not distributing on the streets." I wiped my forehead and the back of my neck again. I tossed the soaked towel in the corner. There was a stack of clean ones in the front office where Lola worked.

She was the office manager and one of the old ladies to leadership. Like she knew we'd hate dripping sweat, she kept the air on in the office with three huge water dispensers and clean towels. Very mother-hen like for such a tough old bitch.

"All because Rita asked him to. It's not right that she has so much control over him." Leo spit again. Where was he getting all that saliva?

I pulled a face and turned away. "Not because of her. The Institution crumbled. We had to restructure our business to make sure we don't have any problems. Javier has a soft spot for them. That Rita's friends with their new woman is the least important of the reasons we pulled back from those businesses."

Glancing back at Leo, I curled my tongue over my canine, and leveled him with a serious stare.

"Look, I'm just saying, overseeing the streets is a fuck of a lot easier than watching men break apart cars and rebuild them." His top lip started to quiver like he was scared.

"We've been in this business for years. We're just expanding." Building cars and bikes was actually how I came to be a Dirty Dog. It was in my blood. I couldn't hate it, just the circumstances of the weather.

Did Leo really not know about Rita's Lambo Javier had made just for her? That *I'd* made?

We couldn't have done that without our shop. It had just never been monetized before. The Dirty Dogs hadn't needed it in that capacity.

He laughed, the sound shaky. "Man, what's up your ass? You're usually the fun time guy."

"I *am* the fun time guy, but I'm also the get shit done guy, and the devoted Dirty Dog guy. Take a lesson. It's not all fun and games. This is our life and our responsibility."

Hopping off the warped picnic table, I sauntered toward the bay. Three feet away, the distant sound of engines rumbled. Tipping my head, I listened.

Those weren't ours. I'd recognize them.

Unlike Leo and his buddy Damen, I loved cars. But I specialized in bikes.

These were new school. Probably crotch rockets.

I didn't hate them. I had one of those too. As a lover of all things bikes, I was an equal opportunist to most of the guys' disgust.

Yep. A string of bikes came around the corner, fanning out to make an impressive V as they headed right for us. Shiny leather vests that were probably just taken off the hanger today. Cutesy patches and brand new jeans.

Where were these guys from?

"What the hell?" Leo muttered.

Pivoting on my heel, I turned to face the newcomers. I whistled to signal the guys in the bay, then crossed my arms as I waited for them to climb off their bikes.

My piece was in my holster, easy to get to, but I didn't

want to come at this from violence. It could be innocent, although unlikely.

The Dirty Dogs walking along the roof of our building and surrounding us wouldn't let these men even twitch the wrong way without going down in a bloody mess.

The man up front took off his helmet and shook out his hair.

That was...unexpected.

It had been impossible to see anything about the guy between the clothes, leathers, and helmet, but I'd assumed he was someone local.

Not this ginger giant with pale skin and mountains of freckles. He set his helmet on his seat and walked over, unstrapping his gloves and pulling them off. He didn't smile, not at first. When he was a few steps away, he grinned and stuck out his hand.

"Matthews, nice to meet you." So he was American.

I stared at his hand, not taking it.

His smile dimmed as his men leaned on their bikes, helmets off.

"You must be new here, but this is Dirty Dogs territory," I warned. It was as friendly as this guy was going to get while I was sweating my ass off.

"I know." The grin came back. "We're new, but I did my research. Just like I know you're Esteban, mid-ranking member, generally liked with just enough power and influence to make you dangerous to a man like myself."

He paused. What was he waiting for? There was nothing in that nice set of pretty words that made me want to respond with anything other than my fists. If I were the fighting type.

I was more of a lover if I could help it.

"Why do you think we'd care?" Leo stepped up next to me, puffing his chest out like a young rooster.

"Leo, lowest ranking member of the Dirty Dogs." Matthews smirked like that was an insult. But all our members were important. It wasn't the sting he thought it would be.

"Watch your fucking mouth," Leo spit.

Fuck, I called that wrong. Extending my arm, I stopped Leo from pushing into this man's space. "Stop before you make me angry," I snapped at Leo in Spanish. Then I focused on Matthews again.

"Why are you here and what do you want? You have one minute."

"I'm just introducing myself. We're new in town, and we've heard you've recently gotten out of...certain businesses. We'll be taking over. I thought it best to introduce ourselves in the light of day. Less dangerous for everyone involved."

I studied him. "Remember I said you're in Dirty Dogs territory?"

He nodded, now sporting a closed-lipped smile.

"You do any type of *business* in Dirty Dogs territory, whether we run it or not, you'll find yourself without a home." I glanced behind him. "And without a few of your buddies too."

That got to him. The almost translucent skin under his right eye twitched.

"We're not going to get in your way. Don't get in ours." That sounded like a threat.

I shook my head. "You don't understand. We've lived here our whole lives. There's an entire network of people you don't want to mess with. We know them all. Even if we didn't want to dirty our hands with you, which would not be the case. We're the Dirty Dogs after all." I lifted one side of my mouth into a cutting grin. "There are a hundred people who would not like your presence here. It'd be best for you to move somewhere else. Try Chile. I hear they have good skiing."

He took a step toward me. "You're not as intimidating as you thin-"

Snapping out my hand, I caught his throat, then spun, shoving him against the tin wall of the shop. He winced and sucked in a sharp breath. That had to burn the back of his head.

Shouts went up behind us, but Dirty Dogs started spilling from the bay doors and coming around the side of the building with their weapons drawn.

"I don't have to think. I know." Shifting my hold, I squeezed to cut off his air supply. He started gasping and I nodded. This was the position he didn't want to find himself in. "This place isn't for you. I'm going to let you go, because I'm the *nice* guy. But if you show your face around here again, I won't stop the Dirty Dogs from going crazy on your bones."

His face turned the bright shade of a pitaya. Once he started to go limp in my hold, I stepped back. He fell to the ground, coughing and cupping his neck.

"You'll fucking regret that," he wheezed.

"Doubt it. There's only one thing I regret, and it will never be setting boundaries with your shiny ass."

Snapping at his buddies, I pointed at Matthews. "You have ten minutes to get him on his bike and out of here. Otherwise, you'll be Swiss."

"Watch them to make sure they actually leave. If they don't, signal the guys." I tapped Leo on the shoulder. He nodded, a fierce look of concentration on his face as I left him there. This was the responsibility he wanted and he wasn't going to fuck it up.

When I stepped through the bay door, Javier was leaning against one of the cars that had been abandoned as the men left to take my back outside.

He grinned and his face became a deep map of criss-crossed wrinkles. The man had never heard of sunscreen and decades of riding bikes in the sun had left his skin rough and leathery. It made his shocking silver hair that much brighter.

"That was impressive." He raised his brows.

I chuckled. "A nuisance. I hate that kind of posturing. I especially hate it when I'm ready for a nap."

Shaking his head, he pushed away from the car. "I just came by to check up on the place. I'm supposed to meet with Andre later about something Rita wants us to do." The fondness for his only child wrapped around his words.

He loved the hell out of her.

I gritted my teeth.

"What's wrong? Rita avoiding your calls again?" He slapped me on the back as he headed deeper into the shop. I walked with him.

"She's a fucking lunatic when she wants something. I just worry about her." I turned my face. Javier was too sharp and he'd see things I didn't want him to see.

But he knew. Everyone fucking knew how much of a hold Rita had on *me*. If I could just pull her head out of her ass, then maybe she'd see it too.

"Rita has a good head on her shoulders. She's making her own way in life, and I couldn't be prouder of her." His voice turned wistful, and I glanced back.

"You don't want her in the Dirty Dogs? Protected and insulated from the crime world?" Because I sure as shit did.

She would always be the Dirty Dogs' princess and that alone put a target on her back.

What she was doing with the Castillo brothers was also dangerous. Maybe not now, but when they started sending out small firecrackers, they were going to start a fire that burned the hell out of Rita because she was reckless after that fuckwad Matías broke her heart.

Javier's gaze dropped to my jaw and I loosened it.

"The Dirty Dogs isn't any place for her after I'm gone. I had hoped..." he dropped his head.

"Hoped what?"

He didn't raise it back up. Instead, he started to sway and after a few seconds, gripped his chest over his heart.

"What's wrong?" I shouted, jumping forward to grab his shoulders.

His face scrunched in a grimace. "Do–Doctor."

Then he seized up in my arms.

4

RITA

"What's wrong with him?" I glared at the doctor clutching the file in the waiting room. I hadn't been able to see *Papá* yet.

They wouldn't let me. They wouldn't *fucking* let me.

"He's out of surgery, and he's doing just fine. Mr. Aguilar just needs time to recover from the anesthesia, Ms. Aguilar." His voice shook on my name. This was the best hospital in our part of town. We sent all of our men here.

This was even the place that treated Parker when he was shot on Dirty Dog property.

He knew exactly who I was. Because of that, he wouldn't lie to me.

The staff would also make sure *Papá* would be given the best care and attention. They knew that the Dirty Dogs were the only thing standing between them and another more vile group coming in and making demands and unreasonable requests. They'd want to avoid as much conflict and death as possible.

Still, I couldn't stand not being able to see him.

"Um, well," the doctor said as he started patting his jacket pockets. "Do you need a tissue?" He pulled a wadded up tissue from his pocket.

I sneered at it. "What the fuck do I want with that?"

"To..." He motioned to my face. "To wipe your face."

"You're crying, Rita," Amorette said softly at my shoulder as she gently cupped my arm.

"Like fuck, I am." I dashed my fingers across my cheeks. "I don't fucking cry. But this prick is going to take me to my father right now. Or else, he'll be missing more than a ratty piece of tissue. Got me?" I pointed my finger in his face, almost stabbing him with my nail.

"Ms. Aguilar! He just needs ten more minutes to wake up! This is procedure!"

I zeroed in on his neck, ready to wring it. They couldn't keep me from my father. They couldn't keep me from the only man in my life who had ever loved me unconditionally.

He meant *everything* to me.

"Doc," Esteban said as he stepped up next to me, trying to take my hand. I yanked it out of his reach and did my fucking best not to look at him. Gritting his teeth, he kept his gaze on the scared as fuck doctor in front of me. "He's in recovery. There's no harm in letting his daughter sit by his side until he wakes up."

"There are processes in place in case we run into any issues–"

"There's no harm in it. I'm sure you can make an exception this one time." His voice dropped into a threatening tone and the doctor started nodding before he shook his head.

"Sir–"

"Call me Esteban."

"Esteban–"

"The next words out of your mouth better be that you'll arrange for a nurse to take Ms. Aguilar back to see Javier, or the *entire* waiting room is not going to be happy." Esteban stressed entire, like the doctor didn't have a clue there were thirty plus men in the room behind me, all waiting for word about *Papá*.

He was loved and respected and every single person here with me would tear this place apart to get to him. That's how much he was loved.

"I need two minutes." The doctor dashed away so fast that his jacket flapped behind him like a cape.

"Can you give us a second?" Esteban asked Amorette.

She nodded, glancing at me before she walked over to where Andre stood in the corner with his arms crossed. The Dirty Dogs gave him a wide berth and he gave not one fuck.

Letting my eyelids flutter closed, I shivered from all the adrenaline racing through my veins. I only needed to see him. That was it. Just to know he was okay. Then I could stop feeling like I was crawling out of my skin.

"Are you okay?" Warm fingers trailed across the back of my neck and I stepped forward, breaking the contact. I didn't need his comfort. I needed to see my fucking *Papá*.

"Fine," I bit out, skating my gaze over his face.

Fire flashed in Esteban's light brown eyes as he leaned closer. "Stop lying to me. You've never been good at it."

I scoffed. "That's a lie all on its own." I wasn't a compulsive liar, but when I needed to be the cover, or mislead crooked assholes for the gang, I did. Without issue.

Esteban gave one tiny shake of his head and came so close, only an inch separated his chest from my arm. He didn't touch me, knowing that would push me away.

"You've never been good at lying to *me*, Rita." His eyes shifted back and forth as he watched me, as if he was trying to work something out.

A warmth started to curl in my stomach just like it had that one night last year. I had been drunk. Esteban had been there. He was a sexy man. Black hair cropped close to his head and a strong, square jaw. Ripped in all the right places with dimples on his cheeks and the small of his back.

He knew how to drive a woman wild, and I needed that. For one night.

Then the splash of cold reality the next morning put everything into perspective. Exactly like *Papá's* life being on the line now.

I didn't respond, instead watching the hall the doctor disappeared through.

"You're not okay."

"What's your point?" I returned, louder than I intended. Some of our people were already watching and a few of the top members rose from their seats.

Shit, I had to be careful. Esteban was well liked. But he was young and hadn't been in as long as some of these men I'd known my whole life. They'd teach him a lesson if he upset me.

He glanced at the men in the waiting room before turning back to me, this time with hurt-drenched eyes. "I know you better than you think I do. I care about you, even when you're a bitch. So I'm going to make sure you're okay. I'm going to make sure you get to see Javier when you want to see him, because that's who I am. Fucking deal with it."

Then he turned and walked to the wall, propping himself up against it as his gaze stayed glued to me. I burned from the inside out for so many reasons. Now wasn't the time to examine any of them.

"Okay, Ms. Aguilar," the same doctor panted as he came rushing out of the hall. "Follow me."

I didn't give Esteban another thought as I followed the doctor through the double doors.

"Mr. Aguilar has just started to wake up. His vitals are good. You can sit with him until we move him to a private room." The doctor scanned his badge and another set of double doors opened. A nurse was waiting and pulled the curtain back on a bay right next to the nurses station.

Good. They were taking this seriously and watching the hell out of him.

I wished they had let him wake up in a private room, but maybe this was better. Safer for him.

"Thank you," I murmured as I pulled the one chair in the curtained area right next to the bed.

The steady beeping from the machines hooked up to him was comforting as I took his hand in mine. It was warm and dry. A reminder that he was still here with me. His eyes fluttered slightly, but he didn't seem coherent yet.

My breathing turned shallow. Seeing him in this bed made it all real. He wasn't invincible like I'd always thought.

I'd just talked to him yesterday. He was fine. Now he was laid up in the hospital and it killed me to see him like this. He'd hate being seen in a gown like this. It didn't scream head of the Dirty Dogs.

Five more minutes passed before his head rolled my way and he seemed to see me.

"Margarita?" His voice slurred and his fingers twitched in mine as if he only now realized I was holding it.

"*Papá*." I scooted to the edge of the chair.

"Wha–what happened?" He tried to glance around, but he couldn't. He didn't have enough energy for that yet.

His skin was sallow and for the first time in my life, he

appeared weak. I sucked in a sharp breath. He needed to get out of here, then he'd be back to his old self.

"You had a heart attack." My voice was so thick, I hoped he could understand me. "They said you had a blockage and it needed to be removed. They did a surgery, but you're going to be okay now."

"Damn," he cursed.

"No more fried food or beer for a while. Doctor's orders." I made that up. They hadn't said that. But they would. I'd watched enough TV to know what they recommended for people after heart attacks.

He tried to laugh but made a pained sound.

"Shhh...don't laugh. Don't try to move." I got so close to the bed, my chest pressed against the rails. "You don't want to cause yourself any harm."

Papá's eyes started to close. "So tired."

"I know." I smoothed my hand over his white hair. "But stay awake just a little longer. For me?"

"I'd do anything for you," he sighed. His eyes still closed but they reopened a few seconds later. "I thought Matías would help me."

My chest squeezed uncomfortably. *Papá* always had a soft spot for Matías. I had too. It was like fate that I'd loved the man my father had taken under his wing. Until fate broke my fucking heart.

How could *Papá* talk about Matías *now*? When I was here in front of him?

I wasn't jealous. I knew *Papá* loved me more than anything in the world. But the one disappointment I'd ever had for my father was when he refused to cut off his relationship with Matías when he kicked me aside.

He'd sighed and smoothed his hand over my hair like I was ten years old all over again.

"There are some things you're lucky enough not to understand."

That was all he'd said on the matter.

I'd hated him for days. Maybe even a few weeks. Then I realized how stupid I was.

Right now, with my own heart threatening to stop in fear, I wished I could take it back. Spend a few more hours with him, just in case.

But he was okay. I was being overdramatic.

"Matías was supposed to be one of us. I wanted him for you..." *Papá's* words were still slurred. The pain meds or anesthesia or whatever had him out of his mind still.

I could cut him off. Shut the conversation down. Or I could ask questions, get information from him that he'd kept from me.

Yet, I sat there. Frozen. Wanting all the answers, and fighting a building fury rising in my gut.

How fucking dare that asshole steal these moments with my *Papá*. He loved Matías like a son, and then Matías had fucked off and faked his death. *Who did that?*

Someone who didn't give a damn about my feelings. Who only cared about his precious brothers.

I turned my head to the side and pressed my lips together. This was the exact line of thinking that led to me cornering Parker in our club. It was useless thinking that would only get me in trouble.

This kind of attitude festered and I was better than that now.

Yet it still fucked with my head.

"We need him, don't we, Rita?"

I snapped my head back up. "What for?"

"Posers. They're going to be an issue. Matías would take care of it."

"We have a whole gang, *Papá*. A whole fucking gang to squash any problems." My hands started trembling.

Was there trouble coming and no one told me? Esteban wanted to talk a big game about knowing me so well? I'd shove my sharp, high heel up his ass when I walked out of here.

"If he hadn't died..."

"He isn't dead. Remember? He called Amorette."

"He is, or he would have come to see me. We're his family too." There was so much certainty in his words that I wanted to kick Matías over the cliff myself.

I'd grilled Amorette about what happened a dozen times, reliving the pain with her until she got the call from her sister.

"What do you want, *Papá*?" I released a slow breath. Would I do anything about it?

"I want Matías to take my place. I want him where he's supposed to be. Where I always planned for him to be."

Jerking up, I breathed through my nose as my eyes burned. What fucking shit was this?

Whatever tears I'd shed dried up like the Sahara desert as all the scorn, embarrassment, and anger welled up to take their place. My brain sizzled with all the reasons I shouldn't walk out that door and jump on a plane.

But I wasn't rational. I itched to track Matías down and demand answers. Then force him to come back and make this right with *Papá*. All *Papá* ever did was support that motherfucker. He gave Matías a safe space when he wanted to escape his psycho father.

Matías was from a rival group. When *Papá* found him, he could have and maybe should have taught Matías a lesson and sent him back to Vicente as a strong message.

Yet, Matías just spit on *Papá's* kindness by faking his death and staying away when he didn't fucking need to.

The nurse poked her head around the curtain. "Miss. I need you to step out for a few minutes so we can check him over."

Nodding, I stood and exited the curtained-off area. Without waiting for a nurse to accompany me, I walked back to the waiting room.

My hands trembled by my sides and my brain was electric with a rush of thoughts. *Papá* was in the hospital. He was weak. This stint in the hospital and his recovery would mean trouble for Dirty Dogs. That was how our world worked.

How long would *Papá* be around if he was starting to have health issues? My chest tightened.

He wanted Matías to show up for him? I would damn well make sure it happened.

Amorette had the answers I wanted. Esteban too. There was so much shit that I needed to yell and ask and demand, but right then, I had tunnel vision for one person only.

When I crossed through the doors, Amorette saw me before anyone else. Pushing away from Andre's chest, she took a step toward me.

"How is Javier? Is he okay?"

I shook my head and held up a hand. "He's okay. Really chatty, unfortunately." Her face softened in relief as Andre came up behind her and placed his hands on her shoulders.

"What's wrong?" he asked.

Amorette tipped her head as she studied me. "You don't look so good."

"When was the last time you spoke to Matías?"

"We haven't. You know that." Amorette furrowed her brow.

"Strike that. When was the last time you checked up on him?" They had hired a private investigator to figure out where in the world Matías was. We never spoke on it after that because I did my best to forget he ever existed, but they *had* to have found him.

And kept tabs on him.

Amorette and Andre exchanged glances then checked the room. All the Dirty Dogs were listening. Of course they were. Their President was in recovery, and their princess was livid and losing it. People tended to get stabbed when I was in my feels.

But that didn't mean they didn't care about Matías. We'd spread the word quietly through the club that he was alive. He had more friends in Dirty Dogs than either Andre or Amorette realized.

"We can talk about this later," Andre said in a commanding tone.

"Nope. Sorry, man. But I want to know right now. Do you know where he is?"

"Why?" Suspicion entered every line of his face and body.

"Because Javier wants to see him." *And I want to smash his balls in.*

"We know where he is." Sweet little Amorette was a jewel.

"Good. I want his location."

Esteban edged up on the side, his face carefully blank. "What are you thinking?"

"Don't know me so well now, do you?" I smirked. Glancing at him, my smirk died into a flat line. He pressed his lips together as his gaze roamed my face.

That's right, asshole. I'm going to fuck your life up after I grant Papá's wish. You just have to wait your turn.

"Why do you want it?" Finally Amorette started to question my motives.

"Don't worry. I don't want to hurt him. I'm just going to drag his ass back here so he can tell Javier exactly why he's never contacted him again."

I didn't bother telling them all the other things I would do when I got there.

5

MATÍAS

Present Day

"I'll see you tomorrow," João called as he dipped his head. As a third generation owner, he stayed the longest, worked the hardest, and remained the humblest man I'd ever met.

"Yeah." I waved back, then wiped excess sand off my arm. Today had been a packed tour, and it had taken over an hour to carry all the tandem kayaks up from the beach.

I loved the cliffs. Strangely enough, they reminded me a bit of home. But today was one of those times I hated them. The climb up with kayaks was a bitch.

Henry popped up from the stairs and I doubled my speed.

I'd barely shaken him off in the caves, and I had already spooked myself enough. I didn't need him needling me or bringing up things better left in the past.

Chills attacked the back of my head, and my head shivered. Leaving everything behind was best.

Andre wanted the Institution, which I heard wasn't the

Institution anymore. If I'd stayed, I'd only be in the way. The legitimate heir sticking around would make it more difficult for my brothers to rise to power.

There was nothing left for me there anyway.

I'd fucked up the one good thing I had, but in no reality did it make sense for me to live in the shadow of my past.

Selfishly, I wanted to break free of that black cloud. Start over. Live a fresh life where *I* made all the decisions. Where *I* was the only one responsible for my own fuck ups.

Instead of jumping in my car, I headed for the cliff where the seagull was caught.

It didn't take long to find where it was. I'd made it my priority to map out the cliffs from the water and on land. Especially after I'd had my own fucked up experiences.

The fishing lines were here, but the bird was gone.

Releasing a breath, I turned away. Either it had lived, or it had died. There was nothing I could do about it now.

Letting my mind wander on autopilot, I stopped at the grocery store to pick up fresh bread and some different meats. I could at least feed my neighbor before I went to bed.

The apartment I'd found was small. A one bedroom and a far cry away from what I'd grown up with. At times it felt comforting, and others it suffocated me. I kept waiting for my body and mind to acclimate to my new normal.

The law of human nature meant I'd eventually get attached to this type of living over what I came from.

I climbed the stairs, bags hanging from my fingers as I made my way up. Pedro lived on the top floor. I think he liked it like that so less people came to visit him. A very different mindset than most of the Portuguese people I'd met.

I knocked on the door and waited.

"*Já abri!*" he yelled, then his voice was followed by someone else's voice. A feminine one. One thing about the homes here, if they were built more than ten years ago, the walls were thin as paper and the insulation was non-existent.

Which meant I could hear the other voice very well.

The blood in my veins froze as my body locked up. That wasn't right. No one knew where I was. I made sure to cover my tracks and when I handed Grace the note, I didn't stick around for questions. I booked it away from her like my ass was on fire.

"Matt!" Pedro yelled louder and there was shuffling like he was trying to get up.

I jolted and used my hand to twist the doorknob. He had arthritis and it was hard for him to get around. That was what I told myself as I walked into his apartment. It had nothing to do with needing to know if I was right, if the other voice was from my past.

My eyes adjusted quickly to the darkened apartment as the door slammed shut behind me.

The physical feeling of blood draining from my face left me lightheaded and swaying as I faced Pedro sitting at his kitchen table with Rita.

Rita Aguilar. The love of my life and the woman I'd left behind.

Sitting at the table, she looked as if no time had passed at all. She had her legs crossed as her toned thighs peeked from under her tight dress. Her feet were in sharp, stiletto heels, just like she always wore.

I swallowed as I let my gaze work its way to her face. Her breasts were about to pop out of her top and she was so fucking sexy, she was every man's fantasy.

When I got to her face, my head and chest felt like they were going to explode from the sudden pulse of heat.

She was as gorgeous as she ever was with perfectly done make-up, puffy, sexed-up lips, and bold smoky eyes that stared daggers at me. Even her curls were glossy and full.

This was what the devil looked like before he came to drag you to hell. Like a dangerous woman who'd cut your heart out and eat it because you couldn't be what she wanted.

One of her brows raised in a mocking gesture. She moved her head back and forth in a motion that screamed, *well? What are you going to do now?*

I was going to fucking pretend this wasn't a big deal to Pedro. Then get my ass out of here.

"Matt," Pedro chastised. He didn't say anything else, because my Portuguese was horrific and he didn't like wasting his breath.

"*Desculpe*," I muttered and set the bags on the counter behind him. I pulled out the bread and meat. "*Para jantar*," I said. Then wadded up the bags in my hand. I almost threw them away, but stopped. I'd save them for next time.

Pedro hummed.

When I turned, Rita still had her gaze locked on me. I couldn't hold her stare. I recognized every single emotion sliding through her eyes and each one gutted me more than the last.

Hurt. Anger. Outrage. And the last one. Hate.

What I didn't see was love.

That was what I wanted. What I had wanted for a long time. Then I'd thrown it away.

"*Preciso*..." I mashed my lips together as I thought about the words. They were so similar to Spanish but so different. "*De sair.*"

Pedro motioned to Rita. "*Seu amiga?*"

"*Não*," I barked. When he raised his brows, I shook my head. "*Sim, mas não. Desculpe.*"

I fled that place like dogs were biting my ass. I laughed, but there was no humor in it. It could be argued that was true. Rita was a Dirty Dog to her core. Something I'd always been jealous of.

The Dirty Dogs were like family. The Institution had been an adult version of The Hunger Games.

Hopefully, my brothers learned a thing or two and would do everything different.

I took the steps two at a time, ignoring how my heart beat harder with every step I got further away from her. Like the sorry muscle was angry with me for leaving a second time.

Yet, I couldn't do this, not today. Fuck, not ever.

The quick, rage-filled taps of Rita's heels started on the staircase before I had the key turned in my door. Fuck.

She followed me. Then again, I knew she would.

I would rather do this in my apartment than in front of Pedro. Even if he and all our other neighbors could hear us.

"Matías," she snapped.

"Rita," I returned as I pushed my door open. I barely stepped through when she knocked the door even wider, pulling the knob from my hand. It banged hard against the wall.

"You think this is funny?" She raised her voice as I turned around. I'd moved far enough into my apartment that she could shut the door. Rita didn't bother with the lock. Maybe that meant she wouldn't be staying long.

Dear God, I hoped she didn't stay long.

"Why would I think you showing up here is funny?" I

raked a hand through my hair. It was a tell, but the only one she'd get.

"Because your sorry ass is smirking." Rita gestured to my face with red tinting hers.

I wiped my hand over my mouth. Damn it. My lips were formed into a slight smile. Not for the reasons she thought. She had always been angry. A quick trigger. A loose cannon. Her barging in and banging my door against the wall was exactly like her.

As comforting as it was painful. A reminder of what I'd once wanted for myself.

"What are you doing here?" I asked calmly.

She backed up, shaking her head as her mouth fell slack. The hurt pushed the hate out of her eyes, and I winced. I didn't want to hurt her. That wasn't what I'd ever wanted.

But what good would it do to say that? It would give her false hope and make me feel like shit.

"You don't care. You really don't give a shit about me? About us?" She stared at me a second longer before her top lip peeled up and her nose wrinkled. Even her hands balled up into tight fists. It was a quick transition from hurt to fury, yet the process happened so slowly, I clocked every change in her body language.

As much as I hated to admit it, I soaked it all up. Every single fucking detail. Once she was gone, it could be the last time I ever saw her. I had to make this time count for something.

"What do you want me to say?" I breathed through my nose to keep my voice calm. It was almost impossible when I wanted to scoop her up in my arms, drop her on the table, and fuck all her emotions right out of her until only a bundle of sated sweetness was left behind.

"I want to know how you fucking survived being shot and falling over a cliff!" she screeched.

Flinching, I turned away. Just like upstairs, I couldn't hold her gaze.

"How? How did you do it? Did you plan it? Was that what you wanted all these years? An opportunity to leave us all behind? Nevermind how much we did for you? The history between us? We still had your fucking back once you left! You know how hard that is to swallow knowing you left me on purpose. Twice!"

Her eyes were red and the pain rolling off of her was so palpable, all I could do was move away from her. I'd done this, and I didn't want to face the consequences of my actions. Why should I have to when it was better for everyone that I left?

"How?" She followed me. Then her palms crashed into my chest. "How, Matías!" She pushed me again.

I caught her wrists, and finally faced her. *"I almost died!"*

Our chests expanded and contracted at matching, brutal speeds.

Silence descended between us and time seemed to slow. It didn't matter if she knew this.

Softening my voice, I said, "I did almost die. I would have, but a fisherman saved me. He pulled me from the water when I was barely breathing. It took months after that to heal, to fight infection."

Somehow, I'd also had just enough brain cells to cut out the tracker Doc had placed under my skin once upon a time. Otherwise, all of my efforts to escape would have been in vain.

But now Rita was here...

I rubbed the spot on the right side of my chest where the bullet had passed through.

Rita closed her eyes, then sucked in micro-breaths. She didn't like hearing this.

"Why, Matías? Why did you not love me the way I loved you?" Her hands sifted in my hold and when she opened her eyes, they were glassy.

So many fuck-ups in my life were because of Vicente and his drive for power and entertainment.

This one? Hurting a good woman? This was all my own doing.

Maybe I could have handled our break up differently. Not been such a coward. I should have, but there was nothing to do about it now, except to tell her the truth and hope she left it alone.

"Vicente wanted you dead," I said, my voice strained.

Her head jerked back and some of her fire returned. This woman, she flipped between emotions like channels on the TV.

"You can't be serious," she whispered, her nails starting to dig into my chest where they rested.

"Every single decision in my life has been driven by that man. To keep the people I loved safe. I would die before I saw Vicente kill you."

"He's dead now, Matías. He has been for a long time." Disbelief colored her words.

"Then Valentina was a problem for everyone. I wasn't going to make her yours." She had to understand that I would make every choice all over again. For her.

"She's dead too! For a long time, Matías!" Each word was louder than the last. Her curls bounced as her temper soared.

"I know that!" I gripped her wrists, pressing them deeper against me.

"Then why didn't you come back for me?" She screamed, trying to jerk her hands away, but I tightened my hold.

It was fucked up, but I reveled in the touch of her skin. I needed the contact for just a little longer.

"Because I couldn't!" I shouted. Fuck. I didn't lose it like this. Rita did. I was the voice of reason, the mask. Collecting myself, I pulled her arms around me, forcing the hug. She let me, but not without a heavy dose of suspicion in her eyes. "Andre and the others were taking over the Institution. If I'd stayed, more people would have died. Loyalties would have been divided."

"They'd never let that happen. It wouldn't if you'd just stood together," she argued.

I shook my head. "The Institution isn't like the Dirty Dogs. Men would have fought just because they could, if they thought it would gain them more power. Or if they thought I was the ticket to the ways of the old Institution."

"You're delusional." She tried to step back, but I cupped her cheek and she froze. Her nostrils flared as she dropped her gaze to my throat.

"No, I'm not. They needed me gone to take the head of the Institution. I needed to stay gone to figure out who the hell I am. As much as I wish it wasn't true, everyone is better off without me there," I said softly.

Her gaze snapped up. "You wanted to leave," she accused.

"I had to."

"Because you didn't want to live the crime life anymore." A statement. An accusation.

"I couldn't keep watching the people I cared about die!"

"You cared about Amorette! You found her sister for her! You knew she'd make contact and tell them you were alive! You *care* so fucking much about Amorette and your brothers who, for years, never gave a shit about you. What about me?" She yanked herself out of my arms and slapped her chest. "What about the Dirty Dogs?" Her voice started to shake. "What about Javier? We were there for you! Always fucking there for you!"

I pressed my lips together. "So what? You think just because Vicente's dead, everything is magically fixed? People aren't territorial or money hungry anymore? If I came back to the Dirty Dogs, that would have started a different kind of war."

One I would never allow. I cared too fucking much about all of them. About Rita.

"It was better to make a clean break. To let you forget me!" Did she think that was easy for me? To constantly walk away from what I wanted? What I needed?

I was making this new life for myself because it was the best I could do for *them*.

Fuck, my entire life had been a black cloud. For a second, yes, I enjoyed what it felt like to breathe without looking over my shoulder. I fucking enjoyed it.

But I never would have come here if it wasn't for her. For Javier. For my brothers.

All I did was make decisions based on everyone else's safety.

"Javier had a heart attack, Matias." Rita threw her hands down toward the floor. "Who did he ask for when he woke up? You! He said you should be there. That you had to really be dead, otherwise you would have come back to see him. To see us." She spun as my world expanded and contracted to that moment.

Javier was more like a father to me than Vicente ever was. He was the reason I was alive.

If he'd had a heart attack...

He was going to go out in glory. In the heat of a battle, not because of some fucking heart attack.

My vision wavered and cotton filled my ears.

"He's okay?" I asked, but the words sounded far away.

Glancing over her shoulder, she nodded. I released the breath I'd been holding.

Then her phone buzzed.

We stared at each other for a few seconds. Then in slow motion, she pulled it from her bag.

She didn't have to tell me what happened. I didn't have the courage to ask what I already knew.

Her face crumpling said it all. Then her wail. I rushed to her, gathering her in my arms as hot tears fell on my arms.

"No, no, no. This isn't right. This isn't happening. We have to go back, Matías." She dropped her face against my shoulder. "We have to go back."

"I can't." I gulped.

"What do you mean, you can't?" The question was a cry all on its own. She didn't understand. I didn't know how to make her understand.

"It would undo everything I've done for you. For them. I can't." My own eyes misted over. I couldn't fall apart. I needed to be strong for Rita until I could get her on a plane.

"You're really doing this?" It was almost a plea. "Come back with me." A desperate order.

"I can't." My fingers flexed against her back.

Then she lost it. Tearing out of my hold, she was a tornado, destroying everything she could get her hands on.

The cheap paintings on the wall. The glass on the table. The wooden chairs.

"I wasted the last three days getting here! I wasted the last precious hours with my *papá* for *you*? For nothing?" Her voice was so deep with grief, the boom of it echoed in the cramped space. Even the furniture crashing against the floor wasn't enough to overshadow it. "You're not worth it. You never fucking were. I–I can't stay here."

She raced for the door.

I had words stuck on the tip of my tongue. *Don't leave. You can't be by yourself right now. I need to help you get to the airport.*

Yet, I was glued to the floor, and my mouth sealed tight. She was better off without me.

Wasn't that the lie I'd been telling myself for years?

6

ESTEBAN

"I'm staying." I raised an eyebrow at Ricco and dared him to argue with me. He was Javier's oldest friend and second-in-command of the Dirty Dogs. Not that that meant shit with how we ran, but it was what the world saw.

"Kid," Ricco sighed, shaking his head at me.

"Ricco," I warned.

"He's passed out. He's doing fine. He won't wake up until morning. Javier will feel like a little bitch if he thinks we have to babysit him. It will fuck with his head. Make him worse than he actually is."

"Don't give a shit. I'm staying. If Rita can't be here, I will." She loved Javier more than herself. It was fucked she'd even leave to get Matías, but something Javier said made her think that he wanted him here.

He probably did. It was no secret that Javier viewed Matías as a son. But Rita needed to be here with her father, not tracking down an asswipe who went to extreme lengths *not* to be here.

"Suit yourself. But Esteban..."

I already had one foot in Javier's private room when Ricco placed a hand on my arm. Glancing back, I met his stare with a cool gaze of my own. He wasn't going to talk me out of this. No fucking way.

Take Rita out of it. I cared about Javier too.

"We all know you fucked Rita–" I sucked in a sharp breath. "But it was just that. Fucking. Everyone but you, knows that."

My top lip curled. This was what he wanted to say? Right now?

"What the fuck is that supposed to mean?" I stepped back out of Javier's room and let the door close.

"Listen, you're a fucking fantastic Dirty Dog. You have been from the very beginning, but you're still a kid–"

"I'm twenty-four years old, Ricco. I'm not a fucking kid."

"And Rita is twenty-seven." He let that settle between us like his words would flip a switch in my head.

I scoffed and turned for the door. "Doesn't matter. We're not together, and it goes against everything in the Dirty Dogs for you to stick your nosey ass in my sex life."

"Not when it comes to Rita. She's as much a Dirty Dog as you are. More. I'm just looking out for you."

Waving my hand, I opened the door to Javier's room, slipped inside, and shut Ricco out.

My nostrils flared and my forehead throbbed from the mild headache Ricco only made worse.

I didn't need that shit. Neither did Rita or Javier.

Releasing a breath, I rolled my head from shoulder to shoulder, forcing the tension from my body. Once it was as gone as I was going to get it, I took the chair next to Javier's bed.

He turned his head my way and gave me a sleepy-eyed look. "Ricco's a fucking Mary Sue with that shit."

I snorted. "You heard him?"

"The dead heard him." He grunted as he tried to scoot up in bed. I bent forward to help but he shooed me away. "Get the hell away. I don't need help. I'm fine."

He said that, but he ended up staying in the same spot with his head resting on the pillow. He was a sharp old man. Loyal as they came, and quick on his feet. Old as shit too.

For a man who ran a deadly gang in South America, he also had a sweet look about him. Like he was someone's happy grandpa.

"Yeah, yeah." I humored him and flopped back in the chair.

"Ricco's right, you know."

I sighed. "Not you too. I'm here because you're here and Rita's not. I care. Get over it."

"Not that." He mashed his lips together and closed his eyes. "The other thing."

"What other thing?" I asked, but made it clear in my tone, I'd rather not have this conversation at all.

"We all know you fucked my baby girl."

What? I scrunched my face up. "I'm not talking about this," I seethed. "Unless you want to rehash your public fucks in the club." There were many, and I'd witnessed more than I liked to admit.

His chest compressed with his loud exhale. "She's always liked you. But you're not Matías."

I couldn't blink. I didn't twitch.

The only thing I could do was sit there staring blankly at him. He actually just said that.

Javier pulled the rug from underneath me and idly watched me flailing on my back like he hadn't hit me in the gut with his fucked up truths.

"Matías was her one. *Fuck*." He coughed, and grabbed his

chest. Not in danger of another heart attack. Probably from the tender muscles. "Damn, he was my one too."

I ignored the disbelief coursing through my body. I kicked aside the doubt his words were creating inside me and focused on how insane his words were.

"What the hell, Javier?" I finally found my voice. "You can't hold onto someone when they don't want you." *I* fucking knew that. "And what does that even mean, he was your one?" I parroted back to him.

"I wanted him to lead the Dirty Dogs. Steal him away from Vicente."

Gripping the ends of the armrests, I fought the urge to shake some sense in him. Every muscle in my body was strung tight.

"Why? We don't need him," I gritted out. It was harsh, but the man jumped ship at first convenience. He was nothing. No one.

"Yeah?" He asked sardonically. "Did you get any messages today at the shop?"

I stuck my tongue between my teeth, almost biting it off. Javier wanted an answer and I couldn't avoid it forever. "A nice flower arrangement with a sarcastic get well soon card," I bit out.

"What else did you hear?" he prodded.

Javier knew all this already. "The new gang is setting up shop on the corners."

He nodded. "And I'm laid up in this hellhole. It's a weakness we can't afford. Just Matías' name is scary to motherfuckers like that. Hell, he wouldn't even have to do anything. Just being head of the Dirty Dogs would be enough to keep away all the fucking posers."

What the hell was it about that guy? Was his dick made

of gold? That might work for Rita, but what *the fuck*? Javier too?

"He's a coward, Javier. He left. Broke Rita's heart. He's not worth shit," I spat as my head felt increasingly stretched from the pressure inside it.

"You don't understand how the heart works. Not Rita's."

I jumped out of my chair. I couldn't believe this shit. "Is this what you want for her? Someone who will leave her over and over again? Someone who's too afraid to take her back when she needs it? To keep her safe when she fucks up?"

"And that person is you?" He glanced up at me, the edges of his dark irises cloudy from age.

"Damn straight, that's me. Whether she wants me or not." I heaved, losing my cool. "I fucking love her. Is that what you want to hear? She wants Matías' dick? Ricco's? Some fucking guy in the Bastard Brothers' company? I can't do shit about that. But doesn't it make you feel better knowing someone like *me*–" I thumped my chest. "–is looking out for her? Always?"

This wasn't what I had planned when I walked in here, but this aching need to get his approval, even if it was only on the surface level, clenched in my gut. I needed him to tell me I was good enough.

Shit. I'd never thought about it but now that it was out here, I needed it.

All Javier did was look up at me with a ruthless sort of pity in his expression. His lips tugged down into a frown like he was measuring his words before he told me how much of a failure I was.

But I wasn't. I was far from it.

I worked my ass off for the Dirty Dogs. I won deals,

delivered punishments, solved problems the old assholes tinkered over for years.

"It's not you, son."

I closed my eyes. Javier was like a father to me. The man must collect fatherless sons for a hobby.

"Rita loves Matías. She always has."

"And you?" I opened my eyes and glared at him, refusing to let him see how his words seared me to the bone.

"He's the son I never had," Javier said softly. "If things had been different, he would have been the next President."

"It doesn't matter to you that he fucked off for selfish reasons?" I shouted.

"It matters because he's not here. I can't change the way it should have been."

"Fuck that. You can't live in the past. Placing all your hopes on one man and forsaking every opportunity after it, is stupid. Let go of the fucking past," I growled as I leaned over the bed. "Ricco was right. You don't need a babysitter. You're just fine. You'll always be just fine, right old man? Maybe the next time you wake up, Matías will magically appear. For you and Rita."

I stormed out, barely able to see where I was going from all the anger clouding my brain and vision.

Fuck, I'd never been this pissed.

He thought I wasn't good enough? That Matías was the magic bullet that was going to save the day?

Delusional was what he was. Fucking rocked in the head.

Matías was a selfish coward who only really cared about his brothers. Fuck everyone else.

I passed a handful of Dirty Dogs on night watch. Several tried to call out to me, but I ignored them.

Outside, I gulped down fresh air like water and hopped

on my bike. As soon as I kickstarted it, I ripped out of the parking lot. My body buzzed too much to head home, so I took the scenic route to clear my head.

It worked, for the most part.

By the time the sun was high in the sky, I was exhausted and drained just enough that I was numb.

The thoughts were still there.

I was only good enough for Rita to fuck.

I wasn't good enough for Javier.

Matías was the golden child, and for what? Doing absolutely nothing.

"Shit," I muttered as I climbed off my bike and pulled off my helmet. At least I was tired enough to sleep off the rest of my anger.

Javier didn't think I was good enough for shit? Fine, whatever. I was still a Dirty Dog.

I walked to the side door of the compound. This was my home as much as my house was and I'd be fucked if I let anyone scare me off.

As soon as the door opened, shouts and cries came from inside. I didn't think twice, just started running toward the main room.

What the hell? Some of the wives were here.

They were crumpled against their men or on the couches. Several of my brothers stood off to the side, blank eyed. Others hugged and buried their faces in each other's neck.

"What happened?"

Ricco glanced at me. "You didn't check your phone," he said. I pulled it out as he hustled my way.

There was a message sent out to the club chat.

Ricco: Javier passed. Blood clot.

That was it. All they'd written.

My head got light and I stared at the floor. My phone slipped from my fingers, busting against the concrete floor. Then in a swell of self-hatred I bellowed and turned to the wall.

I punched that motherfucker so hard, my knuckles split. The pain felt good. Like I deserved it.

I was an idiot. I should never have left his room. Why'd I let his words get to me? He hadn't said anything I didn't know. About him or Rita.

Yet, I made my choices, and I let my anger get the best of me and walked out.

And Rita...

I yelled again, getting all my rage out as I slammed my fist into the wall a second time.

"Stop, kid." Ricco pulled me back. But I was a beast. I fought him off of me, then the next Dirty Dog. Then the next.

Each time I clipped one of them with my hand or elbow, I felt a little more human. With the speed I was taking hits, they needed this too.

All that kept flashing across my face was Rita's beautiful pert nose and perfect face. Her devious cat eyes that held nothing back. And how devastated she was going to be.

We couldn't tell her.

How could we fucking not?

I flopped down on my ass and draped my elbows on my knees. We had to tell Rita. Catching my breath, I reached over and grabbed my phone. The screen was hard to see through the new cracks.

Me: Rita, baby...

I sent the message. Then without giving it too much thought, I broke the news. As quick as I could.

It took a minute, but she read it.

More than anything, I wished I could have been there with her.

I STOOD on the tarmac with my sunglasses shielding my eyes. For once, the heat coming from the pavement didn't bother me.

My thoughts were too consumed by Rita and being there for her.

Somehow, I'd gotten Ricco to tell everyone else to fuck off and let me be the only one to get her.

She'd appreciate that. Rita thought she was so badass, and in a lot of ways she was. Yet she was also as soft as any woman I'd met.

How many times had I heard her say tears were for weak people? *She* didn't cry.

But she'd be crying today. If not when she landed, as soon as she stepped off the plane. Because shared grief burst through the strongest of walls like a motherfucker.

Once her eyes met mine, she'd lose it.

And I'd catch her. Just like I always had and always would.

The distant sounds of the plane coming in started buzzing in my ears. Nice of Andre to let her use his private plane. He'd even sent her with his best pilot. It made for a quick return home.

No matter what I thought of them, he had my gratitude for taking care of her.

It was more than Matías had ever done for Rita. I just had to make her see that so she could move the fuck on.

The plane stopped not far from me. After five or ten

minutes, the door opened, and the stairs were attached. Then Rita stepped foot out of the plane.

She was stoic with her body armor on. That was her thing. Protecting herself with her skintight dresses and wicked high heels. It was an obsession as much as it was a crutch.

Her gaze locked on the steps as she descended and I walked her way, reaching the bottom of the stairs when she hit the last step.

Then she looked up, and her bottom lip trembled. Her eyes were bloodshot and swollen, lacking the heavy makeup she regularly wore.

"Esteban," she whispered as she doubled over.

"Shh..." I gathered her in my arms and lifted her against me. Her body wrapped around mine and I carted her away from the plane as she cried into my neck. "It's going to be okay."

"It's not. He's gone. *Papá* is gone. And I fucked up by leaving." It was almost a wail.

"It's okay. You were trying to give him something he asked for."

"Did he know he asked for that? I left before he was fully awake." Desolation was so thick in her voice.

Shit, it was hard to hear her beat herself up. I got it, but I didn't fucking like it.

"You did what you thought was right. He knew where you were. He loved you and knew you loved him."

I sat down in a chair outside the small private airport, arranging Rita on my lap. She cupped the sides of my neck and stared deep into my eyes. So much heartbreak stamped across her face. Even the tears caught in her lashes were devastatingly sad.

"I hate him, Esteban." Her brow furrowed and she bared her teeth. "I hate him so fucking much. I told him to come back with me, that *Papá* was dead and he just...he just...argh!" Another flood of tears fell, and I guided her head to my shoulder.

"Stop it. It's not worth it. You don't need Matías. You have the Dirty Dogs, and you have me."

She cried harder.

We needed to go. There were arrangements to be made, but I sat there holding Rita. She needed this more than anything else and I'd be damned if anyone stopped me from giving her what she needed.

7

MATÍAS

The liquor wasn't nearly as strong as the pull of home. Yet, it hadn't stopped me from finishing off half the bottle as I sat here in the most uncomfortable wooden chair I'd ever used. It wasn't even the right size, but the furniture that had come with the apartment was seemed miniature. My feet even hung over the end of the mattress.

The silence was a farce as the neighbors turned on their TV, coughed, or flushed the toilet. The noises were a reminder that there were people living their lives while my ass was glued to this seat.

My mind was alarmingly blank as I stared at the glass on the table. I slowly spun it around with my hand.

I'd been in this exact spot for at least a day . My phone had buzzed. Probably João, wondering where I was. But after the first hour, that had stopped.

Someone knocked on my door at lunch. That was most likely Pedro. I didn't move a muscle and eventually, the stairs creaked as he returned upstairs.

Nothing moved me. If given the chance, I could stay in this spot until I took my last breath.

That was what I wanted, wasn't it? To disappear and make everyone's life easier?

What was easy about that? What was right with it? Fair?

I barked out a laugh, then jumped. I startled myself with the break in silence.

Without any thought behind it, I picked up the glass and threw it against the wall. The high-pitched shatter accosted my ears as the pieces flew everywhere and liquid dripped down the wall.

Salty liquid entered the seam of my mouth and I used both hands to wipe my face. Fuck, I was crying.

I hadn't cried when Vicente died. I definitely hadn't shed one goddamned tear when Valentina died.

But Javier? That ripped my heart out of my chest. I could feel it now, like it had been a ghost hiding inside me all along.

But was it because he died, or because Rita used his last days to come get me?

She missed his passing because of *me*. Because he wanted to see me.

What was so fucking important that I had to stay away? Who was I protecting? Them?

Or myself?

It didn't make sense anymore. Did it ever?

Memories floated up to the surface of Javier over the years.

Him clapping me on the back, when I helped him iron out a deal. Javier sitting in silence with me after I had to watch my brother Grey whipped at the post when there wasn't a goddamned thing I could do about it.

Whenever I had to witness a new atrocity at Vicente's

hands, Javier offered a place to gather my thoughts and collect myself.

Then there was the conversation I had with him after my brothers' girl, Amorette, stabbed one of the Dirty Dogs.

"That fucker had it coming anyway." Javier shrugged. *"I'm glad she took care of the issue for me. Saved me a hell of a headache."* He'd laughed, then sobered up. *"I'm glad to see you with your brothers. It's the one thing you've always wanted."*

"You mean you weren't ready to welcome me into the Dirty Dogs?" I laughed it off as a joke.

He held my stare. "Matías, you're a Dirty Dog regardless of whatever shit you're doing with your brothers. You have our support. Doesn't mean I don't wish things were different." *Shaking his head, he'd walked away.*

The fuck of it was, the Dirty Dogs had come through for my brothers. It wasn't easy at first. I'd heard there were rumblings because they blamed them for my death, but in the end, they showed up when they were needed.

Unable to hold my head up any longer, it fell, my chin hitting my chest.

Rita? Even when she was furious with me, she gave it all away with her eyes.

I'd heard she'd befriended Amorette. She did that for herself, and because of the kind of woman Amorette was, but I'd bet she'd done that for me too. Because she thought I was gone.

Everyone in my life who mattered showed up for me over and over. In big and small ways.

Who did I show up for? No fucking one. But I'd tried my best, hadn't I?

Yet, I'd let Vicente and then Valentina dictate every decision I made.

They were dead. *They're dead.*

"You're fucking dead!" I screamed at the floor.

A jolt of electricity shocked me as a new purpose settled over me. Rita was right. I was letting the dead dictate who I could and couldn't love. I loved my brothers, regardless of how they viewed me. I loved Rita, even though I didn't deserve her. And I owed it to Javier to be there when they laid him to rest.

I raced to grab my phone and fired off a text to Andre. He'd meet me. If nothing else, he'd have my back if I needed it. Of that, I was certain.

Then I spent the next two hours cleaning out the apartment. It was pitiful how meager my belongings were, a testament that I didn't belong here.

Before the next morning, I chartered a private plane, and headed back to the place I'd never thought I'd go again.

Home.

~

"Sir," a woman said. "Sir."

I bolted upright, glancing around. The windows were shut, but I was surrounded by luxury airplane seats. All of them empty, but it was enough to remind me of where I was and where I was going.

"We're landing in twenty minutes." She pointed to the seatbelt and walked back up the aisle.

My heart thudded almost painfully, partly from bursting awake, and partly from nervous anticipation.

This was going to go really well, or really fucking poorly.

I headed to the bathroom and quickly cleaned up so I could return to my seat and buckle in. I could use a shower, but that could wait until later.

Once they opened up the plane and I stepped out, a

black SUV was waiting and a man who might as well have been my twin stood with his arms crossed. We were both the spitting image of Vicente, even though we had different mothers. Thick, dark hair, tan skin, and amber eyes. Only Andre was anal about everything, including his impeccable suits.

The wind picked up and fluttered said suit jacket.

I was really here.

Instant relief hit me square in the chest. Tossing my duffle bag over my shoulder, I sped up. I couldn't stop the grin from forming when I got close. Andre, the control freak, kept his level expression.

I hadn't expected him to be ecstatic when I came back, but I didn't care. I was happy to see the bastard. No pun intended.

"Hel–" I started to greet him, but I couldn't finish the word before his fist met my mouth.

"Ow!" I hollered, twisting away and covering my face. I dropped my duffle bag too. "What the fuck?" I yelled.

He waited for me to collect myself and stand up. When I turned around, he grabbed my shoulders and pulled me in for a hug, slapping my back hard. "It's good to have you home, you *pendejo estúpido*."

I returned the hug weakly. "That was an asshole thing to do," I gripped, but somehow, I was still grinning. When he stepped back, he mirrored my expression.

No matter what kind of shit storm I was about to stir up, Andre was happy to have me home.

That felt good.

The doors on the SUV opened and when I glanced over his shoulder, my grin morphed into a smile so wide, my cheeks hurt.

Parker leaned his elbow on top of the car by the front

passenger seat, smirking. He hadn't changed a bit. Still wearing his hair buzzed short and mischievousness ingrained into every inch of him. Lafe sat in the backseat but his head was turned our way. He wasn't smiling, but he wasn't not smiling either. It was a weird sort of calm I'd never seen on Lafe before.

He'd been an addict for years. All because of Vicente. But he'd never had the gaunt look about him. Grey and Andre had done a good job of feeding him proper meals to keep weight on him.

Then there was Grey walking around the back. "It's good to see you." He pulled me into a hug.

Where Andre and I took after our father. The other three took after their mothers. Their separate mothers. Not only were they my half-brothers, but they were each other's half-brothers.

Lafe's mother was Scandinavian, giving him light blond hair and blue eyes. Grey's mother had been Russian. Giving him darker blond hair and green eyes. But where Lafe had always carried a tortured look, Grey had the sharp features of a fighter that would stab you while you were down and smile about it.

Damn, it was good to see them all again. I hadn't expected them to have changed so much without changing at all. Leadership looked good on them.

I had a little more enthusiasm with Grey's hug, but I was still confused. When did we become a hugging family?

Parker appeared on Andre's other side and threw his arms around me. "I wasn't going to hug you, but since you said that, I figured I better," he snickered.

Dammit. I said that out loud.

Leaving one arm around my shoulders, he led me to the back door Grey had exited.

"I'd get out to greet you, but we can't leave our little bug alone," Lafe said as I peered into the SUV.

In the middle seat was a rear-facing car seat with a tiny baby inside. She was maybe five or six months old. Turning her head, she kicked her chubby little feet and grinned as she slobbered on two of her fingers.

"I'd like to introduce you to Cossette Black. Meaning little thing or people of victory. Take your pick." Parker shrugged. "Both apply."

I leaned inside the car to get a better look. She was gorgeous. Soft blond curls and bright blue eyes. Such rosy, fat cheeks. Reaching out, I touched the apple with the pads of my fingers.

She gurgled and started repeating some kind of sound over and over again. Lafe smiled and dabbed her face with a white cloth.

"She's stunning," I whispered as I flicked my gaze to Lafe, then twisted my head to Grey. There were only two brothers with blond hair. Amorette had black. "She kept Amorette's last name?"

"Well, dear brother..."

My heart contracted. Parker had never addressed me like that before, although that was how he spoke to the others.

"There are four of us, all with different last names. It would have been a bloodbath if Amorette had picked one of our last names for the baby."

"What about the father's last name?" I choked out, still caught up with him addressing me so familiarly, without any sarcasm.

Lafe lightly pinched her chin. "We didn't know the father at the time of the birth. So Black worked just fine." He didn't elaborate anymore.

"Here, take the front seat. Grey will slide in the second backseat and I'll sit next to my little victory." Parker tugged on the back of my shirt to pull me out of the seat.

I climbed in the front seat and waited for the others to get situated. "Where's Amorette?"

"With Rita," Andre answered nonchalantly as he put the SUV in drive.

I turned to look out the window, not wanting to reveal how just the mention of her name affected me.

"Ready to tell us the story yet?" Parker tapped the back of my headrest.

"Fuck off," I growled. He laughed.

"You did come back for Rita, did you not?" Parker said with a smile in his voice.

"What are you laughing about? Javier is dead," I snapped, then pinched the bridge of my nose. "I'm sorry. I didn't mean it like that."

The others were quiet for a beat.

"We didn't know him like you did, but of course the family has our condolences," Andre said as he flipped on the blinker. "We were starting to build a nice alliance and I only have good things to say about him."

"Except for when he thought we killed Matías to take over, you mean," Parker added with a snort.

"Parker!" Lafe yelled.

"It's fine." I raised my hand. I had allowed myself one contact, and he'd shared with me everything that happened. If Javier had seriously considered going to war with them over my death, I would have come back.

"But you're here for Rita. You can't lie to us," Grey chimed in from the back.

I twisted in my seat. He never got involved in these kinds of conversations. He held his silence more than the others.

"Why are you avoiding the question?" Andre asked, shooting me a quick look before taking his attention back to the road.

"I'm not." I stiffened. But fuck, I was.

I did come back for Rita, but if she didn't want me...I wanted to lick my wounds in private.

"Come on. We're all family here. We can't help you if you're not honest with us," Parker said in a light tone. Then it turned severe. "For once, be honest."

I swallowed the hard lump in my throat and shifted in my seat. "I came back for her," I whispered. "For Javier too. Because she came to find me and missed Javier's passing."

"We know. What else?"

"You know?" I faced Andre.

He dipped his head once. "We know. We gave her your location when she asked."

"You..." I curled my fingers into tight fists on my thighs. If Andre hadn't given her my location, she might have stayed with Javier. She wouldn't have broken in my arms when she found out about his death. She would have been–

"Whatever you're thinking, stop. She would have gone looking for you if we didn't give her your location. She's a bulldog when she wants something," Parker reasoned. He was right.

Releasing my breath, I tipped my head back. I wasn't even surprised they knew where I was.

"I love her." The words tore from my throat, but once they were out, I felt better. Lighter.

"Good. Admitting it is the first step. The funeral starts in an hour. We have just enough time to fill you in on a few things and get you changed. Did you bring a suit?" Andre took control, just like he'd been born to do.

I was supposed to have been the next leader of the Institution. But I didn't want it. I had never wanted it.

And perhaps, that was why I ran too.

"No. I didn't need a suit to be a tour guide."

"But you had access to a private jet," Parker pointed out.

"I accessed my accounts when I decided to come back. I hadn't touched them before then." I twisted in my seat. They probably knew that.

"Smart," Lafe muttered as he played with Cossette's toes. He was a man obsessed and I was happy for him. For all of them.

"Tell him about what's been happening in the Dirty Dogs," Grey said, leaning his forearms over the seat behind Cosette's car seat.

"Yes, let's get down to business." Parker rubbed his hands together.

They filled me in on some things I hadn't heard, and by the time we got to the funeral, I'd made up my mind.

I was staying. For good. This time Rita was going to be mine, the way she always should have been mine.

Once we were out of the SUV, Grey strapped Cossette onto his chest in a baby carrier. With me leading in the center, they fanned out behind me.

We walked into the Dirty Dogs' compound as a unit.

8

RITA

The Dirty Dogs had clubs, shops, and other businesses, but the compound was our safe haven. Where we could just be ourselves. Sometimes with our families and sometimes with our friends if they were trusted.

It was fitting that we had *Papá's* funeral here.

The back courtyard was decorated by some of the women. I'd overseen it all. Making sure it was classy and tasteful, but still screamed Dirty Dogs. It was harder than you'd think it was to hit both aesthetics.

Soft music played in from the speakers set up in the corners and there were tables of snacks on the side along with a few kegs.

Papá's casket was close to the building, in the center. It wasn't open.

I couldn't handle that.

"This turned out nice," Amorette said from beside me as she surveyed the crowd of Dirty Dogs.

"What? Because we can be well behaved?" I asked wryly.

Her shock was a nice distraction from the gaping hole in my chest.

"What?" Her head popped back. "No, of course not. I mean, the events Vicente threw in the Institution were lavish and pretty similar to the upper echelon of the US, I'd imagine. The two times I've been to a Dirty Dog club, it was..."

"Wild?" I supplied for her as I linked my arm through hers.

One side of her mouth twisted up. "Sure. We'll go with wild. You were there for one of the times." Amorette glanced up at me, her eyes sparkling.

I groaned. "Please don't bring that up again." We'd gone months and months without reminding me about that night with her and Parker. Then I mentioned it, and now her. Why was it on our minds so much now?

Ricco met my gaze from across the yard. He excused himself and walked toward me with his head down.

"Rita," he murmured, pressing a kiss to my forehead. He'd been like a crazy uncle when I was growing up. I'd never really been sheltered from the Dirty Dogs' ways. I'd always been aware of how out of control and free they were.

Ricco had been a staple in those memories, both because of his ruthless defense of the club and his silly antics to make me smile when I was a child.

"Hey," I said softly. I wasn't one to ever be at a loss for words. If I didn't have anything to say, I had an expression chocked full of attitude to share. Except today, none of that seemed appropriate.

"The boys and I have everything sorted for the club, so I don't want you to worry about anything."

I pinched my brows together. "What do you mean?"

"We're going to hold a vote for the next president. You can be present if you want, but I'm telling you, no matter what, you're going to be taken care of." He rested a meaty hand on my shoulder and squeezed in what he probably thought was a comforting gesture.

It wasn't comforting.

I twisted my head to the side and tried not to lose my shit.

Another president. Javier was no longer the head of the Dirty Dogs. I was still a fucking Dirty Dog and he thought I would need to be assured of that.

My breath came faster and I struggled to control my emotions.

"Rita?"

"Get the fuck away from her." Esteban. His hand slipped around my back as he turned me into his chest. Usually, I'd step away, not show any of my private life to the club, but right then, it felt good.

"Kid, I'm just letting her know–"

Esteban's body shook as if he was shaking his head. I just buried my face deeper into his chest.

"I know what you're trying to do," he said quietly. Firmly. "But now isn't the time to get into the politics of the club."

Ricco made a short noise like he was gearing up to argue, but he sighed. "Fine. Rita, *cariño*, if you need anything, let us know. Every single one of us would bend over backward for you."

Esteban rubbed a soothing hand up and down my back and I let myself get lost in the motion. I didn't cry. I'd already sobbed a million tears and I was done. I *wanted* to be done.

When Ricco was gone, I raised my head. Amorette was still next to me, watching with concern.

She was the sweetest.

"You've got to be fucking shitting me," Esteban growled as his arms tightened around me in a hug. It was hard to twist around, but I managed.

Holy shit.

"Is that?" My jaw slackened.

"Matías." There was a light note in Amorette's voice I couldn't place.

There was no lightness inside of me. None.

It didn't matter that Matías was as darkly handsome as he'd ever been in a pressed black suit. It didn't matter that he had his brothers around him how he'd always dreamed of. It didn't even fucking matter that they all looked intimidating as hell even though Grey had my precious little pearl strapped to his chest.

The only thing running through my mind was how this was Matías' fault.

It was irrational, but I needed someone to blame. The stinging fire burning inside my stomach and chest said Matías was the one to get it all.

It hurt to look at him, yet I couldn't tear my eyes away.

Esteban grunted and I glanced down. I loosened my hands and stopped digging my nails into his forearms.

"Don't think about it," Esteban whispered in my ear.

"What is that supposed to mean?" I snarled. This anger was a breath of fresh air. I wanted to lean into it. Revel in it. Fan it enough that it pushed any grief out of my head and heart.

"You have that look about you that you get before you fuck somebody up. Now's not the time."

I glanced up at him through my lashes. He really was beautiful. Rugged, and handsome like any playboy. But it had been his top tier flirting and playfulness that drew me in that night.

Esteban had an ease about him that everyone liked. A charm that drew people in like magnets.

All of that was gone now as he glowered at Matías. Our shared energy hyped up my already wild emotions and when I glanced back at Matías, I raised myself up to my full height.

On four-inch heels, I was only a few inches shorter than him.

His regret was in his eyes as he stared down at me. For a second it tugged at my heartstrings, but I focused on how my love for this man had done nothing but cause me pain.

This was the last straw. I was done with him.

"What are you doing here?" I asked.

Around us, the crowd was murmuring. Some excited, some shocked. It wasn't a secret Matías still lived, but no one had expected him to come back in such a public way.

"Making things right." His voice was calm, just like he always was. I used to admire his ability to remain so unbothered, but now I wanted to rip his tight control to shreds.

"What thing is that?" I asked, then cocked a hip and pursed my lips. I did not want him here, and there wasn't a way I could make that clearer.

"Being here for Javier."

I swallowed but held his lying gaze.

"Being here for you," he finished softly.

"I don't want you here," I spat.

"Rita," Amorette murmured as Matías blinked swiftly. He wasn't sure how to respond to that.

Did he not think that was a possibility? That he would come here and I wouldn't want to see the face that broke my heart over and over again? That everything would magically go back to the way it had been years ago?

Like fucking hell.

"You don't have to leave," Esteban started and I stiffened. Who was he to say that? "But you need to let Rita have her space."

We had a crowd now. Outside of us, the music was the only thing in the background. Everyone was waiting to see what would happen with Matías.

Matías didn't even give Esteban the courtesy of a glance. He kept his gaze glued to my face, his eyes constantly flicking back and forth between my eyes.

Gritting my teeth, I wrapped my fingers around Esteban's forearms, being careful not to get him with my nails. He just pulled me tighter against his body.

A curl of guilt rose in my stomach but I forced it away. I'd done nothing wrong and I refused to let my fucked up emotions make me feel otherwise.

"Is that what you want?" Matías was always so fucking cool.

Even when he walked into his neighbor's apartment, I wanted the satisfaction of catching him off guard. Of throwing him for a loop. But the man had acted as if he expected me there every single fucking day.

Then in his apartment when I'd found out about *Papá*...

In his apartment, he'd caught me when I fell, but that was it. He didn't care enough to leave with me. He hadn't shown any reaction at all.

So what was this? A bout of guilt that made him come running? A weak-ass excuse.

Tears swam in my eyes as I directed all my hate his way. I wanted him to feel how much I didn't want him anymore.

"Stay, go, I don't fucking care, but don't come near me." I

pulled myself from Esteban's arms. He reluctantly let me go, trailing his fingers across my stomach before letting his hand fall away. It was intimate. Something a lover would do.

That was the exact moment Matías seemed to realize Esteban was even here. His gaze snapped to Esteban, and for a few moments, they were locked in a deadly stare down.

A dark smirk curled Esteban's mouth, so different from the carefree smile he usually showed the world.

"What? You thought your toys would stay yours when you weren't here to play with them?"

"You fucking–" Matías dove for Esteban, but Andre caught him around the stomach. Swinging him around, Andre and Grey pushed Matías back. "She's not a fucking toy."

Esteban hadn't even flinched. He had been ready, as if he expected Matías to attack. Loosening his shoulders, he nodded. "You're right. She's not. Rita isn't a toy. She's not disposable, and she damn sure isn't forgettable. All things *you* seem to forget. Don't worry, the Dirty Dogs know exactly what she's worth."

Some of the crowd whooped. Some boo'd. There was a divide between who was happy with Matías' presence and who wasn't.

Stepping back from his brothers, Matías yanked his suit jacket down in quick, harsh motions. "Not for a second did I ever think any of those things about Rita." He met my gaze with a steely look. "Never."

Then he spun and sauntered toward the wall. Parker kissed Amorette on the head and followed Andre to the spot Matías claimed.

Grey and Lafe lingered.

Releasing a breath, I smiled at Cossette. She frowned, her little brain understanding this wasn't a happy place.

When I touched her foot, some of her sunny exuberance returned and she gave me a toothy grin.

"It's a good thing he's back," Amorette said out of the corner of her mouth.

"Mmhm."

"Leave it alone," Grey warned Amorette.

She tipped her chin up, but didn't say anything else.

It was time to start the funeral.

The way Dirty Dogs celebrated life was probably different from the rest of society. We partied hard and told stories around the fire.

Glancing up, the sun had just gone down and the stars were starting to come out.

I walked toward the makeshift platform. Someone handed me a bottle of liquor as barrels were rolled out. Once I was above the crowd, I whistled.

"It's a sad day when Javier Aguilar is no longer with us. He was a great man. A great leader. And a great father." My voice broke at the end. Esteban sidled up to the front of the stage, watching me with a steady support I hadn't known I'd needed until that moment. "Tonight is a celebration! Of his life and his memory! Light the barrels!"

Men tossed lit pieces of paper into the barrels that had been prepared specifically for tonight. They went up in flames and the crowd cheered.

"Until the sun comes up, the Dirty Dogs do what we do best! Fuck it up!" I raised one fist in the air, and used the other to bring the bottle to my lips.

The liquor was warm, adding to the burn as it went down my throat.

When I dropped my head, Ricco and Esteban were there to help me off the platform. As much as I tried to ignore him, Matías was in the crowd, with a perfect line of sight to me.

People crowded around him, clapping him on the back, welcoming him as if he'd never left. Yet his eyes never left me.

Something told me he'd find me before the night was up.

9

RITA

"No, I can't," I forced a smile and pushed away the bottle. Every Dirty Dog wanted to have a drink with me in honor of *Papá*.

I was moving quickly past buzzed and if I didn't call it quits, I wouldn't be able to remember anything from tonight. Even in my relaxed and numbed out state, I wanted to remember.

Yet, I enjoyed the soft humming under my skin. It was warm and built a wall up around me that even the darkest parts of sadness couldn't penetrate. I fucking loved it.

Sweat rolled down the back of my neck and I twisted my hair up into a messy bun. Not securing it, just holding it in my hand as I tried to cool down. It was a hot summer night and the barrels only added to the stifling air.

Esteban pressed a cool beer bottle against my nape and I gasped.

"It's hot. Why don't we go inside?"

I nodded. That sounded like a fucking fantastic idea. "Let's get out of here."

We took two steps toward the door, but Leo, one of the

new guys, called Esteban's name. He cursed under his breath. "I'll be right back. Wait for me?"

"Hell no. It's hot." My words weren't slurred. That was a win. Yet when I walked inside by myself, I teetered to the right. "Fuck," I muttered to myself.

It wasn't that much cooler. There were a couple old air units, but we didn't use them that often. With such a massive garage space, it was a waste of energy.

And it was gloriously empty. For once, everyone was outside having a hell of a good time, exactly like *Papá* would want.

Papá. I sucked in a breath.

No. I wouldn't go there. I wanted to enjoy this break from emotions for a little longer.

Passing the stairs up to the rooms, I headed toward the makeshift bar. When *Papá* had remodeled this place, he had a set of counters added in the back. They were in a separate room and not really a kitchen, although there was a sink.

The only times I could ever remember the Dirty Dogs using them was for potluck cookouts.

I sighed when I flipped on the light. Bottles lined the counter like someone had been collecting them and bringing them in here instead of tossing them in the trash.

At least it was cooler. Someone had turned on the air so instead of Satan's asshole, this room was set to a hot breeze in hell.

Walking to the sink, I was going to run the cold water to splash over my face. I didn't make it there.

"Rita," Matías said softly behind me.

I jumped, spinning around. "Jesus Christ! You scared the shit out of me!" I pressed a hand against my chest, willing the suddenly out of control muscle to chill out.

"Can we talk?" He watched me with sad, puppy eyes.

"Fuck off." My voice was strong as I flipped him the middle finger.

"You came to bring me back. I'm back. For you." He took a step forward, determination etched into every line of his body.

At some point, he'd lost the suit jacket, and his sleeves were rolled up. The veins in his tanned forearms stood out and my traitorous thoughts were trying to tell me what a good idea it would be to trace them with my tongue.

"I changed my mind." Pulling back my shoulders, I dared him to argue.

Shaking his head slowly, he took yet another step forward. "It doesn't work like that. You can't stop loving someone just like that."

That calm facade the liquor had tricked me with, cracked. Peeling my top lip up, I sneered at him. "It's not just like that, asshole. Didn't you ever hear that you can't truly love someone who doesn't love you?" I made a show of glancing up and down his body. "You said all the right words and did all the wrong things. I finally wisened up to the fact that you don't love me. You never did."

Hell, now that I thought about it, he hadn't even said the right words. I'd supplied what I'd wanted to believe. I was such a fucking idiot.

I turned back toward the sink, but he caught my arm and twirled me around.

"That's a fucking lie," he seethed as he glared down at me. His black eyebrows knitted over furious amber eyes.

"Oh, it is? You could have fooled me." I shrugged, like it was no big deal. "You only kicked me to the side for your brothers. And the one thing you did after you faked your death? You made *another* woman's dream come true." My voice cracked, dammit.

The numbness crumbled as I opened myself up to a house full of memories reminding me exactly how I felt when I'd found out he'd tracked down Amorette's sister.

The betrayal, the pain, the worthlessness.

I hadn't mattered to him at all. He'd cared more about making another woman happy than me. I hadn't even warranted a goddamned email.

"Fuck." I dashed my hands across my face, wiping tears that sprang up quickly.

Matías' gaze was glued to them as fury and guilt warred on his face. I shoved him away from me and it caught him off guard enough that he stumbled back a few steps. "Get the fuck away from me. You hear me?" I screamed. "I don't want to fucking see you. I don't want your pity. Your regret, or whatever else you're trying to do here. You should have stayed in Portugal! That's what you wanted right? A life away from me?"

"That's what you think I want?" He yelled, throwing one hand out. "You think I wanted to leave you? I did it to fucking *save* you! You're the only good thing that ever happened to me!"

"Then why did you find Grace for Amorette?" My voice was a screech, clawing against the sensitivity of my own ears. "Why not call me? Why not take me with you?" I slapped my hand over my mouth.

What was I doing? Even if he'd offered, I wouldn't have gone with him. Would I?

All my dumb ass did was hand him ammunition about how much I loved him. He was a man. He would use this against me somehow.

At one time, I wouldn't have thought Matías would hurt me.

But he'd proved me wrong. He showed me I had to take

care of my heart with *everyone*. My instincts weren't to be trusted.

He fucking broke my trust in myself.

"Rita..." His voice was strangled. "I...*fuck*," he sighed. "I didn't think that would hurt you."

"You didn't think I would find out, you mean." I nodded succinctly. "Because I. Don't. Fucking. Matter."

"Rita!" he snapped.

Matías picked me up and set me down on the counter. Bottles went flying as if he'd cleared them with his arm. Maybe he had.

I couldn't look away from his eyes. He was livid and his left eye twitched. I'd never seen him like this.

I'd never seen him anything close to angry with me. I wanted more.

"Admit it. You wanted to fuck Amorette."

"No," he ground out.

"Admit it!" I leaned close to his face so our mouths were only a breath apart. "You wanted to be part of that fucking brotherhood so bad, you wanted her too. I bet you were glad you'd already tossed me aside."

His hand snapped around my throat and he growled. My back hit the wall and he forced his hips between my thighs.

My eyelids fluttered and my breath quickened.

"The only thing I have ever wanted for myself is you! You were *mine*, Rita! Fucking mine and the only reason I walked away was because I loved you too fucking much! Javier knew that! Why do you think he didn't kill me on the spot?"

"Don't bring my *Papá* into this!" I kicked out my legs but it was useless. He was too firmly stuck against me.

"It's true and you know it! Javier loved you so much, if I didn't have a hell of a reason for breaking your heart, he would have gutted me."

The tears fell freely. I didn't try to wipe them away. Let him see how much he hurt me. That felt almost as good as his anger.

"And Amorette? Why find Grace?" I slapped my hand on his chest and shook it. "What did she have that made you want to take care of her so much? What didn't I have?" I ended on a sob, and the next thing I realized, I was pounding on his chest.

"I was fixing what Vicente and Valentina broke! That wasn't for her. That was for my conscience! And yes, for my brothers!"

"You were all I wanted! I hate you!" I cried. "I hate that I love you, you bastard!"

"I love that I love you! It's the one damned thing in my life I don't regret!" He gripped the hair on the back of my head to tip my lips up and he slammed his mouth against mine. Forcing his tongue inside, he fucked my mouth, blitzing my mind with the haze of his kiss.

Matías always kissed me like I was his last meal. The air he needed to breathe.

He pulled back and peppered kisses at the corner of my mouth then along my cheek. "You're mine. You've always been mine. From the first second I laid eyes on you."

His hand smoothed up my thigh. Then he gripped the side of my panties, yanking them down.

Heat curled in my stomach. Lust for Matías was a familiar thing. It was a comfort when everything else in the world was dangerous.

My body recognized him, and I wanted this. I wanted him.

Like I had always wanted him.

I no longer tried to push him away. Instead, I pulled him closer, letting my hands roam over his body. He was more muscular than before. More toned. He fit against me perfectly.

My ass bounced against the counter as he lifted me just enough to clear the panties away completely. He tossed them to the side as he came back to kissing me.

I yanked his shirt apart, sending the buttons flying as I spread my legs wide.

He worked his pants open with one hand. "I need you. I need you so fucking much." He dipped closer for another wet kiss, biting my bottom lip as he slid the thick head of his cock up my slit.

I groaned and dropped my head back. This was what I missed. This connection with him. This shared need.

It had always been different with Matías. It was the one time he seemed to break apart, to drop the mask. Sometimes I'd lie to myself and pretend I was the only one who saw him this way. That he really was all mine.

Shoving my hands inside his shirt, I closed my eyes at the feel of his hot skin.

This was real. He was here with me.

Matías knocked my hands away to yank the top of my dress down, freeing my tits and trapping my arms. He dipped his head and sucked a nipple into his mouth as he thrust inside.

Tossing my head back, I yelled.

He released my nipple with a pop. "I love your tits. Your ass. I swear, if I believed in such things, I'd think you were made for me. Everything I love about a woman wrapped up into one package. You." Moving to the other breast, he left suck marks across my sensitive skin before raising back up to look me in the eyes.

His hips pistoned against mine, our skin slapping together.

"You remember what you said to me in the club?" he panted, dropping his head so his lips brushed mine.

I groaned as his change in angle hit just the right spot. "No," I breathed. I tried to move my arms, but he tightened his hold on my dress.

He smiled against my lips and tingles shot from my core. I was close. So fucking close.

"You said I smelled like yours." He chuckled under his breath before grunting, his hips crashing harder.

Ignoring his words, I tried again to break his hold. "I want to touch you," I whined.

"Not this time. Next." He used his arms to jerk me forward, meeting him thrust for thrust. The motion was just enough to rub against my clit. The sparks turned painful as they spread across my lower stomach, and I let out a soft cry as I started to come.

"Ah, fuck," he grunted, thrusting even faster. Matías let go of my dress, and I could finally move my arms as he wrapped me up in a tight hug. Resting his head on my shoulder, he groaned as he shivered.

My heart raced and the sweat on my skin started to cool. Everything in the room became stark in the harsh fluorescent lights overhead.

"I love you, Rita. I love you," he whispered against my neck. "I'm sorry I never told you before. It will be different now."

Whatever was left of my buzz evaporated.

It *was* all different now. We were at *Papá's* funeral.

Oh, God. "Get off me." I shoved him away from me, then hopped down. "I can't believe I just did that." I searched the floor for my panties and when I saw them discarded on the dirty concrete, I snatched them up.

I couldn't put them back on. But the wetness between

my legs was a reminder I didn't want. I tossed them in the trash and grabbed a paper towel, frantically cleaning myself up.

"What's wrong?" Matías tried to touch me but I twisted my shoulders to avoid him.

"Get the fuck away." I couldn't even look at him. "I can't..." I struggled to breathe. "I can't believe I just did that."

"Rita," he said in a tense voice.

"Stop! Don't you get it! You're the reason I missed–" I couldn't stay here. Chucking the paper towels in the trash too, I fled the back room.

His footsteps followed behind me, so I picked up my pace. If I could make it outside, the Dirty Dogs would help keep him away. Even the ones who liked him. They loved me enough to protect me against him.

I burst through the doors, and instead of getting a wash of calm, I was faced with out of control shouting.

Up ahead, Esteban pushed through the crowd, heading for the source of the commotion.

I ran after him. The Dirty Dogs were out of control, but I couldn't make sense of what anyone was saying.

Ricco saw me and started shoving men out of the way so I could get through. Together we made it to the front.

At the gate to the property was a small group of bikers. Their weapons were drawn and pointed at the Dirty Dogs.

On the ground at their feet was a body, a dark pool of blood spreading underneath him.

Next to him, flowers scattered the ground.

"What's going on here?" Esteban shouted at the Dirty Dogs. Leo and Damen were huddled together, squaring off with the bikers.

"I just got a call that these pendejos are working the corners in our territory. Then these guys show up with a flower arrangement." Leo spat on the ground, practically vibrating from rage.

"We were coming to pay our respects." One of the men called as he reached down to feel for a pulse. Shaking his head, he stood up just as another bike roared around the corner.

The newest man came to a stop, pulling off his helmet in jerky motions and shoved it at one of his guys as he crouched down. His red hair was pale orange under the lights from the compound. When he stood up, he motioned for his men to pick up their friend.

He searched the Dirty Dogs before his gaze landed on Esteban.

Did they know each other?

Then it clicked. This was the trouble *Papá* mentioned. I wanted to slap my forehead. How had I forgotten about this?

"I tried to do this the nice way. But if he dies..." He pointed back at the man now cradled in his friend's arms. "All bets are off. This won't be a friendly negotiation for business you no longer do. This will be war."

The Dirty Dogs called out obscenities and insults. Most were too drunk to realize what kind of situation this was.

The bikers ignored it, maybe realizing that tonight wasn't the time, or maybe just afraid for their friend. In seconds, they were gone.

I wasn't a doctor, but I'd seen enough gunshot wounds. There was next to zero chance his friend would make it.

The Dirty Dogs didn't even have a president to lead us and we already had a war on our doorstep.

10

ESTEBAN

The roar of the bikers' motorcycles faded into the background, leaving us surrounded only by the sounds of music from the jacked up speakers and the crackling of the fire still burning in the barrels.

I could barely see straight after what I just saw. And I wasn't talking about this fucked up mess in front of me.

Some of the seriousness seemed to sink in as no one said a word.

Except for Leo. Fucking, idiot Leo.

He bounced on his heels. "We gotta hit them hard so they don't–"

I snatched him up by his T-Shirt and shook him, using every bit of strength I had to give him whiplash. "*Do you know what you just did?*" I shouted in his face.

Leo blinked, his eyes glassy from a night of binging liquor. "They're trying to take our territory." He raised his chin with mutiny in his eyes. This *pendejo* didn't understand anything about club life. Damen never should have brought him in.

"Who gave you the authority to make a kill in the name

of the gang?" I seethed. Even on the worst days, the Dirty Dogs did not kill without leadership's approval. Fights? Couldn't help it, but no outright murders.

"Who are you?" He spat to the side. "Just some mid-level Dog. Your word don't mean shit."

I wanted to squeeze his neck, to rip his head off, but I couldn't even fucking argue.

Shoving him away from me, I kept hold of his Dirty Dog vest, yanking it from his body.

"What the fuck!" He started to charge me.

The Dirty Dogs were crowded around us now. Ricco stepped up next to me and Damen pushed through and caught Leo's arm.

"You're right. I'm mid-level. I earned my place by being smart. Thinking with my head instead of my ego." I held his jacket up. "You're the low-man. After what you just did, you shouldn't even be here."

Matías pushed through the crowd and I gritted my teeth as my entire body became one giant muscle spasm.

He wasn't even back ten minutes and Rita jumped on his dick. Grey and Andre were at his back. The rest of the brothers took their girl and baby home hours earlier.

I pointed at him with the hand that held Leo's vest. "It was great to have you here to celebrate Javier with us, but I think it's time you go. This is Dirty Dog business." I glared at Matías.

I wanted him to know exactly how much I hated his ass.

His brow furrowed. "Rita–" Matías started to turn toward Rita standing across the circle, watching Leo and me with round eyes.

"Rita has not one goddamned thing to do with you. Call her tomorrow."

Damen whispered in Leo's ear but Leo didn't want to

hear it. He kept trying to shake Damen off. Leo was going to make a scene and I wanted Matías gone.

"Javier would want him here," Ricco said next to me. Some of the men in the crowd chimed in.

The tops of my ears burned as I glanced from Rita to Matías. Had she even been aware that I'd stood in the door as they'd fucked on the dirty counter? That's how the Dirty Dogs treated their pussy, not their wives and daughters.

I couldn't look at Rita anymore so I focused all my attention on the asshole I wished I could fuck up. Andre and Grey pulled themselves up, gearing for a fight. I wouldn't give them one. Not the kind they were after.

"Would he want a man here that treated his daughter like a whore?" I raised my voice so every fucking one in the crowd would hear me.

The tension was already high. When my question fully penetrated, they erupted into chaos. Men knocked into Andre and Grey. Joel, the third in command, tried to dive for Matías but Grey punched his shoulder, forcing him back and away from Matías.

Ricco placed two fingers in his mouth and gave a sharp whistle as Rita ran for Matías.

Fuck that.

I stuck my arm out to stop her in her tracks. Rita hit my arm and cut her eyes at me.

"What the hell are you doing, Esteban?" She *allowed* me to stop her. Her chest pushed against my arm lightly. Enough that to anyone else, she'd appear to be trying to get by me. If she really wanted that, she would already be at Matías' feet right now.

A smile threatened to break free. She had second thoughts, and I'd given her a chance to think about what she was doing.

Turning away from Matías, I caught her hips and pulled her toward me. "What are you doing?" I kept my voice low. The chaos reigning around us was enough to hide my words. "You fucked him on a sticky counter. He doesn't care about you. Not like you want him to."

Her eyes fluttered shut and the pain on her face hit me square in the chest. "I know."

Jesus Christ, that hurt.

"Get your hands off of her!" Matías had broken free of his brothers and the crowd. He grabbed my shoulder. I ducked half a second before his fist would have connected with my face.

For the first time tonight, pleasure shot through me. I couldn't wait to get my hands on this motherfucker.

Dropping the vest and letting go of Rita, I planted my shoulder in Matías' stomach and tackled him to the ground. I got one punch to his face. The sound of my fist hitting flesh did wonders to replace the sounds echoing from that back room.

Matías caught me under the chin and my head snapped back.

Shit. I let myself get distracted and he caught me off guard enough that he flipped me. It didn't last long before I got him on his back again. We were a tangled mess of arms, legs, punches, and jabs.

It felt just as good to take the hits as it did to deliver them.

Then I was lifted off of him, one Dirty Dog on each arm.

"Stay the fuck away from her," Matías growled, blood tricking from his nose and lips.

I licked the blood off my teeth and grinned. "Yeah? What are you going to do about it? Run off again? It will just make it that much easier for her to forget you ever existed."

He nearly vibrated with rage and his face twisted up.

"Just leave." Rita stepped between us, keeping her back to me and facing him.

"Rita," he said quietly, almost beseeching.

"Don't. Just. Don't." She sucked in a deep breath. "Esteban is right. This is Dirty Dog business and you and your brothers, no matter how much I like them, don't belong here."

Matías opened his mouth but Andre slapped his shoulder and whispered in his ear.

"Fine." He straightened his torn shirt. That was his first rookie mistake. He should have known from years of coming around Javier and the club that you don't wear a suit to a Dirty Dogs event, not even a funeral.

We were bikers, for God's sake.

Sometime while we were fighting, the crowd lost their bloodlust. As if an actual fight sobered them instead of hyping them up.

I watched the three of them leave, and once they were through the gate, I turned around.

It didn't matter that Matías had left. *I* was still jazzed. I wanted blood and I knew exactly where I'd get it.

"Ricco," I said without looking at him, leaving all my focus for Leo.

"Yeah, kid."

"We have a traitor on our hands."

"That's fucking bullshit!" Leo exploded.

Damen tried to calm him down. "Stop. You fucked up," he snapped at his friend.

"*I* fucked up? You're all a fucking bunch of pussies." Leo shoved Damen away.

You could hear a pin drop. That was how quiet it was after Leo insulted every single person here.

"What?" He raised his hands out to the side. "I made a stand. For the club. Those bitches are coming for *our* business and *our* territory. You want to sit with your thumbs up your asses? Fine. But I protect what's mine."

Rita started laughing. Ricco started to step forward, but she held a hand out, stopping him. Her raspy chuckle still filled the air as she took slow, methodical steps toward him. Her heels clacked against the pavement.

"What was your name again?"

I raised my brows. She knew his name. She knew everyone here.

"Like you don't know my name." Leo rolled his eyes as his face heated. He was trying to save face. Whether it was from her mild insult or how every single man and woman zeroed in on him and he was finally realizing exactly how much he fucked up.

"I know you're the last recruit in. I know you wear the vest, but you haven't earned it. And I know there's no place in the Dirty Dogs for your stupidity." Rita never raised her voice as she went toe to toe with him.

"Your opinion doesn't count," he spewed, but his eyes were wide as he flicked his gaze from one side to the other.

"Who told you that?" She tipped her head, curious.

"Everyone knows it. Even Damen–" He barely got his name out when Damen pushed the side of his head.

Leo popped over, stumbling several feet.

"Keep your fucking mouth shut," Damen growled.

"That's interesting. I didn't realize you didn't care about my opinion." Rita tipped her head to the side.

I stepped up behind her because no way in hell was I letting her be that close to Damen without me. His reaction to the few words Leo spoke said all I needed to know.

"What's interesting is that we've now got a gang war on our hands." Damen tried to change the topic.

Others shouted, but Rita raised a hand again. "I want to know. What's the big plot? You seemed happy enough when *Papá* was alive."

Damen pressed his lips together as he studied her. Then as if he figured it wasn't worth keeping anymore he shrugged.

"I was. But now he's not and we have to figure out who the next leader will be."

"We talked about this," Ricco said as he worked his way over to Damen.

"What the fuck, Ricco?" I asked. He was having conversations about leadership without the whole club?

Ricco glanced back. "You know we have to have a vote."

Rita laughed again, this time I winced. It was a nasty sound that scratched the back of my neck like brittle nails.

"Funny how *Papá* is fresh in the ground and you're all fighting like dogs over a bone." She dropped her head and rubbed her forehead. "Get lost. Get some sleep. Tomorrow, when we've sobered up, *I'm* calling a meeting. Twelve sharp in the compound."

She started to leave, but Leo finally righted himself.

Her steps slowed and she stared at him. "Except you. Until further notice, this is *my* fucking club and you don't have any place in it."

That's my girl.

Rita was Dirty Dogs. And she was going to clean shit up if they let her.

"I don't answer to bitches." Leo crossed his arms.

Rita paused her walk, and I froze from bending down to pick up his vest. This idiot didn't have a lick of self preservation.

"I can't help you. You're a lost fucking cause," Damen muttered as he melted through the crowd.

"Now, you see. *Papá* didn't raise me to believe I was less than a man. Are you saying that I'm not powerful in my own right?"

Picking up the vest, I joined Rita.

"That's because he babied you. No other woman in the gang gets the same treatment."

"Hm. Ricco, do you shit talk your old lady?"

"Hell, no."

"Robby, who runs your house?" she called.

"You know Stasia does!" he yelled back.

"Seems you're the only one who thinks that way. That tracks, because you're a danger to the club. No one shares the same asinine opinions as you." She tapped her full, red lips. "Dirty Dogs. This man, this *cabrón*, could be the reason we lose some of our brothers. He took that decision away from you. He thought he knew best. He's no longer a Dirty Dog anymore." Leo stiffened and his face mottled with purple. "The question is, after this disrespect, do we let him run and chase him down, or kill him on the spot?"

Every bit of color blanched right out of him.

"Kill him," I tossed in.

"Let him run! I need a good chase!" Due, my best friend, shouted. I couldn't make out all the votes. Everyone had an opinion.

Rita listened, then out of nowhere, her hand snapped forward and she held Leo's balls in her hand. He whimpered as her nails dug in.

"I don't mind a little blood, and unfortunately, we're safer without you on the run. Who knows what kind of trouble you could cause us." She gave a twist and he cried out.

I winced.

"Dirty Dogs?" Rita projected her voice.

We answered back with a savage bark.

"Take care of him." She squeezed so hard, Leo's eyes bugged out and his mouth fell open on a silent scream. When she let go, he collapsed to the ground.

The crowd parted for her and then descended on him. Grunts competed with the thumps of punches and kicks they delivered. Leo never made a sound.

Following after Rita, I tossed his vest in one of the barrels. It hurt my heart to burn the leather, but it was tainted now.

"Rita, wait up!" I jogged to catch up with her. She was already halfway up the stairs.

"What?" She didn't have the same sass she had outside. It was as if the testosterone from the men had held her up and now she was just depleted. Dark circles started to ring her eyes, and her mouth was set into a severe frown.

Rita was devastated and even still, she was the most beautiful thing I'd ever seen.

"Sleep in my room."

She cast me a suspicious glance, but I held up my hands. "I'm not going to try and fuck you. I wouldn't." I wouldn't dishonor her or Javier that way and the way her expression changed, she recognized it for the dig it was. "But we don't know what kind of shitstorm this is going to turn into. I want to make sure you're safe."

Releasing a sigh, she nodded as she pushed some of her hair out of the way.

I passed her and led the way. Once we reached my door, I unlocked it and let her in. Cool air washed over us.

"This feels nice." She hummed.

"I installed an air unit. I'm not like those other fuckers. I need cool air to get my beauty sleep." I turned the bed down and waited for her to climb in.

She didn't take the invite. Shifting on her feet, she eyed the bathroom. "Can I take a shower?"

To wash Matías off, she meant. Or I hoped.

"Yeah." I nodded toward the bathroom. Not everyone in the compound had their own, but I'd built a whole-ass bike as a trade for this room.

Once she was out and dressed in one of my shirts, I was already down to my boxers. I took a breath to fully appreciate how good she looked in my clothes. Then I sighed and lifted the covers. She climbed in against the wall, then I slid in after her.

This wasn't the first time I'd shared a bed with her, but at least this time I was sober. I wanted to remember every second.

Her head rested on the pillow as she stared up at the ceiling. "I'm surprised your room is so clean."

I scoffed. "You mean because I don't treat the room like a bachelor pad and fuck my way through bitches in here?"

She giggled softly. "I'm just surprised."

Rita grew quiet and I closed my eyes. "Get some sleep. Tomorrow is going to be a shit storm."

There was a tension in the air like she had something to say, but when I turned toward her, she shook her head.

"What?"

"I don't know why it couldn't be you," she whispered as she covered her face with her palm.

"Ouch," I whispered back, rubbing my chest.

"Shit! I'm sorry. I shouldn't have said that."

"No, don't apologize. But Rita, you've never given me a chance." I pulled her hand away so I could see her beautiful face.

"You want that? A chance?"

"More than any fucking thing."

She started to lean forward like she was going to kiss me but I placed a finger on her lips. "I can't. I saw you with him and I..." I groaned and flopped back on my back. "Try again tomorrow."

She was quiet, then there was a soft, "Okay."

Somehow, I fell asleep quickly and the next thing I knew, someone was banging on my door.

11

RITA

Bang! Bang! Bang!

I jolted to a sitting position as images of Parker on the ground and Amorette hovering over him scrolled one after another through my head.

Pressing my hand against my chest, I sucked in a deep breath. My heart was beating so fast, I couldn't count them if I tried.

Esteban ripped open the door to his room. "What?" he barked.

The memories dissipated and I was left staring at Esteban in all his glory. I never appreciated him how I should have.

Standing there with a lazy tent in his boxers, he was a work of art. Delicious tan skin that stretched taut over corded muscles. A strong jaw and full lips that could smirk better than the devil himself.

Yet, it was always his charm that got to me.

Not for the first time, I thought, *why couldn't it have been him?*

He was so uncomplicated. The man lived and breathed

the club like *Papá* had. He was sexy as hell, and made me feel like a queen.

I liked him, more than liked him, I'd simply been stuck on Matías for years. There was history there that was hard to erase.

Except, now when I looked at Matías, the fifteen minutes in the back room excluded, all I felt was resentment.

"Oh shit, I didn't realize Rita was in here." Due poked his head in and gave me a chin nod. Esteban straightened up and stepped into his line of sight.

"What do you want?" Esteban asked again, methodically enunciating each word. He was close with Due, more than he was to any of his brothers. It was odd how detached he sounded.

Due cleared his throat. He was also one of the officers, like Esteban. He wouldn't let Esteban pull rank on him, but he seemed to allow him this moment of anger.

When creating the Dirty Dogs decades ago, *Papá* had wanted to keep it simple. He'd installed three Vice Presidents to help him with the heavy lifting. They had the same title but they were still ranked by responsibility. There were six officers to run projects and oversee businesses. They didn't have autonomy to dish out punishments or make decisions, that was all *Papá* or on occasion the VPs, but they kept the gang running.

Then there was everyone else. All one-hundred-thirty-nine of them.

A great legacy.

"Leo's head is gone."

"So fucking what?" Esteban griped.

"So, we didn't take it. When I left the yard last night, Leo had been strung up as a traitor."

I tried to call up some empathy for the guy. He was

young, probably Esteban's age or a couple years younger, but he was an idiot who put every single Dirty Dog's life in jeopardy.

So there was no empathy. And when I'd walk by his body, I'd work damn hard not to spit on him for dishonoring *Papá's* day.

"Fuck," Esteban mumbled and tipped his head back.

"The VPs are calling the officers to do a search."

"Fuck them. Leo's head is the least of my concerns right now. I'll join you when I'm ready." He started to shut the door, but stopped when he caught Due staring hard at me. "And stop whatever thoughts you're thinking."

The door rattled when it slammed closed, and Esteban turned to face me.

He stood with his arms loosely by his sides, his chest rising and falling, his stomach contracting as my gaze moved down his body.

Now his half-erection was a full-on monster.

Desire curled in the pit of my stomach.

Turning my head, I swallowed hard.

"You can look, Rita. You can always take your fill any way you want it," he said softly.

I flicked my gaze back to him and the same dark desire filled his eyes. I bit my lip. Attraction was never the issue between us.

He'd just been a baby. Only a handful of years younger than me, but for a man in his early twenties, that might as well have been a decade.

"I don't want to hurt you." My face was aflame.

"You won't." He was so sure. So confident and cocky.

I wanted that. I wanted that kind of love, where I didn't have to worry about hurting him or him breaking my heart.

I wanted a man who wanted to shout to the rooftops that I was his.

Crawling out of bed, I pretended like I didn't want to climb him like a tree. "I have to pee." I rushed past him to the bathroom and took care of business.

When I came out, he had pulled on a pair of worn, dark jeans. Sitting on the edge of his bed, he rested his elbows on his knees and stared at the floor. Even like this, his body just begged to be licked and sucked.

Lines crossed his forehead when he glanced up at me.

I stopped in the middle of the room.

What the fuck do I do now?

I should be sending a text message to Amorette to let her know I needed some days off to take care of Dirty Dog business. She'd understand.

The meeting today was going to be a headache. I could be getting ready for that.

But I imitated a mannequin.

"I need to go check out what happened to Leo's head." His words snapped me out of my thoughts.

"I need to get ready for the meeting in..." I bent down and grabbed my phone where it lay next to my dress. At a whopping five percent. "One hour."

He got up and walked close to me. He wasn't as tall as Matías but he still towered over me when I wasn't wearing my heels. Esteban brushed a lock of hair away from my face. His gaze was confident and far too calm for my mess of emotions. "What do you want to happen, Rita?"

"What do you mean?" I asked, my voice barely more than a whisper. His dark chocolate eyes softened as he twisted his lips to one side.

"At the meeting. With the club. Between us. Take your pick."

I winced. I didn't fucking know. Last night when I called for the meeting, I'd been incensed. *Papá* started this club. It was his legacy, and they were making decisions and trying to assure me *I* wasn't going to be pushed out.

It was mine too.

His brows tipped up in the center, revealing a quick flash of hurt before he smoothed his expression out.

"Esteban..." I started. What did I say?

"It's not a big deal. I knew when we fucked, it was meaningless for you."

"It wasn't meaningless," I said, tone hard. "It was one of the best nights of my life." It had been. A great escape. A slew of fantastic orgasms. Everything I'd needed in that moment.

"Then what's the issue? You're stuck on Matías?" He shifted just a tiny bit closer.

"No. Yes. Fuck!" I tossed my hair back, thinking. "Yes, I *was* hung up on him. But you—us. You're a joker, the fun time guy. You get girls to drop their panties just by smiling at them and I..."

"You what?" He raised a brow, mocking me.

A fresh wave of anger ignited in my stomach.

"You think you're one of them? Just dropping your panties because I smiled at you?" His words were cutting.

"No, it's just....You're young, Esteban." Matías' maturity and strong silence had been like crack to me. So mysterious and addictive, thinking I was the one to get under his skin. Until I learned I was just another hopeless casualty of his whims.

I knew now, at least, I believed him, when he said it was because of his father. But then the question was *wasn't I worth fighting for?*

Esteban's hands snaked around my waist and he yanked

me against him, letting me feel just how much he wanted me. "I'm twenty-four. Not a fucking baby. I know what I want."

My heart pounded in my ears as I placed my hands on his chest. I almost didn't want to ask, but I did anyway. "What do you want?"

"You, Rita. I've always wanted you." Instead of the hard and fast kiss Matías delivered last night, Esteban lowered his head slowly, keeping his eyes locked on mine.

Then he brushed his lips against my own, teasing me.

That was all it was. A tease, before he pulled back. "I have loved you since the first time you strutted your ass in front of me in those high heels. You had so much attitude, so much confidence, and I wanted it all for myself. Only to watch you walk straight into Matías' arms." He worked his jaw.

"I'm sorry," I whispered.

"Don't be sorry. Give me a chance."

"A chance for what?" I just laid *Papá* to rest, I just fucked Matías, I had a club threatening to fall apart. How could he want me when I was so clearly fucked up?

"A chance for me to show you just how serious I am. That's it."

I closed my eyes. I did like Esteban. We had explosive chemistry. And the best way to get over someone was to get under someone else.

"I just don't want to cry anymore."

"I thought you didn't cry," he said, a smile tinting his words.

I snapped my eyes open. "I don't."

"Right." He released me and stepped back, his signature smirk sliding over his lips. "I'm going to figure out what's going on. You go get ready for the meeting. I'll see you in an hour and don't forget."

"Forget what?" I pressed a palm against my stomach, shocked at the sudden flood of butterflies.

"That I'm going to show you just how serious I am." Then he grabbed a Tee off the back of one of his chairs, pulled it on, then dropped a kiss on my forehead as he passed me. "Don't forget to lock this. I don't want any other fuckers stealing my air unit." He tapped the doorframe then he was gone.

It took a minute for my brain to start working. Then I picked up my clothes, holding them to my chest.

I could search his room. See what he was all about. I glanced around, noting the bare dresser, the now made bed. Everything was neat and clean. Nothing showing his personality. But that wasn't that strange.

He could save all his secrets for his house.

Deciding against snooping, I left, locking the door and heading straight for my room. I passed a few men, and lifted my chin, daring them to question why I was leaving Esteban's.

They nodded or looked away, not giving me any issues.

Inside my room, I dropped my clothes in the hamper and plugged my phone in with my spare charger I kept here. I didn't stay here as much as the others but I at least kept the essentials.

Before thinking too hard about it, I called Amorette.

It rang a total of four times.

"I heard you had an eventful night."

Was she trying to be smart? I didn't detect any anger, or sarcasm in her voice.

"I fucked Matías," I rushed out. Completely throwing my reason for calling out the window.

"Wow," she drew out, and then a door shut in the background. "That isn't that surprising, is it? You told me he was your one."

Red crossed my vision.

"That was before he cost me the last few days with *Papá*." Fuck, this wasn't her fault. Taking a breath, I cleared the anger from my thoughts. "I wished I hadn't. It just happened. I was drinking and he caught me at a bad time."

"I can tell you, he looked a mess when I left for the office this morning. Swollen and bruised too."

As if on autopilot, I immediately felt bad for him.

No, fuck that. He was the one who caused everything that happened last night. I needed to remind myself that he left me twice as I shored up my wall, brick by fucking brick.

"That's his fault. Did Andre and Grey tell you what happened?"

"That he didn't want Esteban to touch you? Yes. I guess he never found out you had a one night stand with him?"

"Why would he? He had already tossed me away." I sat on my bed and rested my back against the headboard. "I stayed in Esteban's room last night."

"Okay..."

"He wants a chance. He said he's serious."

Silence. Complete dead air on the other end.

"What are you thinking?"

"That your love life is complicated. What do you want?"

I wanted a world where Matías wasn't a giant asshat and hadn't faked his death. "I want to never see the man again. As for Esteban," I sucked in a breath. "I think it's too soon for me to get wrapped up in a man, but I want to see what happens."

"You want to see if he can make you forget why you love

Matías so much?" There was no judgment in her voice, but there was a note of something.

"You want me with Matías?"

She hesitated. "I just think Matías came back for a reason. But if you're set on this, I'll support you no matter what."

Thumbing the hem of Esteban's shirt, I thought about it. "I don't have time to figure out what I want. Not right now. But I do know it's not Matías." Pulling the shirt down, I stretched my legs out. "I was calling to tell you I need a few days away from school. I have some issues to take care of here."

"Anything we can help with?" She was instantly alert.

"No, just club business. I'll let you know when I'll be back."

"Okay, call me if you need anything."

We hung up, and set my phone down. Just that small conversation lightened the load on my chest. It would take time to come to terms with my decisions and how they fucked up my own life, but for now, I'd take every lift I could get.

After going through my routine, one minute before noon, I was walking down to the club hall.

Whenever there was club business, we always held the meetings here. For the same reason we had our other parties here. It was club only, unless you had an invite.

The club was already assembled and someone or some-ones had pulled out all the metal chairs. At the back of the room, a long table was set up on a temporary platform that was two feet off the floor. Just high enough for *Papá* and the leadership to sit where everyone could see them.

Their conversations died as I approached the table. Ricco, Manny, and Joel, the VPs were on one end. The Officers were at the other. All except Esteban. He stood behind *Papá's* chair with his arms crossed.

His expression was grim, yet his eyes darkened in a different way as he watched me walk toward him. Those butterflies started fluttering harder with every step. He was going to do something. I just didn't know what it was.

Stepping forward, he held out his hand when I was at the stairs. I took it and climbed the two steps up.

Then he yanked me into him as he threaded his hand through my hair at the back of my head as he kissed the shit out of me. I was so shocked I didn't do a damned thing. When he pulled back, he thumbed the corners of my mouth like he was fixing my lipstick.

Shaking myself out of the haze he'd placed me in, I turned toward the table. The guys were looking at me with a mixture of confusion, hope, and anger.

The anger was strange, but fuck 'em. With the Dirty Dogs, I'd find out what got them hot and bothered in a matter of minutes.

Esteban pulled *Papá's* chair out, and tucked it underneath me as I sat down. The crowd held much the same expressions.

Ricco stood before I had a chance to greet everyone.

"I'm glad you're all here. You too, Rita. It's come to our attention that someone took Leo's head, and we know where it went." He glanced around. There weren't many looks of surprise.

"Damen delivered it to the new club this morning, hoping it would be enough of a deterrent for a war." Ricco pressed his meaty fists against the table. "Which is the exact type of behavior that got Leo killed."

What the fuck? I was supposed to be running this meeting. I opened my mouth, but Ricco kept talking.

"Which brings us to today's meeting. We need a vote. Who's going to be our next president."

"Ricco, this is my meeting," I said calmly.

He glanced at me. "*Cariño*, this is a Dirty Dogs meeting. You're a Dirty Dog, but you're not part of the gang."

"Like fuck I'm not." I bent forward. "My father created this club. He built it up with his blood, sweat, and tears. He never hid that from me, or the business. I've run just as much of the club as you have."

Ricco stiffened. "You have your business with the Castillos' girl now."

"They're not the Castillos. Call them the Bastard Brothers if you don't address them by name. And I can do both." Looking out over the crowd, I laced my hands on the table. "We do need to have a vote. And I'm throwing my name in too."

A bomb could have exploded underneath us and no one would have noticed.

"You look like right shit." Parker fell into the chair across from me. They'd moved into a new place, a proper mini-mansion, and decorated it the complete opposite of Vicente's home.

This place was classy, yet built for comfort with darker tones and colorful art. There were quite a few pieces appreciating women. I wonder who had sourced those...

Sarcasm. It was Parker using his resources from his art heist business.

For all that the Institution was a thing of the past, they'd kept many pieces alive. Like Grey and his fights. Parker and his art. Andre and his spy and law enforcement contacts. It was really only Lafe who had completely rewrote his story.

He was opening clinics and managing healthcare businesses with our old friend, Doc. Of all of the brothers, he was now the cleanest.

"Fuck you." I pressed the squishy, half-melted ice pack against my face. It was better than a bag of frozen vegetables and prettier too. The pink and green color scheme screamed newborn baby. Although, what Cossette needed this kind of pack for, I had no idea.

Grey sauntered into the kitchen in his workout clothes, grabbing an apple off the counter. "It wasn't his best moment. Which, while you're here, Matías, we're hitting the gym. I'm going to teach you how to knock a man out instead of tickling his chin."

I shifted in my seat, glaring at him through my exposed eye. The obnoxious crunch of his bite into the apple only irritated me more.

Lafe laughed as he carried baby Cossette into the kitchen. "Good luck. He whipped all our asses when he felt like we needed to brush up on our skills. It's really just an excuse to beat us into the ground."

Grey smirked as he cut his gaze to Lafe. "It's hard to find good sparring partners. At least with you three, I know it's going to be a good fight."

"Give my sweet little thing here." Parker plucked Cossette from Lafe's arms as he walked by. "You hog her too much."

This was surreal. It was like Amorette was off being the working mom and these four *pendejos* were the ridiculously dangerous stay at home dads.

"I don't have time to train with you. I'm heading straight over to the compound as soon as my head stops throbbing."

Yesterday had been bittersweet and wretched all at once. It had been the closure I didn't know I needed, to be there for Javier's funeral. It had also been a breath of fresh air to see the ones I cared for after so long.

When I followed Rita into the backroom, I hadn't expected to fuck her. I also hadn't imagined even on my worst days how she would react to me finding Grace.

Fucking hell. If I could take it back, I'd do it all differently. I would never purposely hurt her like that. This was going on my new list of things not to do to protect Rita's heart.

That look in her eyes...

Damn. I rubbed my chest.

"Why is he glaring at the table salt like it spit on his toothbrush?" Parker stage-whispered to the others.

"I think he's realizing just how bad he fucked up by faking his death." Lafe touched the feather-soft curls on Cossette's head.

"No. I'd do it again." No matter how many times I argued with them, I couldn't make them see that what I'd done had been the right decision *at the time*. Except for Rita.

There went my fucking heart squeezing again.

"I should have contacted Rita, or come back sooner." Or taken her with me. That was the kicker. I'd been so messed up and down on my own worth, I hadn't ever thought that would be a possibility. "I need to go."

"What? To take your pound of flesh out of Esteban for fucking Rita?" Parker asked slyly as he leaned back in his chair.

"They haven't fucked." I waved a hand. "He's just a flirt." It had just been bad timing for me when he put his hands on her.

The guys exchanged looks.

"What?" I narrowed my eyes on them.

Grey shrugged. "Not our business."

"That did not answer my question." I leaned forward, tossing the icepack on the table. My eye and jaw were swollen and mottled. Holding the ice on it any longer wouldn't make it heal any faster.

"Look," Parker started, then Cossette added her opinion in a high-pitched babble. "Shhh...Let Daddy slap some verbal sense into your Uncle 'Tias."

This time, my chest twinged with warmth. I'd never had this kind of connection before. It was alien and welcome.

"I'm not saying they fucked..." Except he raised his brows like that was exactly what he thought. "And if I knew they had, I wouldn't tell you." I gritted my teeth. That was as good as a confession. "But Esteban *hates* you, according to Amorette. And when I've seen them together, there was a familiarity there."

"Esteban did hold her like he knew her *very* well," Grey added in his two cents.

That was enough. I couldn't sit here any longer and listen to their theories. I needed to see Rita and get some things straight. She needed to know I was here for good. For her.

Esteban needed to know that I was back in the picture.

"I'm going."

My pocket vibrated and when I pulled my phone out, I had a text from Ricco.

Ricco: Club vote in twenty. I'd like you to be here. Javier would have wanted it.

Closing my eyes, I breathed through my regret. I hadn't come running back when I first found out about his heart attack. This time, I would go.

"What's wrong?" Lafe asked, leaning against the counter.

"I need to be at the compound." Not opening myself up for anymore conversation, I booked it out of the kitchen. I grabbed a set of keys from the keyring by the door, and left. They'd have to fight me later if they were pissed I took one of their cars.

～

THE SHOUTING WAS LOUD. The compound wasn't built like the mansion, but the insulation was decent. I shouldn't be hearing them this much outside.

With the Dirty Dogs, especially after last night, this only meant trouble.

Picking up my pace, I slammed into the front door to the main hall. It banged against the wall, but only a handful of people noticed.

Ricco and Esteban were in each other's faces and the Dirty Dogs in the metal chairs were yelling obscenities and pumping their fists. There was even a fight breaking out in the corner.

Rita sat at the table, glaring daggers at Ricco. Her mouth set and her brow furrowed like she was trying to figure out how she wanted to jump in. Her fingers were curled on the table like she wanted to claw someone's eyes out.

Then her gaze met mine and I pulled up short. No matter who her thoughts were on seconds ago, now that she saw me, I was the center of all of her anger.

"Rita cannot be President," Ricco argued.

"Why fucking not?" Esteban returned.

Joel, another VP, tried to wade between them. He'd always been passive. A peacekeeper for when the Dirty Dogs got their shit in hot water.

"Calm down. We have options. There's no harm in letting her be part of the vote."

"You're just sure you're going to win." One of the guys in the crowd shouted. "You've wanted the top spot since Javier started talking about stepping down."

Joel jutted out his chin. "We need a leader who's not hotheaded like Leo or Damen."

"He's right," Ricco growled, still nose to nose with Esteban. "Which is why I called Matías here."

Rita shot up out of her chair and Esteban had some kind of sixth-sense, reaching behind him and cupping her wrist, tugging her to him. She went grudgingly, though her gaze was still locked on me.

I couldn't feel the shock of his words through the vision of Esteban and Rita together. Now that Parker's poisonous words were stuck in my head, I could see it all too clear.

Maybe I'd always seen it.

Esteban just hadn't been on my radar. He was young. Almost a decade younger than me, and a flirt. That asshole had just been biding his time.

He glanced back at Rita and his eyes softened in a way that spoke of history.

I'd never considered myself a jealous man. Yet, right at that moment, if I had had my gun in my hand, Esteban would be on the ground. As it was, I had to curl my fists to keep from reaching for it.

Then he followed her gaze to where I stood and a fiery hate burned in his eyes that was clear to see in the light of day.

He also sported bruising around his mouth and eye. Good. I was glad I wasn't the only one with a physical reminder of that shitshow last night.

"Matías, I called you here for Javier," Ricco said as he took the opportunity of Esteban's distraction to step back.

That brought me crashing back to reality.

The Dirty Dogs quieted down, though some still murmured.

"We need to vote for the next President. Joel wants a shot. Tiago does too." He nodded to one of the officers standing in front of the table facing the crowd. "And Rita wants in. But you have always been Javier's pick."

Esteban's face purpled as a few Dirty Dogs clapped me

on the back. Some yelled for me to leave. A few called for Ricco to step up. There was no consistency. They were divided into too many corners.

"Why do you need to have this vote now?" I asked, soaking in every inch of Rita, avoiding the places Esteban now touched as he molded himself to her back.

How had I never noticed them together before? When did it start?

"Because, you fucking *cabrón*," Esteban spat, none of the light-hearted flirt I'd seen before. "We got a note ten minutes ago from Matthews, the leader of the new club in town. Their man died. He doesn't give one fuck about Leo's head. Either doesn't trust us or believes that we're responsible as a whole."

Rita's eyes widened. She hadn't known that.

"You don't need a vote for president. You need to plan on how you're going to protect yourselves."

"The best way to do that is to have a leader." Ricco glanced out across the men in the room. "The Dirty Dogs need a president. Otherwise, we'll have just as much in-fighting as planning."

Some of the men started to form around me, like a show of support. Hope.

What the hell was this? I wasn't a Dirty Dog. I had been a stray Javier had taken in from time to time. I didn't want this either. If I did, I would have stayed with my brothers to run their new business.

"Why do you think Javier wanted me to lead?" I couldn't help but ask. It was ridiculous.

"Because he told me," Ricco said softly as the blood drained from Rita's face.

I stepped toward her, but Esteban shifted her so she was behind him. It didn't last, she jabbed him in the side and moved in front of him, but the message was clear from both of them. I wasn't welcome.

"That was his plan from the first year he knew you. He saw the potential in you. In your name. And..." Ricco's gaze flicked to Rita then back to me. "He had other plans that fell apart."

"We need a vote." Tiago stepped forward. I'd interacted with him from time to time. He was solid, but too much of a hothead. He'd drive the club into the ground if he was given the reins.

"What makes you think you deserve it? If we vote on men in the club, they need to be the VPs." Due shoved Tiago's shoulder lightly. Not enough to show actual aggression but to get his attention.

Tiago scoffed. "There are no rules saying I can't toss my name in. I've sweat and bled for this club too. And I have visions I think the VPs are too old to have. We need fresh blood."

There were boos and scoffs tossed from the Dirty Dogs. He at least didn't seem to be a contender.

"We do need a vote." Rita pulled away from Esteban and took her seat. "Sit down. We'll run this the way *Papá* has always done." She glanced at me, I tried to hold her gaze, but I couldn't.

Damn it. I needed time alone with her.

"Matías, come up here." Ricco pointed to the extra chair. Either it was Esteban's or he'd added an extra chair for me and no one had noticed.

"No." I slowly shook my head.

"No?" His brows popped up and Rita tilted her head. Even Esteban frowned at me.

"I'm not a Dirty Dog. I won't run your club. I'll help in any way I can. For Javier. For Rita," I added in a softer tone.

"But I'm not going to steal the head spot for myself. What I will do, is back Rita."

I walked toward the platform as the last few Dirty Dogs took their seats. The only one left standing now was Esteban.

He eyed me as I climbed the two steps up. He was positioned directly behind Rita, and he didn't budge when I got closer.

That was fine. I didn't want to hash anything out in their meeting anyway. I stayed to the side, but still behind Rita.

She pulled her shoulders back and faced the men. "I am a Dirty Dog. That means something to me. I will honor the position and do right by the club. If I'm voted in." Those last words seemed to tear from her throat.

Rita didn't believe she had to be voted in. But she was following the club rules.

"All in favor of Tiago," she called. Only five men raised their hands, one of them being Tiago. He made an ugly sound in the back of his throat as he jumped up and kicked his chair back, then stalked out of the main hall.

Rita released a breath. "All in favor of Joel."

Roughly half the Dirty Dogs raised their hands. That meant...

"All in favor of me."

The other half raised their hands.

"We need to count." Ricco called for the men to raise their hands again and counted.

It took several minutes, but the answer came back just like I figured it would.

Sixty-eight for Joel and Sixty-eight for Rita.

Deadlocked.

"We're calling a break." Ricco wiped his forehead. "We

have work that can't be put off any longer. We'll hold another meeting at the end of the week."

"What about the club? They're a threat." Esteban placed a hand on Rita's shoulder and I had the urge to rip it off.

The VPs exchanged glances. It wasn't often they had to make decisions like this. For the most part, the Dirty Dogs had operated with few issues or challenges. So much different than the Institution.

Joel raised a finger. "I can work with Rita on a plan. If she's voted in, I'll still be her VP. If I'm voted in, I'll know everything that's gone down."

"Fair enough." Ricco pounded his fist on the table twice and the room started to clear out.

Rita stood, and I tried to touch her arm. "Rita."

Esteban knocked my arm away and I raised my fist, ready for another fight.

"Stop."

I glanced down. Rita placed her hand on my chest, almost over my heart. Could she feel how fucking hard it beat for her?

"We need to talk."

"We don't. I need you to get out of my sight." Then she walked off the platform with Esteban two steps behind her.

"Matías," Ricco said next to me. "I'm glad you're back."

"I came back for her." I wanted there to be no doubt about my intentions. I didn't spend my life fucking up for all the wrong reasons to give up when I finally had the right one.

"Matías...." I glanced at him, and he too was watching Rita and Esteban.

She glanced back right before she disappeared through the door. Her expression was blank like she didn't give one fuck about me.

I pulled in a long breath through my nose. "Did I miss that? How could I have fucking missed it?"

Ricco must have known exactly what I was talking about because he sighed and scratched his bearded chin. "No. He's always had a thing for Rita, but he never let it show when you were around. She never acted on it until you broke things off."

I whipped toward him. "She acted on it?"

Even though Parker insinuated he knew things I didn't, I had hoped he was wrong. This confirmation hit my chest like a ton of bricks, forcing the air from my lungs.

"Fuck," Ricco groaned. He took in the now empty room and stepped closer to me. "She fucked him one night as far as I know. We saw them disappear together, and that was the only time we saw it...Until this morning."

Spinning on my heel, I started walking away.

"Matías!" he called.

I didn't answer. I couldn't. I needed to destroy something and if I stayed here any longer, it'd be Ricco.

Grey was getting a sparring partner after all.

How could Rita go to bed with him after we'd fucked?

13

RITA

I tapped on the keyboard of my computer, outlining a ridiculously boring email. I wasn't sure why I even bothered. It wasn't like Amorette wasn't going to go over it and legalese it anyway.

There was a knock at the door. Instead of yelling for the person to come in, I rolled my chair out and stood up. Smoothing my dress down, I walked to the door.

It was a cop out for more time. It didn't matter who it was, I just needed more time.

The last few days had been exhausting and I was running out of fucks to give. Why did I even want to be President of the Dirty Dogs? It had never crossed my mind before *Papá* died. Yet, as soon as he was gone, I knew I had to take his place.

My brain and heart were in agreement. They demanded it.

"Yes?" I placed my hand on the doorknob and waited. I didn't always lock it, but I did today.

Carnage Industries was as secure as they came. Amorette's men made sure of it. Add in the school next door, and Jesus himself couldn't break through the gates uninvited.

But a girl needed her privacy, and I needed time to process my mess of a life.

"It's me," Amorette said.

I twisted the knob to open the door. She wasn't someone I wanted to see either. Mainly because I didn't want to see the judgment on her face after what I told her on the phone. Amorette was the master of judgment, even though she said she didn't judge.

She absolutely did.

With the door open a handful of inches, I sucked in a breath. There was Amorette all right. And Esteban stood behind her, raising one taunting eyebrow at me.

"Seems this man was loitering," Amorette remarked drily. Then she excused herself, giving me a slight smile to let me know she wasn't irritated that he was here or that I was avoiding her.

"Hey," I said as I stepped back and opened the door.

He started to come in, but I held up a finger. "You know what, hold on."

I grabbed my keys and phone from the desk and joined him in the hall. He watched me silently as I shut and locked the door. Call me paranoid, but I'd seen Matías here this morning and I didn't want him to ambush me in my office.

When I faced Esteban, we had a moment of mutual appreciation. My body buzzed under his appreciative gaze as it swept my body.

Like always, he was dressed in ripped jeans, a white Tee and his Dirty Dogs vest.

"Shouldn't you be at the shop?" The chop business was still fairly young and Esteban was heading it up due to his love of all things bikes. Cars were his second love.

"Due is handling it. While we're waiting for Matthews to make a move, the VPs and officers thought it would be best you have someone protecting you." He shoved his hands in his pockets.

"And naturally that person is you?"

"Naturally," he repeated, smiling. Damn it, his dimples popped out. I was a sucker for dimples.

I didn't have any smart comebacks. I wanted to blame it on life and stress, and how I couldn't think around him. Different from how Matías made me feel, and that was the most intoxicating of all.

"Are you kicking me out?" His gaze flicked to my shut door. "Is that why you shut and locked your office door? Afraid of what will happen if we're alone?" He pressed his lips together to suppress his smile.

Those dimples were still there.

Damn.

"I slept in your room without any issues controlling myself." I sniffed as I started walking down the hallway. He'd catch up.

He chuckled under his breath, giving me a full-blown *show me all the beautiful white teeth* smile. "That was because I respected your space. I wasn't trying to fuck you."

"Hm," I hummed, suddenly flustered.

"Where are we going?" He easily fell in step beside me.

"You've never been here before. I thought I'd give you a tour."

His eyes softened and he nodded. "I'd like that."

I took in the hallway, trying to see what he'd see. I'd gotten used to it now, but I remember the first time I walked the halls. The understated opulence took me off guard. I imagined it was similar to what Amorette was used to in her high-profile law firm.

The Dirty Dogs owned some nice clubs, but they were nothing like this. Even our best club still had a level of grittiness to it that was both thrilling and sexy. Everything a nightclub should be.

"The hall back that way is where the rest of the offices are for Amorette and her guys."

A hint of anger slid through his eyes even though his smile didn't dim. "I know. Amorette walked me past them."

"You saw him, didn't you?" It was weird to ask, but that had to be what flipped his emotions.

"Yeah," he grunted. "I saw him on his way out."

Okay, this wasn't going to turn into a complaint fest about Matías. He was still here, and I'd been dodging his calls left and right. The one line he hadn't crossed was showing up at my house.

Yet, I wouldn't put it past him.

"The school is in the next building. Where we keep all our little badasses." I grinned. Those girls were going to be something when they grew up.

He studied me as we rode the elevator down. "You're not concerned with them getting killed on jobs?"

I shook my head. "That's always a possibility. But women get hurt everyday by men. This way, they'll be trained not only on how to defend themselves, but to go on the offensive, how to quickly leave a situation, and cover their tracks if they need to."

The elevator dinged and I led the way to the school.

"That's actually pretty smart."

"We thought so." Going through the gate, we could already hear sounds of Olga putting the girls through hell. *Papá* should have had Olga training the Dirty Dogs. She was hell on the ego.

The middle group of girls were with her today.

Several called out to me, and I waved. I wanted to check on Molly and this walk with Esteban was a perfect opportunity.

We moved inside the school, heading for the gymnasium. While a lot of their training was held outside, classes and exercises were run in the gym.

"The classrooms are on either side of the hallway. We cover regular courses, such as math, English, science. Then we also have guest teachers on poisons, repairs, electrical wiring. Anything that we think might be useful to get them out of a tight situation." I shrugged. "Or finish the job."

He whistled under his breath as he passed the lab used for poisons. He eyed the hazard signs with appreciation. "I'm impressed. How many classes have you sat in on?"

"All of them," I snorted. "I like to have a full and secret arsenal too."

We reached the end of the hallway, where there were two doors. The one on the right led to the theater, and the one on the left the gymnasium.

"That way is where the girls take dance classes–"

"That's a deadly skill?" he snarked.

I smirked at him. "Grace is a skill. I've been taking those classes too. The girls love when Amorette and I join in." Amorette hadn't been able to do many of the classes while she was pregnant or right after, but now that Cossette was getting bigger, she attended one with me a couple weeks earlier.

She was perfectly poised and petite, like a tiny elfin fairy. Until she couldn't get her feet right, then she was an angry-faced pixie.

"Shit, you got me." He raised his brows, glancing at the theater door.

"But we're going here today." The girls should be in the

practice segment of their class. A perfect time for me to pop in. Esteban would enjoy this too.

I pushed the door open and stepped inside. The gym was warmer than the rest of the building but still severely cooler than outside. Those poor girls with Olga were sweating to death.

The youngest group of girls were in here. I spotted Molly right away, where she stood off to the corner. Her group seemed to be ignoring her and her dagger stares.

I sighed as I approached the teacher.

This class was run by Jewel, a world-class motocross racer. She specialized in both dirt bikes and off-road motorcycles.

"This is the class I should be in." Esteban rubbed his hands together as we walked between the groups of girls working on learning the anatomy of their bikes. Once they knew the parts, their functions and why they were important, then they'd start taking lessons.

This class was held twice a month and it was quickly becoming a favorite.

"I knew you'd like it." I turned to Jewel and smiled. "How are the girls doing?"

She grinned. As a spunky American, she had so much bubbliness, the girls instantly took to her.

"Great. They're catching on really fast. Almost faster than the mid-level girls." She glanced out over the groups, an obvious look of pride on her face.

Esteban joined one of the groups, asking them questions. An eruption of little girl giggles pierced my ears and he shot me a lopsided grin.

Stepping closer, I lowered my voice. "What's going on with Molly?"

Some of the exuberance leaked out of Jewel. "I'm not

sure. She's not in trouble today. But there's something going on with the girls. They've pretty much just been snubbing her. It's making her angry."

I glanced over and Molly was still shooting all her ire at the backs of two girls in particular.

"Can you keep an eye on it? Let me know if you hear anything?"

"Absolutely." She nodded.

Walking over to Molly, I waved my fingers to catch her attention. This girl was absorbed in her hate stare. She flicked her gaze my way and her face lit up.

"Ms. Aguilar!" She hugged my waist. Some of the other girls peered over curiously, but no one made an attempt to come over.

There were only a few who felt comfortable enough to show me affection like this.

Esteban noticed where I was and excused himself from his now substantial crowd of tween admirers. He jogged over and stopped a few feet away.

"Who is this badass?"

Molly pulled her shoulders back. She definitely liked his attention too. Or being called a badass. If I was right, it was a combination of both.

"This is Molly. One of our newest girls."

He must have seen how she was separate from her group because he crouched closer to us. "What's the deal? Those girls messing with your vibe or something?"

I laughed. It was weird to hear Esteban speak so...teen girl.

She shrugged, shooting me a look. Molly opened her mouth as the door opened again.

This time it was Parker and Matías.

Matías instantly zeroed in on me and I narrowed my

eyes. That motherfucker. He found me so quick, I'd bet that was the whole reason he was here.

Parker wore a shit eating grin as he strolled through the girls. Now he was a favorite. Most of the girls left their assigned bike to jump around him.

Matías got caught up in the circle but the girls didn't seem to even know he was there. That would at least hold him for a few minutes.

"That asswipe," Esteban muttered under his breath. "You want to leave?"

"Absolutely not." He wanted to chase me? Fine. I was still checking in on my girl.

Esteban didn't say anything. He turned to Molly and touched her shoulder. "Now that your group's bike is free, I'll show you a couple secrets I bet the teacher hasn't gone over." He winked and Molly swooned. I'd never tell her. She'd hate it.

He walked her over to the bike and crouched down. "You like bikes?" he asked.

"Yeah, they're not bad." She bent over, placing her hands on her knees.

"Not bad!" He slapped a hand over his chest. "You wound me." Shaking his head, he pointed to a screw like plug. "Rita tells me you all need to know how to get away fast. You see this? It's the spark plug." He twisted it and popped it off. "It's what starts the engine. You unhook it, which should be easy to do, then they won't be able to follow you. But if it's too hard to twist off..." Esteban trailed his fingers over a line. "This is the fuel line. Cut it, and they'll have a really fucking hard time coming after you too."

Molly stared in wide-eyed shock at Esteban.

I laughed. He'd just ignited a crush and I doubted he realized it.

He shot me a sly smile and I rolled my eyes. Oh, he knew. The man knew exactly how girls responded to him. There was just something so magnetic about his personality.

Not able to help it, I glanced over.

Matías had just separated himself from the girls surrounding Parker. None of them paid him any attention at all. He could have been a ghost as he wove between them with his unblinking gaze locked only on me.

I started backing up before I even realized what I was doing.

"Rita?" Esteban stood up.

Fuck this. I wasn't ready to talk to Matías yet. As much as I loved him, and it bit my ass to admit I couldn't turn the feelings off just like that, I also didn't want to look at him. Not after what I'd let happen at *Papá's* funeral.

It had been one of my lowest points and I walked away from him with so much hurt, I just couldn't do it.

Not right then.

"Sorry, Esteban. I'm not going to talk to him today."

Then I did what I said I'd never do. I ran.

And it wasn't fucking badass at all.

14

MATÍAS

P arker was soaking up all the attention from the class.

All except for one girl.

Whoever she was, she was Rita's favorite. It was obvious in her smiles and the way Rita glanced at her.

While Parker caused a scene with his smartass jokes and sarcastic smirks, Rita was having a hell of a time in the corner with Esteban and the girl.

Crowded around the bike, Esteban spoke quietly, head bent toward the girl, who looked at him like he was the best thing since underwear. Even Rita seemed mesmerized by what he was saying.

I strained to hear what he was telling them, but all I could hear was Parker's voice and feminine giggles. Nothing from that side of the room.

Somehow, the girls made a complete circle around both of us. I couldn't get through if I wanted to.

Then Esteban smiled at Rita and she melted.

I couldn't take it. Knowing they'd slept together.

Knowing I pushed her to that. Or that she'd been avoiding me since the night of the funeral.

Suddenly, there was an opening right in front of me and I took it. Sidestepping another girl, I made it even farther away from Parker and closer to Rita.

She glanced up, and her jaw set.

That was fine. I'd take her anger any day over her absence. What kind of fucking hypocrite did that make me?

She said something to Esteban, then like a hole in the bottom of a boat, all the steel and anger leaked slowly out of her face. She turned away, as if looking at me physically pained her.

My heart was breaking right in front of me and I couldn't get to her fast enough. A couple girls stepped in my way, but not to get my attention. They didn't notice me at all as they huddled together and whispered about how cute Parker was.

I was five feet away when she started backpedaling and then she was gone. Running from the room and heading out a side entrance.

"Fuck," I cursed under my breath and started to sprint after her.

Esteban popped up in front of me, and I almost bowled him over.

"Not a fucking chance." He planted a hand in my chest and knocked me back.

At first, I didn't acknowledge him, dead set on getting to Rita. Making sure she was okay, and letting her know once and for fucking all that I was here to stay.

I wasn't going to run. I wasn't going to leave her behind. Not again.

Never again.

Dodging to the side, I tried to get around Esteban but he stepped in my path again. As the door slammed behind Rita, I moved my attention to Esteban. His brows were dark slashes over his eyes as his top lip peeled back from his teeth.

"Did you hear what I said?"

All of the despair and regret that stretched inside me like gum, filling up even the darkest crevices, started to recede as my body vibrated for a different reason.

Like the other night, all my thoughts turned to putting this kid on his ass. She wasn't meant for him. She was mine.

"If you don't get out of my way, I'll make you." It was low, but a gasp from a girl close by meant it wasn't as quiet as I thought.

"Threaten me all you want, but you're not going to chase after Rita when she doesn't want you." He shook his head.

His words only threw fuel on the fire raging in my gut. My instincts said that this man was the reason she didn't want to see me. He was why she ran out on me.

Logically, I knew that wasn't it, but his face was right there.

"That's not your call." I sidestepped again.

He followed.

"I will fucking lay you out. You're in my brothers' business. You don't have anyone to back you up. Move."

He laughed like I told a joke. Then he spit on the floor. "Doesn't matter if I have my club here or not. Rita's a Dirty Dog before she ever worked here. I'll protect her to my last breath."

"Because you want her. Not because she's a Dirty Dog," I said bitterly.

His mouth kicked up at the corners. He enjoyed this. Delaying me. Every second that Rita got farther away, singed my mind. Yet I craved to put Esteban in his place.

"Okay. We'll say it's both."

"She's not yours," I spat. Fuck, she wasn't mine either. But she was going to be.

His smile started to die. "Keep telling yourself whatever lies you want, but she isn't yours."

Again, I tried to get around him and he blocked my way. I made an agitated sound in the back of my throat. "What the fuck do you want?"

"What do I want?" His voice rose and he crowded me. "I want you to disappear like you did before. I want you to fuck off to another country and leave Rita alone. She doesn't deserve your brand of fucked up. You want to make her happy? Do what you always do, you fucking coward, and *run*."

I reared back, but before I could let it loose, Parker caught my fist. "Not in front of the children." He tutted. "Take it outside, boys."

Spinning toward him, I threw an arm out toward Esteban. "You're not going to kick him out?"

He eyed Esteban. "Unfortunately, no. Rita's fond of him and Little Love is fond of Rita. As much as it pains me, this is a lover's spat you'll have to figure out on your own. I will however ask that you both leave." He raised his brows.

"Fuck this," I muttered and pushed past Esteban. He didn't try to stop me. Probably because Parker told us to leave and no matter what club he was part of, you didn't ignore one of the Bastard Brothers on their property.

As soon as we went through the side door, which dropped us into a back hallway, he gripped my arm and spun me around.

"What is your problem?" I yelled in his face. "I'm not running. I'm not letting her go. You can fuck off! You're just a kid who doesn't understand anything."

"I understand plenty! I know you care more about your brothers and their woman than Rita. I know you had more fear for your father than you had love for Rita. It all comes down to that, doesn't it? Everything matters more than Rita!"

Each word pelted me, and I couldn't stop the flinches. As grim as he was, satisfaction slithered through his expression.

"I'm not letting her go. I won't. And I'm not explaining myself to you." I started to turn, but an ugly part of my soul had me twisting back. "And you? What about you, Esteban? The guy who can't be taken seriously because he's such a flirt? The guy I didn't even have on my radar because you didn't fucking matter. The only reason you made it to Rita's bed was because I had to step back–for her safety." He tensed and that same sick satisfaction that he probably felt settled in my stomach like hot acid. "Whatever you think this is between you two, it's not real. She's using you to get back at me, or hell, maybe to get over me. If that wasn't the case, she wouldn't have fucked me the other night."

There was no change in his expression. None.

He knew it. Or suspected it, and it didn't make one bit of fucking difference to him.

I wasn't lying to him. I had always known who he was since he joined the club. I liked him in a distant sort of way. Yet, as long as he stood in my way to Rita, I had no pity for him. He was the obstacle to my happiness, and Rita's.

I hope Rita's. I swallowed.

But if Rita truly didn't want me, I would leave. For her.

That wasn't true for the same exact reason I explained to him. We would not have fucked if she felt nothing. She would not have begged me to take her.

It was on me to make this right, and that was what I was going to do.

When I left this time, he let me go, staying on my heels every step of the way.

My brothers hadn't had this building before I left. Am and Rita hadn't been in business together. But when Andre brought me here, I knew how valuable this building was. Since coming back for Rita, I'd learned this place like the back of my hand.

Not only to have a better chance of catching Rita, but because I didn't have anything else better to do. Part of me also liked seeing where Rita spent most of her time.

The first place I looked for her was her office. It was locked. Not surprising.

I headed to the garage next. Esteban stayed with me the entire time. Instead of starting a fight, I let him follow me. It was more important to find Rita than it was to trade verbal jabs with him.

Parker was right, we couldn't fight here. Rita would hate that more than me tracking her down. She cared about these girls and she wouldn't want them to see us scrapping on the ground like scum.

"Damn it." I pulled my hair on the sides of my head. Her car was gone.

I pulled the keys out of my pocket and got in the car I'd taken over since I came home. My brothers didn't seem to mind. They had plenty to go around.

Esteban jumped on his bike and followed me.

What? Did he expect me to try and hurt her? Or did he want to play hero in front of her?

Grinding my teeth, I watched him stay on my ass in the rearview mirror as I drove to her house. She was close to Dirty Dogs territory. Between the few apartment buildings they owned. It gave her a sense of privacy while still protecting her.

Her garage was closed, but there was movement through the front window. She was home.

I parked on the sidewalk right in front of her house. Slamming my door shut, I jogged up the steps. Esteban stopped behind my car but he had to take off his helmet and get off his bike. I had at least ten seconds before he tackled me.

Fuck, he was already coming for me.

Turning around, I picked up the pace but skidded to a halt.

Rita opened her door. She hadn't been here long since she was still dressed in the tight sleeveless dress that hugged her curves in all the right places. Her hair was still down in thick glossy curls. Even her lips still had that vibrant red she loved.

That was the thing with Rita. She loved dressing up. But she loved being comfortable more. Whenever she was home more than five minutes, her armor all came off. Did Esteban know that?

I didn't dare look away. She was too much of a vision. I couldn't take my eyes off her if I tried.

But it was the pain that got me. Rita watched me with so much pain and hate twisting on her face it stole my breath. This wasn't what I wanted.

"What are you doing here?" she seethed.

"You've been avoiding me," I said, my voice thin and raspy as I carefully moved closer.

Esteban had stopped running behind me and now he was breathing down my neck. Probably waiting for the word from Rita to eject me from the property.

"So you show up at my house? It's not like you to force yourself on a woman." She crossed her arms and cocked out a hip.

I grimaced as memories assaulted me. Of what my father had condoned. What my uncle had done. What I'd witnessed and loathed my *entire* life.

The hardness in her expression wavered but she firmed it back up.

"What do you want?" she asked the very question I'd thrown at Esteban.

"To talk." I pulled my shoulders back and sucked in a deep breath. This was it. She'd give me five minutes to lay it all out. Then I'd make her see how this was different. How I wouldn't make the same mistakes I had before.

A cattiness I'd only seen a handful of times flickered over her face. Her gaze moved to Esteban behind me and then back to me.

"You want to stay? I'm not in the mood to talk." Before I could process what she meant, she crooked a finger at Esteban and motioned him closer. He went, like the fucking dog he was. He stopped on the bottom step, and she cupped his face like he was precious.

Dipping closer, she kept her gaze on me as she pressed her lips to his. It was a sensual slide. So fast, it was over almost before it started.

I schooled my expression. Everything Vicente had taught me came down to this moment.

My stomach rolled but I would not show it.

When she stepped back, she pulled a disgusted face and shook her head.

"Get out of here. I need to take care of Dirty Dogs business and it's no place for you."

She went back inside, leaving the door open. Esteban slipped inside after her. Neither of them glanced back as the door shut.

I did the only thing I could do. With my head held high, I walked back to my car, and drove the fuck away from here.

15

ESTEBAN

My lips tingled from the kiss and the back of my neck warmed in satisfaction from slamming the door in Matías' face.

He thought he did something by reminding me that Rita loved him and not me. Fucking *cabrón*. I knew that.

But it was what I was willing to do that made all the difference. I could make Rita love me. Show her that I was the right man for her. She might not love me today, or tomorrow, but she lusted for me.

That was enough for me until she did. By then, Matías would be a long forgotten memory.

Rita stopped in the center of the room, then whipped around to face me. Her brows pinched together and her mouth was slightly parted as she stared up at me.

"What's wrong?" Everything fell away except for the obvious upset on her face.

"We have to go to the compound. Tiago is dead."

What the fuck? I almost had to reach out a hand to steady myself. It took a minute for her words to process.

We didn't have deaths like this. Not since we fought with the old Institution.

"We have to go. Come on. I'll take you." I grabbed her hand and bolted for the door, picking up her keys on the way.

This was big. Huge. If this was the work of that new club...

It really had meant war.

I glanced back to make sure she had her shoes on still. She did.

Outside, Matías was already gone. Thank fuck. The last thing we needed was for him to try and stick his nose in our business. He would too. If he saw us leave in a rush, he'd follow.

I scooted Rita to the side and locked her door, then led her down the path to my bike.

"Here, put this on." I handed her my helmet. It would be a little big but it would work. I'd already ordered her a helmet, it just hadn't come in yet.

"It's yours."

"Baby," I said, sliding it onto her hands then cupping the sides of her neck. "You're more important to me than this helmet, this bike, or even my own self. Wear it."

Then we were off. She molded herself to my back, and if it wasn't for the looming dread, not knowing what was going to happen next, I'd have savored our first ride.

We arrived at the compound all too soon and inside, there was already a good portion of the chairs taken up. More guys trickled in as some of our club girls brought water, more chairs, then scurried back to the kitchen.

Rita took her hand from mine as she pulled back her shoulders and held her head high. "What happened?" she asked as she strode toward the table on the platform. Whatever she was feeling at her house and on the way here, she masked it.

As fucked up as it was, my cock twitched.

Then I remembered why we were here.

Joel stood in front of the table as his gaze tracked every person who entered the room. Almost like he was counting them. Hell, maybe he was.

There was a somber mood in the air that seemed to be boiling just under the surface. We needed retribution, and each man here wanted to be the one to deliver it.

"Tiago was dropped at our gates thirty minutes ago. No one saw who did it and it was just outside of the cameras." Joel crossed his arms and stared at the floor.

"We know who it was!" Due stood up. He was usually pretty level, but not today. His face was mottled red and his fists were clenched tight.

"We can't let this stand," Roddy, a ten year member shouted from the seats. He was a lunatic on the best days.

"You're right. We can't." Joel nodded. "We need a plan of attack. The Dirty Dogs are not to be fucked with."

"Wait." Rita walked next to Joel, facing the men. "We can't just go half-cocked. We don't even know for sure that it was them."

"Don't we?" Joel returned, a hint of a snide tone lacing his words. I glared at him for his disrespect but he wouldn't look at me.

"Rita, it was the new club," Ricco said softly from his seat. His face was drawn tight, and his shoulders bunched up. "Shit, we have a club after us and we don't even know their name." He looked at the rest of us. "Do they have a club name?"

I shook my head. They hadn't introduced themselves with a club name. Only Matthews. No one else knew either.

"I need five volunteers." Joel glanced around the room. Fifteen men instantly lifted their hands.

"You can't do this! Not yet!" Rita raised her voice, panic rising.

"Why not, Rita?" Joel was starting to lose his patience. "Tiago is currently on the back table, beaten black and blue. He's almost unrecognizable if not for his tattoos. He was murdered. And we know who did it. We have to strike back fast before they really do come for our asses."

"This would be a suicide mission. I'm not saying we shouldn't retaliate, just that we need to wait. We need more information." Her voice started to shake as her wide-eyed gaze moved from one volunteer to the next.

"Who else would it be, Rita?" Ricco asked, trying to force her to back down. "Carnage Industries?"

"No! Of course not–"

"The Movement?" He pushed.

"You know they don't give a fuck about us," she shot back. But she barely finished her sentence before Joel talked over her next.

"If we don't hit them now, we could lose more men. They could pick us off one by one. Do you realize that?"

"Stop fucking trying to patronize me!" She raised up as high as she could on her toes, getting right in Joel's face.

"Then make decisions like a Dirty Dog! Javier would have hit them hard. We have to make a stand for our territory. Our pride." Joel touched his nose to hers.

As soon as he said Javier's name, Rita backed down. She tried not to show it, but she wavered. He'd made her question herself.

Fuck that. I didn't belittle women, and I damn sure wouldn't let him do it to her. I waded in the middle, forcing Joel away from Rita.

"I'm with Rita. We didn't see who it was and we don't have enough information. The only thing you're doing is igniting a war that may or may not be on our doorstep anyway. We can wait ten fucking hours for someone to do some goddamned research."

I pointed at Joel and Ricco. "This emotional manipulation bullshit stops now. You have an idea. Say it. Don't try to make Rita or anyone in the club think it's the right idea just because Javier would have done it. And you're fucking wrong anyway. Javier would have done his homework to see who dropped him off at our gates."

"Twenty-four hours," Due said slowly. "Twenty-four hours. If we don't have an answer then, I'm riding to their place. I'll ask questions, and if I'm not satisfied, I'll do what I think is necessary. On my own."

Due wasn't close with Tiago, but he was as rage filled as the rest of us.

I shook my head. "Due, man, we don't need anyone going off on their own–"

"I'll go." Rita's voice was loud and clear. "If you can't figure out who dropped him in twenty-four hours, I'll go question them."

"I'll go with you." Joel straightened up.

"Fuck that, you'll try to undermine her like you did here and that's not the look we need in front of those assholes." I shook my head. "I'll go with her."

"Then take Matías," Ricco said.

"Absolutely not." Rita backed up, affronted.

"Rita, his name does more than ours does. If these guys did their homework like they said they did, his presence will help. That is what Javier wanted." Ricco eyed me, daring me to argue, but fuck. I knew for a fact, *that* at least, was true.

"Fuck," Rita muttered under her breath as she twisted

away from us. I almost jolted forward to steady her, but she started heading for the door in a fast clip. "I'll be back to see what you've found in twenty-four hours."

"Due, pick two guys and start checking the area for clues," I called over my shoulder as I chased after Rita. Ricco and Joel protested, but it didn't matter. Due would do it because I asked him to, even if Ricco and Joel sent someone else on the job.

He was loyal to me before the VPs. The Dirty Dogs had just never had a reason to split ourselves.

"Rita!" I called as she reached the top of the stairs.

She didn't stop. Her feet moved quickly toward her room. I sprinted the last several feet so I could catch the door before she slammed it shut.

"Please, Esteban. I need a few minutes to myself." Rita wouldn't look me in the eye. Her gaze was locked on my chin as she shifted and fidgeted, acting like she was going to crawl out of her body at any second.

"Nope, that's not what you need." I pushed the door open far enough for me to slip through. "You don't want to chat? That's cool. But you're upset, and you shouldn't be alone."

The perfume of her room wafted over me and I was assaulted by memories of the best night of my life.

Rita at the club dancing her ass off. Me disengaging from my partner and sliding up behind her. At first, I thought she was going to push me away, but when she glanced over her shoulder, her glassy eyes sparked in recognition and a sultry smile softened her face.

"Esteban..." she said, but I couldn't hear her over the music. She turned and grabbed fists of my shirt as she started to grind on me, dancing to the erotic beat of the music.

One thing turned to another, then we had shots...

Another round of dancing before we found our way to her room.

"Esteban."

Snapping back to the present, I took in the space. It was exactly the same. Luxurious bedding on an expensive mattress even though the walls and flooring were jacked, just like the other rooms in the compound. Yet somehow, because it was hers, it just seemed feminine, sexy.

I dropped my gaze to her questioning one. "Hmm?"

"Where did you go?"

"Nowhere. What do you want to do? We can talk or sit in silence. Your choice. Just not alone."

Somewhere in the span of minutes, she'd gone from upset, to a confident badass, then waffling with her emotions written across her face and body.

I didn't know what bothered her the most, but I had my guesses. She'd experienced so much death in a short time, and it was getting to her.

She shook her hands out as she started pacing. "I don't want to sit. I have all this nervous energy inside me. I can't get my brain to stop."

"What's going on inside your head?" I asked softly, leaning my ass back on her dresser.

She tossed her head back and laughed, but the sound was stretched, distorted from her usual exuberance. "So fucking much. While they were talking about sending guys downstairs, the only thing that went through my head was no, we'd have ten more deaths, and I can't deal with that. Not for a stupid reason. I mean, if we have to go to war with those bastards, we will, but I need to know it's not pointless. But then..." She cut her gaze at me as she kept pacing.

"Joel and Ricco made you question yourself?" I supplied.

"They made me feel like a little girl who didn't know

shit. And I do, Esteban. I've seen Javier make a hundred calls for the club. I know how to run it. I know I'm right, but damn. It just–It just made me pause. And that's all it takes, right? For the guys to lose faith in me? A second." She huffed, but then her breathing started turning erratic.

"You're right. We don't need to be sending men off half-cocked to make a statement. That's what kills people." I wanted to make her feel better, but she seemed like she was becoming more agitated, not less.

"What am I doing, Esteban?" She spun and threw her hands out. "What *the fuck* am I doing?"

"You're following in Javier's footsteps. Whether he wanted that or not, I think you're the right one for the job. Joel doesn't have his heart in the right place. He just wants the status. You care about the men more than the club."

"The men are the club!"

"Exactly." I gave her one solid chin dip. "Want to talk some more? I got twenty-four hours for you."

"No." She forcefully shook her head. "I don't want to talk. I want to fuck. I want to forget this agitated feeling that's too much like insecurity. Because that's not me. I'm strong. I'm ruthless. A little bullheaded at times."

I laughed. More like at *all* times.

Smoothing her hands up my chest to rest on my pecs, she glanced up at me through her lashes. "I'm a hell on wheels sex goddess. I want to remember that."

My cock filled up so fast my head spun.

"You made me feel like that. You always have, but that night..."

I peeled her clothes off of her body with so much reverence, I couldn't stop just as much as I couldn't not realize that this was making love. Not fucking. I left a trail of kisses everywhere my fingers went, so fucking glad she had the lamp on so I could engage all five senses.

"You make me feel powerful, Esteban."

I gripped her hips and pulled her tight against my throbbing cock. "Say my name again."

"Esteban..." The warm, throaty voice was my undoing.

She said my name. Not Matías'. Mine. She wanted me. Matías could say whatever the fuck he wanted, but she was mine too.

Sliding my hands over her plump ass, I picked her up by the back of her thighs, guiding her legs around my waist. "You want to forget, baby?" I murmured, staring deep into her big, beautiful, brown eyes.

Biting her lower lip, she sucked in a short, quick breath. Her chest was rising and falling so fast now, stretching the material of her dress.

I loved her body almost as much as I loved her.

"Come on, Rita, baby. You want me? You want me to make you feel like no one else can?"

"Yes," she whispered.

"Yes, what?" I asked as I laid her in the center of her bed. With slow methodical detail, I tucked my thumb in the side of her shoe and slipped her heel off, then moved to her other foot.

"Yes, Esteban."

I groaned. "Everything you say, I want Esteban to be attached to it. I want to hear you say my name over and over again."

"Okay, Esteban." She smirked as I kissed her ankle. This woman was going to be the death of me. Now she was going to say my name just to be a shit.

Whatever, I'd have her screaming in ten minutes, after I stripped her bare.

Pushing her dress up her thighs, I paused when I reached her panties.

Take them off or leave them on until I had her dress off?

She took the decision from me when she spread her legs wide, arching her back and moving her feet across the comforter in a sensual move.

Fuck. I narrowed my eyes on her. She was the very definition of sex appeal.

Dropping to my stomach, I sucked on her clit through the thin material of her panties, and her breath caught. I hummed and sucked harder until a soft moan fell from her throat. That was what I wanted, and this time, both she and I would remember every second of it.

I raised just enough to remove her dress. She lifted her torso to help. Then fell back on the bed with a bounce when it was off. Her tits jiggled in her bra, drawing my eyes.

"That has to go." I opened the front clasp and pulled her bra down to trap her arms. It was a weak trap, but she humored me as I worshiped one breast then the other.

Yanking the bra from her body, I caught her hands and held them above her head, grinding my hard cock against her as I kissed and licked her nipples. I needed them to be that perfect dark purplish pink before I could move on.

I caught one nipple between my teeth and sucked so hard, she arched against me, her hips riding me.

"I want your clothes off," she panted.

"Hmm...Not yet." I scooted back down the bed and cupped her thighs around my ears like the best fucking earmuffs. "I love the way you smell. And you're so wet for me."

She was. Her slit glistened with her arousal. Working her hips forward and backward, it was the most erotic sight I'd ever seen.

I licked every bit of her up, eating her out like she was my favorite meal. She was. And I wanted her to remember it.

"Oh, God." She pressed the heels of her hands to her forehead.

That's it. A little farther. I stuck two fingers inside, thrusting and twisting so slow, it was torture for her. She writhed under my hands and before long, she clamped around me and bowed her back so I couldn't see her face or tits.

She shuddered and shook from her orgasm. I kept eating and fingering her until she quivered.

"No more. No more..." she moaned as she continued to pulse around my fingers. Fuck, she was still coming.

Using one hand, I reached down and undid my pants, freeing my cock. Then I pulled my fingers from her soaked pussy and slammed inside her on a grunt.

Shit, shit. She still contracted around me so tight, I was going to come.

Breathing through my nose, I didn't move as I reached behind my head and pulled my shirt off. Then I shoved my pants down a little more.

Rita whimpered, looking at me through lust-drunk eyes. When she reached for me, I fell over her, molding my body to hers.

Then I moved, rolling my hips in strong yet lazy circles, gasping and groaning just as much as she was.

I raised my head, kissing the shit out of her, sliding my tongue inside her mouth, mimicking the motion of my cock. Her legs trembled around my waist.

That was it. She was close again.

Using more pressure and a slightly different angle, I

ground against her clit, pistoning my hips in short bursts. Then she tossed her head back.

"Esteban!" she cried, her nails cutting into my shoulders.

"Fuck," I grunted, losing it. Jamming my fat cock inside her over and over again as I came. "Say my name," I panted. "Say my fucking name one more time."

I thrust harder, getting every goddamned ounce of pleasure from her as I could.

"Esteban. Esteban, Esteban, Esteban," she whined, lowering her head and meeting my stare.

One last shiver, and I stilled my hips, my heart trying to break out of my chest and into hers.

This was perfect.

This was what I'd make sure I'd never lose.

Rita was mine.

16

RITA

Somehow, I'd managed to fall asleep. Was it that surprising after the way Esteban set my body on fire?

I needed it too. Now, Esteban's fingers trailing up and down my bare back were the gentle wake up I needed.

I let my eyes flutter open and there he was, up on his elbow, watching his fingers. A look of deep concentration made him appear slightly older.

"I'd say good morning but it's after ten pm." There was a note of amusement in his words.

"I know it's night. I can tell from the lack of sun coming through the windows," I grumbled.

Sitting up, I stretched my arms over my head and let out a groan as my back cracked in a couple places.

"You don't have to get up. We still have until tomorrow before we figure out next steps."

"I can't." I climbed out of bed and found my phone. There was one missed call and text from Germaine. And one text from Amorette.

Amorette: I wanted to check in. Want to have a drink?

Before answering her, I called Germaine. He was the head manager at Lucia's, the highest performing club the Dirty Dogs owned.

It was also the most high-end, which compared to Amorette's decor choices, wasn't much.

"Took you long enough!" Germaine grumbled in English. He was German, and did speak Spanish, but it was hard to understand him. He spoke English to anyone he could to make his life easier.

"What's wrong?" I shut myself inside my bathroom to do the essentials.

"We're out of at least five liquors." He rattled off a handful. "We'll have to BYOB it tonight unless you can make a miracle happen. I've already spoken to the other two clubs nearby and they don't have any extra stock."

I closed my eyes and worked my brain. It was coming back online slowly, and it took me an extra minute to think. "There's stock here at the club. I think we have all of those."

"Good! I'll see you in a few." He clicked.

Well, fuck. I stared down at my phone. I hadn't meant to offer to take it, but this was good. It would keep me busy and give me a chance to get my head right.

Me: I have to run stock to Lucia's. Meet me there in one hr?

I finished brushing my teeth then stepped out to fill Esteban in. He was still sprawled back on my bed, his jacked arms tucked behind his head. I shivered at the delicious sight.

It couldn't be said that when I went out, I went all the fuck out.

"I have to take some cases to Lucia's."

"In what car?"

I froze my efforts to find an appropriate clubbing dress. "Shit." That was right. I'd rode here on Esteban's bike.

"It's fine. I have a spare SUV here. I'll drive you." He rolled out of bed without an ounce of irritation.

"What are you doing, Esteban?" I tilted my head, waiting for him to look at me.

He slid his jeans over his toned ass and glanced over his shoulder. "Getting dressed. What I assume you're about to do. Unless you want to make Germaine wait?"

The thought was tempting, but... "I can't. The club's already packed at this hour. Anyway, you know what I mean."

Sighing, he turned around after he'd zipped up his jeans and pulled on his shirt. "I told you. I want a chance. This is me taking it."

I nodded, pressing my lips together. This was fun, and I liked him. More than liked him. But I was so fucked up right now for so many reasons.

Did he understand that?

The seriousness in his gaze as he watched me said he did. He also didn't care.

"You also need a bit of normalcy. And time to just breathe. I'm going to make sure you get it."

I grinned and raised one brow. "So you're going to pamper the shit out of me until I can't live without you?"

"Yup." He stepped closer, cupping my waist and dropping a kiss on my lips. "No regrets." Then he slid past me to go to the bathroom.

ESTEBAN DIRECTED several of the workers to unload the back of the SUV. We had everything I thought we had in inventory at the compound. It was nice, knowing something and being right about it.

These employees weren't part of Dirty Dogs. *Papá* had always handled the gang as mostly above board and he wanted clean people to do that. The guys had a momentary identity crisis when we'd pulled back from some of our other activities after Vicente and Valentina died.

Shit. That could be part of why the men were all fired up to go hard after this other club. They were insulted, their pride had taken multiple hits, and they were struggling to fill their time.

I checked the time. Amorette should be here by now.

"I need to go find Amorette." I touched Esteban's arm.

He worked his jaw as the last worker took the final box. "I'll come with you."

"I don't need a bodyguard in our own club." I tucked my phone in my clutch and waited. I wanted him to come with me. I wanted him to fix that fundamental thing inside me that Matías broke.

"Ask me if I give a fuck," he hummed.

Beaming, I led the way through the back entrance of the club. The blacklights overhead gave everything a dark and sinister vibe. The employees all wore white to stand out in the crowd. Hilarious considering that the Dirty Dogs owned it.

Not all of our clubs had a VIP section, including this one, but we did have a section that was in the corner just for Dirty Dogs. It wasn't roped off, it was simply known as off-limits to the locals.

As I pushed through the sweaty crowd, I craned my neck looking for my tiny friend. She was a bitch to find in these places because she was shorter than everyone and refused to wear anything bigger than kitten heels.

I'd asked her once why she didn't rock taller heels. She'd said she wanted to be able to run if she needed to. Given her chosen men, I understood it.

We reached the bar, and Germaine propped his elbows on the counter. "You're a lifesaver. Tonight is wild!" he yelled over the music.

"No problem." I gripped the wooden edge of the counter and Esteban caged me in with his arms. Warmth pooled in my stomach. This was what I'd always wanted. The feeling that I was the most important person in someone's life.

I opened my mouth to ask if he'd seen Amorette–he'd met her a couple times in the last year, when he pointed to our section.

"Your friends are over there."

"Thanks!" I called, but I was already weaving through hot and sweaty couples.

"Fuck a bitch," Esteban muttered.

I would have asked why, but I wasn't turning around so he could hear me. My path would get swallowed up and we'd be stuck here for another ten minutes. It wasn't that I minded, but as much as I wanted to see Amorette, I hadn't wanted to stay out very long.

Just enough that both Amorette and Esteban saw that I was okay.

Another gap appeared and I cleared it. Then some scrawny ass kid stepped in my path.

"Dance?" His smile was as slimy as his polo. The tourists found us.

"Get lost." I flicked my fingers, but his smile didn't change. He moved closer.

He used his one chance. Shooting out my hand, I cupped his feeble balls, making sure to dig my nails in. At the same time Esteban caught his throat.

I sputtered out a laugh, leaning closer. "If you want to keep your life and your balls, I'd hit up Lorana's. That's where the tourists party."

As if synchronized, we let the kid go, and he wasted no time scrambling back.

I glanced back at Esteban and we shared a smile, before his gaze flicked over my head. Murder entered his expression and he curled his hand around my waist.

Oh fuck. I had a good idea what he was frustrated about. I almost didn't want to turn.

But I did.

There was Amorette, sitting in the center of three of her men, minus Andre, and in the fifth chair was Matías, looking grumpy as hell as he returned my stare.

As soon as our eyes met, I looked away as heat blistered my cheeks. I'd done nothing wrong, but my body reacted like I'd betrayed him. Fuck that.

Moving forward, I switched my attention to Amorette. She had the decency to look sheepish. When I reached her, I nodded my head toward the other table. Smiling at her guys, she excused herself and followed me.

"Why did you bring him?" I demanded once we were seated.

"Grey and Parker didn't want to leave him at home." She gazed at them with too much love. It was going to make me sick.

"I don't want to see him, Amorette." I wasn't kidding.

She shrugged. "So don't look. We're at a different table anyway."

Yeah, she said that, but my eyes had a mind of their own. Every few seconds they wandered to his seat and slid away from his heated stare. He was making a scene with how intently focused on me he was.

Esteban glanced between Matías and me. He seemed torn between staying with me and starting another fight with Matías. Finally, he released the tension in his shoulders and came to stand against the wall behind me.

I sighed. I hadn't realized how concerned I was that they'd start fighting in the club. In our compound was one thing, but in one of our businesses was another. It required paying off a few officials for turning their heads the other way.

We'd had to do that for Parker last year.

"Parker told me about what happened at the school." Amorette flicked her gaze to Esteban and back again. The music wasn't as loud here, but she still kept her voice low so he couldn't hear what she was saying. "Why didn't you call me?"

"And tell you what?" I played dumb. One-hundred-percent.

She reached for my hand and tucked her small hand around mine. "I'm just worried about you."

"Yeah? Well, bringing the man who broke my heart isn't the way to check on me," I snapped.

Amorette pressed her lips together and glanced at Matías. I did too and wished I hadn't.

He wasn't looking at me anymore. He was talking to Ricco and a couple of the guys from the club. They slapped him on the back like a long lost friend. It was hard to see.

I was the Dirty Dog. I was *Papá's* fucking daughter and they all knew he dropped me. Yet they fawned around him like he was royalty.

"I just don't understand..." Amorette trailed off.

"Don't understand what?" My voice changed from angry to frustrated.

"He came back for you. I hoped it would fix things. I want you both to be happy."

I pulled a face. "He was the reason I missed *Papá's* passing."

She faced me. "That's not his fault. Andre or any of my guys would have gone to get him for you. You wanted to be the one to go. That was your decision."

My chest squeezed at the uncomfortable feeling pressing down on it. "You think I don't know that?"

"You *don't* know that!" Amorette tossed up her hands. "Otherwise you wouldn't blame him for it."

I shook my head. "You don't understand."

A roar of laughter came from their table. I recognized Matías' laugh. It wasn't often he laughed like that. I used to savor those moments.

I glanced over as Matías did the same. A bright smile on his face for the first time since he came back and I wasn't the one who put it there.

Not able to hold his gaze, I looked back at Amorette. "I think a night out is more than I can take."

Turning to get Esteban's attention, I was ready to call it quits. I had bigger things to worry about. Like how I was going to win the vote. Actually that wasn't even in the top three. The most important was figuring out how to keep a bunch of man babies from running to their deaths.

"Wait." Amorette leaned over the table, reaching for my arm.

"What?" I'd lost all my good mood.

Someone screamed in the crowd and people started running toward the back of the club. The music cut and men's shouting echoed off the walls.

The brothers surrounded Amorette and I ran from the table, straight for the front. Esteban was hot on my heels.

Ricco called for the Dogs, from right behind me, and when I glanced back, Matías was on his other side.

Several women almost ran into me in an effort to get away but I wove as Esteban pushed.

At the front of the club, Due stood toe to toe with a couple men I didn't recognize. Their new leather jackets gave me an idea of who they were and my stomach sank.

"What's the problem?" I asked, stopping shoulder to shoulder with Due.

He glared at the man in front of him. "Looks like the new gang in town wanted to scout out our club. Not fucking happening."

The man in front of him smiled, not the least bit intimidated. "What? You don't want to make friends with your new neighbors?"

"You don't want to be friends. You made that clear when you killed one of our men."

The man scoffed. "You killed your own man and delivered his head. Don't blame that on us."

"I'm not talking about him. I'm talking about Tiago. He was dropped at our gates today." Due lifted his chin.

I had to give it to the man. He looked genuinely confused. "That wasn't us."

"Don't lie!" Due shot forward but Esteban pulled him back and took his place.

"Tonight, you're not welcome here. If you didn't deliver our man like you say you did, leave as a show of good faith," Esteban said as he placed his shoulder slightly in front of mine.

"You expect us to just roll over anytime your club says? It seems you don't have your shit together and you're holding onto your businesses by your fingernails." The guy laughed and slapped his friend's chest. The three of them were having a good laugh at our expense.

"Your first mistake is assuming the Dirty Dogs aren't lethal. They are." Matías' shoulder touched mine as he made his allegiance obvious. "Your second is assuming they don't have friends."

The guy glanced at Matías, his gaze lingering. He didn't outright recognize him, but he must have thought he looked familiar.

"Who the fuck are you?"

Matías smiled, and it was the one he'd always had for the Institution or his enemies. A crazy and rage-filled show of teeth. "Matías Castillo. You might have heard of me. And if you haven't heard of me, you've surely heard of Andre Medina. Or Grey Morozov, or Parker Adair. Maybe even Lafe Nilsen." He rattled off his brothers like he was reading a shopping list.

The men backed up. It was only half a step, but it was enough to show they did fear the brothers where they didn't fear us.

That was bullshit.

I stepped forward. "You have two seconds to get off of our club property. This is us being nice. We'll pay you a visit and talk to your president soon. Send him our regards."

The men glanced at Matías, then each other. That was all it took for them to leave.

Anger like I'd never experienced before burned through me. When they were gone, I grabbed Matías' wrist and walked him to the back office. The others fell away. I heard Esteban shouting but when I glanced back, he wasn't behind us.

Inside the office, I shut the door and faced Matías. He wanted to have this talk. Fine. We'd have it right now.

17

MATÍAS

God she was gorgeous.

Her cat eyes were so sharp, she could cut a man with just a look. By all accounts, I should have been in ribbons at her feet.

Wild curls floated around her head giving her an aura of ferocity. Yet, she stood there, her body turned slightly to the side, as if it was a mechanism to protect herself from me.

I would never hurt her. Not again.

Her top lip curled and she wouldn't look directly at me. It didn't matter. She was the very image of perfection. At one time, I considered myself lucky that she was mine. The thing was, whether she knew it or not, she was still mine.

And this was my chance.

I glanced around. I'd been in this office before. Not often, but enough to know it hadn't changed at all.

A few cork boards hung up on the concrete walls with old receipts and reminders pinned. There was a shabby desk with a metal chair behind it and two in front of it. That was it.

The Dirty Dogs weren't the savvy business owners my

father had been. They only cared about function and purpose.

I took a deep breath and scratched my temple. "Can we sit?"

Her gaze moved straight to the chairs. Instead of moving, she closed her eyes and took several inhales before letting them out. She'd been fired up when she marched me in here, but now that we were alone, that anger was draining.

That was best. I could never talk to her when she was upset. She was just as bull headed as Javier had been. Worse actually because she was the monster he created.

Fuck, not a monster. Not in those terms and not like my father.

Her brand of crazy was more endearing.

"Rita," I walked after her, making an effort to keep up, which was impressive all on its own. She was a few inches shorter than me in strappy high heels. But she moved in those things like she'd been born in them.

"I don't have time for your shit, Matías." She held her hand up. Some of the men at the club nodded at us as we passed. A few even smirked as they watched me chase after her.

They thought it was hilarious. Most of the time I did too.

Except right now, the club wasn't packed and I had a direct line of sight to her luscious ass bouncing with each step. I struggled to remember what I was supposed to be irritated about.

Then she stopped at the bar and raised a finger to get the bartender's attention.

"I can't believe you've never ridden a bike. That's outrageous." She huffed.

Oh, yeah. She'd thought I was the one out of my depths because I didn't ride bikes. Like that was the base-level requirement to fuck the Dirty Dogs princess.

I never said I couldn't ride, but there was no point in telling *her. If Vicente ever caught me riding with them, I'd be punished worse than my brother Grey for embarrassing him.*

I grabbed her hand and walked her to the back hallway, out of sight of any patrons and any men who could report back to my father.

Caging her into the wall, I nipped her bottom lip. "I can still make you scream my name."

She glared at me in defiance, like she knew exactly what I was trying to do.

I grinned. Rita was the one person I couldn't bluff my way with. Her gaze dropped to my lips and she released her ire. "You want to date me, you have to ride a bike. That's non-negotiable."

Date. Such an innocent word but I savored the meaning behind it, ignoring all the reasons I couldn't take her home with me.

"Why does it matter to you so much?" I nuzzled the soft spot just under her earlobe. It seemed so juvenile she'd care.

"How are you going to integrate into the Dirty Dogs if you can't keep up with Papá or the other men?" She huffed. "We'll have to get you a Riker. You'll be the butt of all jokes for the next decade. Matías Castillo. Son of the notorious Institution leader and trike rider." She rolled her eyes.

I grinned at her ridiculousness. I didn't give a shit what the Dirty Dogs said. Except for Javier. I did respect him.

Sliding my hand under her dress, I nibbled down the column of her throat. Her breathing changed and I realized this was the key. Sex was the distraction she couldn't see through.

I used it to my advantage because I didn't have the heart to tell her the only way out of the Institution was death.

"Hell no." She glanced at the chairs like they were poison.

"Rita," I spoke softly, moving closer until I pulled a chair three or four feet from the other. "I'll sit over here. Please?"

If this was my only chance, I didn't want to fuck it up by starting in a hostile environment. Sitting down, I placed my palms on my knees and waited. Eventually, she huffed out an aggrieved breath, and sat down in the chair closest to me.

Rearranging my features, I remained calm. The last thing I wanted to do was irritate her with some fucked up expression.

"You want to talk? Fine." Her narrowed brown eyes locked on my earlobe. "Whether we're in the compound, at the club, or anywhere, you do not step into Dirty Dogs business. Ever."

I stiffened. Where the fuck had that come from?

"You're not a Dirty Dog, and you made it clear you never wanted to be. So–"

"I only stepped in to diffuse the situation," I interjected, then silently cursed. Fuck. I hadn't meant to talk over her.

"I don't need your help. I don't want it. I don't want anything from you." Her gaze met mine for half a second, then slid to my nose.

What the fuck?

"You don't want me to help, fine. Noted. But that's not what I wanted to talk about." I curled my fingers over my knees. "I wanted to apologize."

She reared back. "For what?" I opened my mouth, but she continued. "Because you've done a thousand and one things to me that you don't have any remorse for. So what *thing* are you giving me an empty apology for?"

The back of my throat burned. "Let me just explain?" When she flat-out turned her face to the wall, I continued. "I love you."

She sucked in a shallow breath, but otherwise didn't move. This was the second time I'd told her I loved her, and as much as I felt like I was trying to stand in a mudslide, I *had* to tell her.

"I love you so damn much, Rita. But I was fucked up. You met my father. At the very end, you saw how he made my brothers' lives hell, and those were his *sons*. His fucking sons!" My voice started to rise and I dropped my gaze.

I needed to get a grip. I would not ruin this chance by losing my cool.

"I loved you enough to walk away." The words settled between us with a soft boom.

She shook her head vehemently. "That doesn't work, Matías. He was dead before you left. You could have told me anytime that was why you stayed away." She laughed. "I would have fallen at your feet because that's how much I loved you, even though I was a dirty fucking secret. But now? I can't accept that. I won't."

I made a sound of frustration in the back of my throat. "I'm sorry, Rita. The best I can say is I fucked up. But you've knocked sense into me. When you left my apartment in Portugal, I had a real look at what my life was like without you in it, and I refuse to live like that. I deserve happiness, even when I convinced myself I didn't. You deserve happiness. I'm here now. I'm not leaving again. There are no more obstacles in my way. Most of all, myself."

Her eyes started to water but she kept them from me.

Nerves wracked my body. Why wouldn't she look at me? I leaned to the side and she still didn't meet my gaze.

Without any of her fire, she shook her head. "No, Matías. You broke something in me that can never be fixed. You picked your family for whatever fucked up reason, over and over again. I lost confidence in myself, I lost trust in my judgment, and *I missed the last days with my* Papá *for you!*"

She ended in a heart-breaking scream. "Whatever you want to do, *stop*. You broke it, and you can't fix it."

"There has to be something I can do, Rita," I pleaded, a note of desperation entering my voice. Scooting to the edge of my seat, I inched as close to her as I dared. "I'm not leaving you again. I will *never* leave you again."

She finally met my gaze, her pupils flaring at the contact. "*I don't believe you.*"

"Then I'll fucking prove it to you," I growled. "What do you want? What will make it right? To show you that you are the most important thing to me in my entire fucking life?"

Rita pushed her tongue up over her front teeth as she glared at me. "There's nothing you can do."

"Then I'll have to prove it to you my way."

She grimaced in anger as she raised her hands, slowly curling them into tight fists. "Why did you even come back?" Her voice boomed through the small room.

"For you!" I yelled back.

"Well don't bother! I've been fucking Esteban." The way she spilled the admission between us, she wanted to make me angry. To push me away.

It did hurt. It stung like a motherfucker, but it was the consequences of my own actions.

"I know," I said through gritted teeth. Forcing myself to relax, I loosened my fingers. "Is that why you can't look at me for more than two seconds?"

Shaking her head side to side in disbelief, Rita stood up from the chair. "You don't even care. You don't even fucking care that I fucked Esteban before I came to Lucia's tonight, do you?"

"Do you want me to be upset?" I asked, working damn hard not to destroy the room in fury.

"I want you to have a fucking reaction!" She leaned over me.

Because she did care. She loved me and she couldn't turn it off. I understood that. There was nothing I could do about my feelings for her except sit in them, let them wrap me up like a warm blanket and hope they didn't suffocate me.

The door swung open as Esteban stepped in. "I don't like what I'm hearing." He shut it behind him. "Say the word, baby, and I'll take him out back and make sure he stays gone for good this time."

Fucking hell. He had a pet name for her? I didn't even call her anything like that.

It reminded me so much of my brothers with Amorette. They weren't afraid to show their affection, but I was fucking terrified.

In my childhood home, affection was a weakness to be exploited against you.

And I made sure there was as little to be discovered about me and Rita as possible.

"Esteban..." Rita's voice took on a devious note. "Come here," she purred, curling a finger.

He raised a brow as he stalked toward her. She sat on the edge of the desk and raised her thighs, spreading them. The movement forced her dress up and exposed her cloth covered pussy.

"Kneel."

He did, as she sucked on a finger, then pulled the gusset of her panties to the side to circle her clit.

I was one tense ball of anger and hate. "You don't have to do this to prove your point."

She glanced at me, never stopping as Esteban curled his large hands around her smooth thighs, leaving kisses on the inside of her leg. He made sure to stay out of the way of the show.

He knew how fucked this was for me, how much I hated it and he followed along.

"But I want to." She faux pouted.

This was the catty side of Rita I hated. *That I loved and hated.*

"I want a reaction and you need to see that I'm not the same woman. You turned me into this, and I enjoy it. I *enjoy* Esteban." She trailed one fingertip down his jaw. "Don't I?"

"Mm. We enjoy each other, baby." He angled his head to lick around where her finger still circled that tight bud of nerves. She moaned as she tipped her head back.

A thousand ants crawled under my skin as I now gripped my thighs so hard, I'd have bruises.

She opened her eyes and glanced at me with lust-filled eyes. Rita was actually getting off on this and fuck me, but my cock twitched.

"Shove two fingers inside," Esteban said in a low tone. Using his hold on her thighs, he pulled her out to the edge. "I want to see how well you fuck yourself."

Insecurities ran rampant inside me. I'd never talked like this to her. Was this what she wanted? Was it lacking with me?

Grinding my teeth so fucking hard, I pushed the thoughts out. Rita wanted this?

She was being a bitch trying to break things with us once and for all. No fucking way would I allow that. Rita wanted to fuck Esteban, I'd have to show her it didn't faze me.

She groaned, her hair falling over her shoulder as she rolled her head forward. Esteban suckled on that sweet nub as he played with her tits, working her over with a confidence I hadn't even known I should have expected from him.

A surge of competition rose inside me. I wanted nothing more than to smack him out of the way and make her scream from pleasure.

I bent forward, then stopped myself.

Rita snapped her eyes open and locked her gaze on me as if she knew what I was thinking.

"Tongue fuck me, Esteban. I'm close." She propped herself up on both hands as she leaned her head back. Her plush red lips parted as Esteban pulled the top of her dress down so one of her tits popped out. He pinched her nipple as he did exactly as she told him to.

He tongue fucked her.

The wet sounds were so obscene, my cock was diamond hard. Waves of blistering heat washed over my body and I struggled to pull in a breath.

Jesus Christ, this was the single hottest thing I'd ever witnessed in my life.

I didn't want to see this. Without a doubt, this image would be burned into my nightmares, yet I couldn't look away. And in that moment, it was all too clear this scene would headline in my fantasies too.

It was Rita. The woman was always gorgeous. But she was divine as Esteban worshiped at her feet. Or between her legs.

This was seven kinds of fucked. I shouldn't be turned on by this. Yet, I was. Rita wanted to scare me away? She was only making me want to fuck her harder. To show her I could make her feel just as good.

Letting out a low mew, she started rocking her hips against his face.

"That's it. You're so close. You're doing so good, fucking

yourself on me," Esteban mumbled before he started fucking her again. "Come for me, baby."

Biting her lip, her fingers flexed against the desktop and her back arched.

"Yes! I'm there, I'm fucking *there*." She moaned so loud, it was the only sound that existed. Soon, it changed to gasps, and then sighs.

Breathing became non-existent for me as the intimacy of her coming became the beginning and the end of my being.

Esteban brought her down gently before placing a kiss on her mound. After Rita stopped moving, he stood, gathering her to his chest like she was his prized possession.

I should be holding her. She was mine. And in this moment, she was his too.

He turned to face me, his mouth and chin still glistening. "Did you like that?" His gaze dropped to my cock. "Fuck," he griped, a dour expression on his face. "You did."

Rita pulled her head back so she could see me. Immediately, she zeroed in on my cock and a soft gasp escaped her.

I knew what they saw. A man filled with so much embarrassment, because as much as I should have run when she started to fuck Esteban to spite me, I couldn't.

My brothers must have rubbed off on me.

18

RITA

I picked up the mug of steaming hot coffee, and used too much force. Coffee sloshed over the sides and splashed against my fingers.

"Shit!" I yelped and dropped the mug in the sink. It shattered as coffee splattered all over the counter. Snatching the towel hanging off the stove, I wrapped it around my hand as I curled over. "That hurt!"

No one was here to care about my cries of pain, but it felt so much better to get them out.

Turning on the cool water, I dropped the towel and held my fingers under the faucet. The pulsing from the burn wasn't so strong now. But when I turned the water off, my skin was still bright red.

Orgasms were supposed to make everything better. That was the shit I told myself over the last week. I'd had more orgasms in that time than I'd had in the entire last year. At least not self induced.

Instead of helping last night, I calmly walked out on both Matías and Esteban, then drove my happy ass home. Happy was sarcasm. I couldn't even fool myself.

My phone buzzed.

A night of terrible tossing and turning and a morning of everything going wrong should have worn my brain out. It didn't. Thoughts of what was going to happen with the Dirty Dogs and the lives we'd lost much too soon played on repeat.

Another buzz vibrated across the counter.

Sighing, I turned it around to see the screen. Ricco.

He was one of my favorites, but the shit he was pulling lately, I didn't want to speak to him.

I answered anyway. "What?" I snapped.

"Rita, *cariño*. I'm just calling to check in on you." His voice was so familiar, it provided a weird comfort even though I was pissed with him.

"Really? Because all you've been doing is undermine me and try to bring Matías into the fold. Did you forget he ran away *twice*? And one of those times he fucked me over?"

"A breakup is not fucking you over," he said, exasperated. "My concern is the club. I want the Dirty Dogs to thrive now that the Institution is no longer there to hold us down. The brothers seem like they're willing to honor their truce with us, but Matías is still the leader we should have."

"The leader you want us to have or that you think Javier wanted us to have?" I pinched my phone between my ear and shoulder and used my left hand, the unburned one, to wipe up the counter.

There was a pause. "Do you think you're the best leader for the club?"

My hackles immediately raised and I froze. "Why are you asking me that? It's clear that you already have your own opinions."

Instead of answering my questions, he hit me with another one. This one the worst by far. "Tell me three reasons why you want to lead? I'm not sure you can name one good one."

"A good one?" Instead of letting my ego take a hit like last night, I straightened up, embracing the anger building inside me.

"We know you miss your father. But you can't hold onto him just by taking his place."

Oh...I was going to fuck his shit up the next time I saw him. Placing my phone on the counter, I hit the speaker button. My hands shook and I gripped the countertop just to steady myself.

"How about because we have shit options. And if you say Matías' name, I will hang up on you. Then there's the fact that I'm more level-headed than any of said shit options. And lastly? Because it's my fucking legacy and I, more than any of you, know the toll the club had on *Papá*."

It was true. He hid his frustration and exhaustion from them. I'd seen it in his house. He'd talked to me about it. Not them. I sat through the majority of meetings and he never showed them a goddamn hint that he was tired from leading the club.

But it was his life's work.

I'd be damned if I let them run it into the ground because their egos were bigger than their cocks.

"What time is the meeting? I haven't been notified at all." We should be meeting in a few hours to go over anything and everything Due found. I'd be there, just in case they tried to wedge me out.

"We haven't decided," Ricco said, but the tone was off.

"You mean you were hoping I'd miss it. I'll be there." Then I hit the red end button. Even if he tried to keep me away, Esteban would make sure I was there.

Esteban. I closed my eyes.

He was proving to be everything I needed and then some. I still felt guilt, especially after using him to hurt Matías. Esteban seemed like he hadn't minded.

And Matías hadn't seemed hurt at all. Well, he was feeling some level of hurt, but he was turned on more. I'd never seen his cock as big as last night when it tented his jeans.

I got a text message.

Esteban: I have to check on the shop. I'll swing by to get you for the meeting.

So there was a time already set. Assholes.

Me: Don't worry about it. I'm going to the compound early.

Tires squealed outside and I ran to the corner drawer. I pulled out a gun and crouched as I moved toward the front door. Gunshots went off next.

Shit. I should have taken Esteban up on his offer last night to come home with me, but I'd needed some time away from both of them.

My house was brick, so I was relatively safe hunkered down close to the floor. When I didn't hear any more noises, I raised up and peeked through the corner of my front window.

Matías stood at the end of the sidewalk, glaring down the street with his gun held in both hands.

What the fuck?

I opened the door, not ready to put the gun down, and poked my head out. "What are you doing?" I hissed.

This was Dirty Dogs territory, but we still had to be careful not to raise too many questions.

Matías didn't look at me right away. He watched the empty street like he believed a threat would pop out at any minute.

Eventually, as my heart left my throat, he turned to me but stared down at the ground. "Fuck," he muttered.

On the ground were two spilled coffees from my favorite cafe and a box of breakfast food splattered across the concrete. The savory smell of rice, beans, and eggs registered.

My stomach growled the same time that my eyelids fluttered shut. He'd tried to bring me my favorite breakfast. Even after I'd fucked Esteban's face right in front of him.

I opened my eyes. No. I would not feel guilty about any of that. His actions had consequences. I just couldn't figure out why he didn't seem to care what those consequences were.

Clearing my throat, I lift my gaze to his eyes. After last night, I could miraculously look him in the eye again. "What happened?"

"I believe the new club was going to try and either shoot up your house or car. Until they saw me." His grin was full of sharp teeth.

"So you shot at them?"

"They were in the process of lowering their windows. If I didn't shoot first, it would have given them an opportunity to not only hurt you, but to kill me." He raised one shoulder. "This way, they were on the defensive and sped away."

Matías sneered down at his wasted efforts. "Motherfuckers." Then sighing, he shook his head. "Let's grab breakfast."

I blinked. "Grab breakfast? After those assholes tried to hurt me."

"You're hungry. When you need food, you always get this crazy look in your eyes." He waved his hand toward my face.

I tried not to grin. There was nothing to grin about, but his statement still set off butterflies in my stomach.

"I'm mad at you, Matías. You should hate me."

He canted his head. "Funny. I don't. And you *should* be mad at me. I fucked up." Swiping a hand through his hair, Matías turned his head for a brief second before swinging hurt eyes back to me. "I did, okay. I fucked up. I could have done a million things differently, but I can't change it. I *believed* I was doing the right thing. The best I could do for you and for my family. I can't change it," he repeated on a broken whisper.

I was still stuck in a bubble of grief and stress and his words made sense, but at the same time, it was like I was in an alternate reality.

The best for me? I started shaking my head, but it was pointless. He really thought that. But it didn't change anything, did it? He broke my heart with the best of intentions, but he still broke my heart. Who was to say he wouldn't do it again?

Like he was shaking off the unwanted emotions, he shook his head and sighed as he walked up to the door. "You're dressed. Grab your shoes and we can go. You want to drive?"

I jerked back in whiplash.

"What is wrong with you?" We never went out to eat before. We met at the compound, our clubs, or under the cover of dark. At the time, I'd thought it was sexy and mysterious. Dangerous and thrilling.

Now, a little older, and fuck of a lot more jaded, I saw it for what it was. I had been a dirty little secret.

Licking his bottom lip, he held my gaze. "I did everything wrong the first time. You were right about some of the things you said last night, but not all of them. This is me correcting my mistakes."

"By feeding me?"

A ghost of a smile slid over his face. "Sure, if that's what you want to take from this."

I started shaking my head and tried to close the door. He stopped it with a hand. I glanced up at him, and his face had sobered to the point of being depressingly sad. "If you don't want to go with me, that's fine. I won't force you. Despite what you think, I would never force a woman to do anything."

A twinge flared in my chest as I remembered one comment I'd made out of spite. I hadn't meant it.

"However, I will not leave. If this new club has their sights set on you, you need to be guarded. I thought Esteban would have stayed with you last night. Yet, when I drove by early this morning his car wasn't here. But yours was." Matías glanced toward my baby in the drive. "Why didn't you put her in the garage?"

I wasn't sure. Which was really fucking telling for where my headspace had been last night.

"Esteban wanted to come but I needed time to myself." I needed to take up for him. I had pushed him away last night so him not being here was my doing.

"Then he should have sat on your porch or had some of the other Dirty Dogs protecting you." Judgment clung to his shoulders as he surveyed the street. He didn't trust the men wouldn't drive by again.

I almost caved.

"I don't want breakfast. And I'm not going to invite you in. Thank you, but I'm leaving in a few minutes to go to the compound." I closed the door quietly and he didn't protest.

My heart fluttered in my chest. This was fucking hard. Why now? What was so different about now over last month? Hell, six months ago?

Peeking out the window, I held my breath. He wouldn't hear me, but he'd be able to see me checking on him.

Like he'd said Esteban needed to do, he sat down on the top step like he did this every day.

Going back into the kitchen, I grabbed a banana and scarfed it down. It was tough. It wasn't anywhere near as delicious as the food at my favorite cafe, but I'd be damned if I rolled over and allowed Matías back into my life with a few pretty words.

They felt good. They might even have started to mend the broken pieces inside me. But I couldn't forget. Actions spoke louder than words, and all this man had ever done was meet me in the dark.

TEN MINUTES LATER, I stepped outside. After checking to make sure no gangs were lurking in the bushes.

Matías hopped up and dusted off his jeans. I took a second to study him while he wasn't looking at me.

He wore jeans and a T-shirt today. An outfit so very different from anything he would have worn before. When we were together, he mostly wore suits or some variations of business casual. I used to get a kick out of it, but now, it was just one more sign I should have paid attention to that we didn't fit.

"See something you like?" he asked mildly.

I stiffened. "Nope." Breezing past, I slid my sunglasses on my face. "I'm just shocked to see you out of a suit."

"I found that suits weren't really my thing. I'm in my new era of figuring out who the hell I am. More importantly, who I wanted to be." He'd said all that so innocently, like he was on some quest in a fantasy book.

He'd never been good with words. He'd been better with threats and deranged smiles when he felt threatened. And this new side of him was getting to me. I couldn't trust it.

The quick reminder helped me focus back on the more important issues for the day. Making sure Ricco and Joel knew exactly where I stood and that I wasn't going anywhere.

I climbed in my car and revved the engine. I'd driven this sweet girl for five years. It was hell on wheels and sentimental. Esteban had actually been the one to oversee it.

It was everything a Lamborghini Veneno should be, but he'd souped it up in all the best ways. Matías got in his car parked on the street and when I pulled out, he followed.

Glancing in the rearview mirror, I floored the pedal and left him in the dust.

Cranking the music, I smiled during the short drive to the compound. It was only when Matías pulled in behind me and got out that my short stint of happiness burst.

"What are you doing?" I faced off with him.

"Attending the meeting." His own sunglasses were black tinted lenses so I could only see my own reflection in them.

"Why? You're not a Dirty Dog."

Another sly smile that was there, then gone. "You see, that's the thing. I'm figuring myself out and there's only one thing I want, outside of you."

His brothers. But that wouldn't be what he was thinking to lay it out like this between us. If he did, he knew I'd claw the shit out of him. That left something he thought was romantic. Or something I had once wanted.

I didn't know whether to melt into a puddle of goo or burst into flames at how he kept pushing me into a corner. He thought he was cunning.

"What's that?" I asked as a form of torture I apparently loved to inflict on myself.

The smile lines deepened on one side as he gave me a crooked grin. "To be a Dirty Dog. I'm here to put in my official application."

"You've got to be fucking shitting me!" Esteban stormed around the side of the compound, grease marking his hands and shirt.

I should have stepped between them, but I was shocked. I knew what he would say, yet I was still shook to my core.

He wanted to be a Dirty Dog? Fuck.

19

RITA

Dirty Dogs started pouring out of the compound. Ricco and Joel coming right behind Esteban.

Esteban was on a mission. He couldn't be stopped as he stormed straight for Matías.

Except Ricco somehow got in front of him and knocked him back. Grinning so wide, Ricco's face was going to split. Joel on the other hand looked like he'd sucked on a lemon.

"Matías! It's about damn time!" Ricco pulled him into a tight hug. Matías seemed mildly uncomfortable as he waited a beat before he patted Ricco on the back.

Shooting a quick glance at me, Esteban seemed to think better of starting another fight and came to stand slightly in front of me, crossing his arms. His T-shirt stretched over his muscles and sweat glistened on the back of his neck.

He was so worked up, the muscles in his arms were spasming. "Don't trust it," he growled.

Joel glanced at Esteban, then at me. I'd been standing there mesmerized but his attention jump started my brain.

"What do you mean you want to be a Dirty Dog?" My

voice was shrill at the end, all of my shock and outrage slamming into me like a semi-truck.

He'd had *years* to make this decision. I couldn't get over the fact that he'd let so much time pass and *now* he wanted to change everything?

"Why shouldn't we trust him?" Joel asked loudly.

Several of the men patted Matías on the back, trying to engage him in some wasted-ass, small talk. Absolutely none of them cared about what Joel had to say.

Joel was well liked and popular in the club, so that was telling enough that it set my teeth on edge.

"He either wants Rita back, or he wants to take the club. I don't trust him." Esteban spit toward Matías.

It didn't reach him but the sentiment was still the same.

The guys closest to Matías made booing sounds like they were egging on the fight while stepping back to avoid any backlash if one did start.

"Doesn't matter what you think." Ricco was too jolly. "It matters that he's made his intentions known. That's the first step." He raised his voice so the crowd of Dirty Dogs would all hear. "Matías wants to be a Dirty Dog!"

Everyone except Joel, Esteban, about three others, and me, whooped their excitement.

"You know the drill! He has thirty days to prove his worth. Then we vote!" Ricco wound his arm up before pointing at the sky.

So fucking dramatic.

My hands shook from the revelation. Matías was pushing hard. Everything was changing and I didn't have a choice but to keep up. I headed toward the compound, leaving the men in their circle.

"The meeting starts in three minutes. You're not there,

you don't get a say in the next steps!" I called over my shoulder.

Esteban and Due fell in line on either side of me. The noise behind us calmed down, and once I took my seat at the table, I realized just how close Matías had been. He was already seated in the closest chair, his gaze soaking me up.

I shifted uncomfortably.

"Do you want him gone?" Esteban whispered in my ear.

"No, it's fine." I held Matías' gaze in challenge. He wanted to fuck with me? I'd fuck right back. I only had to figure out how to do that without sacrificing who I was and what I wanted. Been there before. Done that. Didn't want to do it again. The gang was more important.

We had three quarters of our men here. That was a pretty good amount. Usually meetings were run on half the gang. There were just too many businesses and errands the guys were involved in for everyone to be here.

"Due," I rushed out when Joel opened his mouth. "Time's up. What did you find?"

Joel raised a brow but he didn't say anything.

In the middle of the chairs, Due stood up. He was my age and his dad had been a founding member in the club until he died from a job about a decade ago. He was also Esteban's best friend.

His gaze flicked to Esteban standing behind me.

"Wait." Matías raised a hand and stood up. "Before the meeting gets too far, I have an issue to raise."

"You can't raise an issue without being an official member," Esteban fired at Matías, derision dripping from his voice.

Matías pulled his shoulders back. "You'll want to hear this issue."

"Doubt it." Esteban rested his hands on either side of me at the table, making his claim clear.

Fuck. I should tell him to back up. Just because we were involved didn't mean I wanted my laundry aired out for the club, but I didn't want to either. I enjoyed the claim as much as I didn't want to rub Matías' face in it.

It seemed I'd gotten out most of my spite the night before.

"You'll want to hear this one, and when you do, you'll feel a fool for giving into your obvious dislike of me."

"Who said I disliked you?" Esteban asked lightly. Matías started to respond but Esteban chuckled. "I fucking hate you. Years I watched you lead Rita on. Treat her like a backroom whore and roll over for your father because you were too weak to do anything else. It took you a year before you surfaced again. So you're either here to take over, or to get Rita back. From where I stand, you don't deserve either."

The room fell so silent, you could hear a mouse breathe. If we had mice. We didn't because that shit was nasty.

Matías' eyes darkened and his expression seemed to stretch taut. Not even Ricco or Joel had anything to say to that.

He didn't rise to the bait. Matías turned to the room. "Regardless of what you think of me, I'm here because I want to be here. Sure, because of Rita, but also because the Dirty Dogs is the only home I've ever really known. But I'm still going to raise this issue." His gaze flicked to me. "This morning, there was an attempt made at Rita's house by the new club."

"Rita!" Esteban snapped at the same time Ricco and Joel yelled.

Shit, I should have alerted someone. I almost did, but

Matías had me off-kilter. "Matías was there and within minutes, I left to come straight here."

"Why was he there?" It was spoken so quietly, I could almost pretend I didn't hear Esteban.

"This all feeds into what Due found. Due." I motioned for him to continue his report. He twisted his lips to the side before nodding and standing back up.

"There's nothing to report. None of the neighborhood surveillance caught anything on camera. None of the locals we spoke to saw anyone. As far as everyone was concerned there was no one out of the usual riding through."

I released a long breath. This was exactly what I feared.

"Then we need to go speak with the new guys." I leaned back in the chair, the back of my head brushing against Esteban's chest. His stare drilled holes in the top of my head, but I couldn't acknowledge that right then.

"We need to hit them hard and fast." Joel argued and a few men murmured their agreement. "If they don't exist anymore, then they can't cause us problems."

"No," I returned. "They want us to strike back, I'm pretty sure that's the case. Just like I'm sure it's likely they're the ones fucking with us, but we can't act without knowing for sure."

Ricco sat back and smoothed his fingers down his jaw thoughtfully. "I agree, you should go. Take Esteban with you since he's attached to your hip right now. But you'll take Matías too."

"Fuck no." Joel twisted to glare at Ricco. "I'll go."

"Why, because you want to be president?" Ricco leaned toward him.

"I am going to–" Joel bit off the rest of his words.

"We'll hold the vote later, but Rita called dibs on this job and you'll just work to undercut her or talk over her. That's not going to do us any good with these assholes. Let Matías go. We at least know that both he and Esteban will keep her safe." Then Ricco squinted at me. "And you officially have a detail. You may also need to move into the compound."

"Fuck that," I spat. "I won't run from my home."

"Now who's being an idiot?" Esteban murmured under his breath. Without glancing down, I stomped my foot backward and caught his toes through his boots. They were too thick for my heels to cause any damage, but I got a grunt out of him.

"Then you'll have to have at least a couple Dirty Dogs with you at all times." Ricco's gaze slid to Matías.

"Absolutely not." I pushed up out of my chair. Then I pointed at Matías. "You want to tag along, fine, but this is my job and I call the shots. But–" I moved my glare around the room, ending on Ricco–"I choose who guards me. Not you."

"I am only here to protect you. I'll follow your lead. Always." Matías was so fucking serious. It was written in the way his eyebrows pulled low over his eyes and how his chin was tucked toward his chest.

How could I actually trust him?

"Regardless of if you're voted in or not, you're still the Dirty Dogs Princess. A blow to you is a blow to the gang. We've already been too lax given recent circumstances." Ricco shook his head.

My eyes watered but I blinked to clear those bastard tears up.

"You need a guard, Rita," Joel chimed in. "I'll arrange a patrol. You live close to our apartments anyway. You can decide who stays in your house."

"Fine. Five volunteers to ride with us?" Several men raised their hands and I picked the most competent and badass looking men. "Anything else?"

Joel gave a slow shake of his head. How he studied me sent chills down my arms. He didn't seem to like that I was going to speak to the club. But he couldn't object either. Or at least he must have felt like he couldn't.

The meeting ended and Matías walked up to the table. The men I'd selected to accompany us hung at the entrance to the club.

"I'll be ready to leave in a few minutes," I yelled, and they nodded. Then they turned to each other and started cutting up.

Due walked over with a file. "Here's the location of their headquarters. A brief on the men I could find and anything else I could find on such short notice." He flipped the file open. "They're using a Chinese restaurant as a front. I'd recommend going through the front. That would give you time to chat with them on neutral grounds. It does operate as a legit restaurant."

"Got it." I flipped through, reading as I went.

"We can ride in my car," Matías said as he read with me over my shoulder.

"You can ride behind us."

"Esteban," I sighed. "We can't go and not be united."

"What's your problem? Are you pissed I didn't lose my cool last night?" Matías casually tossed out.

"No, I'm pissed you enjoyed it." Esteban pressed his chest to my arm as he leaned toward Matías.

"Noted. Also not important."

Esteban's body tensed and I shoved him back before he could start another fight with Matías. One was brewing and I'd do whatever I could to stop it. "Not here." Actually, "Not ever."

His cold gaze dropped to me. "Why was he at your house this morning?"

"What? Afraid that she really was just using you?" Matías taunted.

I shoved Matías away too. "Shut the hell up." Then I pulled in a breath and placed a hand on Esteban's chest. "I didn't invite him over. He was on his way up the sidewalk when it all happened."

Some of the tension leaked out of his body. "Fine."

Then he walked away leaving me with Matías.

"He doesn't believe you."

"What is wrong with you?" I whirled toward him.

Matías adopted a mutinous expression. "He's my problem. He thinks he knows everything just because he fucked you."

"He doesn't!"

"I know that!"

We were left staring at each other. One of the guys across the room who was waiting on me, snorted a laugh at something his buddy said and broke the moment.

"I'm driving." Then I walked away too.

I should be kicking Matías to the curb. Esteban was the steady ride or die. I'd learned my lesson the hard way and got burned for my efforts.

Yet, I couldn't send Matías away, and the more I got to know Esteban, I couldn't leave him either. A deranged part of my head said *what if I kept them both?*

20

ESTEBAN

I had to get my shit under wraps. I was a walking, talking, ticking, time bomb.

Last night, I'd done exactly as Rita asked me to do. I dropped to my knees for her. Worshiped at her fucking altar for Matías to see like she'd requested. I wasn't stupid. She wanted to push him away and she used me to do it.

I hadn't given a fuck. I jumped in with both feet to assert my place in her life.

Yet, she'd walked out on us like she couldn't look at either of us.

Then this morning I find out that one, he wanted to be a fucking Dirty Dog. And two, he was there to save her when I wasn't. That shit stung and it swirled under my skin in a toxic cocktail.

Shaking my hands out, I blew out a hard breath.

"Fuck," I muttered. Turning around, I stalked back toward the front where Rita had parked. Because her car only had two seats, she was already in the driver's seat of a club SUV and Matías had taken shotgun.

Gritting my teeth, I yanked open the back door and slid

in. Without thought, I pulled out my gun, and rested it on my thigh pointed at Matías.

He glanced back and raised a brow. "What are you going to do with that?"

"Nothing, as long as you mind your manners." I shrugged.

Rita glanced back and rolled her eyes. "Esteban's harmless."

"That's what you think. That's what everyone thinks, but you haven't seen me angry."

She paused, then nodded. "You're right," she breathed out. "And this is my fault."

"No." Matías grazed his fingers over the back of her hand on the steering wheel. "It's no one's fault. He just has to grow up," he said with a sneer as he cut his gaze at me.

Raising the gun, I pointed it straight at his head. "Watch your fucking mouth."

I had to give it to him. He didn't even twitch. Eyeing me calmly, he leaned between the seat and pressed his forehead to the end of the gun. "You want to shoot me? Go ahead. I think you underestimate how fucked up my childhood was. I was constantly on the verge of murder at my father's hands, just like my brothers."

"Sit your ass back, Esteban," Rita yelled. She wasn't playing. Her voice was firm and cold. "We have a funeral to plan for Tiago and a club to keep intact. We don't have time for petty posturing."

There was a note of uncertainty there. My girl, she knew me as the easy going guy. But right then, she didn't know if I would actually kill him or not. She didn't know how far my hate drove me at that moment.

I didn't glance at Rita as intrusive thoughts battered against me. I could pull the trigger. I could get rid of my number one problem. Then nothing would stand in my way with Rita. She'd forgive me.

Eventually.

Once I made her see how useless Matías actually was.

There wasn't even an ounce of sweat on his forehead. This fucker really didn't care. Or he cared, but he didn't think I'd do it.

"Esteban," Rita snapped, fear coloring my name. Shit, I didn't want that emotion attached to my name out of her mouth no matter the cause.

It was like fighting hell itself to lower the weapon.

"Thank you." She sounded so prim and sassy, if shaky. But I still couldn't look at her. Matías and I were locked in a battle of wills.

He broke the stare first, facing forward and hooking Bluetooth up to his phone. He broke our stare to put on fucking music.

Low notes came out of the speakers and Rita stiffened. "This is my favorite song."

Matías reached over and grazed her hand again. "I know," he said softly, like they were having a minute without me in the backseat.

How could this man, who proclaimed to want her so badly, to say she was his one who got away–or he threw away, not to have attacked me the night before?

He was a bigger man than me because just knowing where his skin touched hers made me want to cut his fingertips off so he'd never do it again. I thought I could wait for her to see me. But I couldn't.

I needed her now and I was going to do everything I could to convince her she needed me more than him.

Giving one slight shake of her head, Rita started the car and put directions on.

"What's the plan?" I gritted out, doing my fucking best not to reach forward and choke Matías.

Twisting her lips to the side, she thought for a minute. "Matthews is the leader. They're American. I've dealt with my fair share of tourists so I can possibly play up their need to treat a woman right."

"That might work, but they could just as easily see you as a non-threat because you're a woman," I said, pressing my back against the seat.

Bikes roared as they surrounded the vehicle. Some of my tension eased. At least we weren't going into this blind.

"The days of thoughtless killings are behind us. We're not the same club we were when the Institution was alive, and we're not going back there."

If Matías thought that was a dig at his father, he didn't show any reaction at all.

"You'll make sure they don't get to that point," Matías assured her.

She made a noncommittal grunt as she picked up speed.

"Remember that time when you stalked me through the streets close to the mansion?" Matías stretched back in his seat, hands grabbing the top of the headrest.

Rita snorted. "I did not stalk you. You have a faulty memory."

"You couldn't get enough of me so you had to track me down. You almost got us caught." There was a smile in his voice and I wanted to puke.

Sneaking a glance at Matías, she fluttered her eyelashes. "I love a bit of trouble now and then."

"What is this?" I tucked my gun away and leaned between the seats. "Do you hear yourself right now?" I turned to Rita.

Red tinted her cheeks. "Shit. I need to focus. It was just a quick distraction that my brain needed."

Matías frowned. "There's a reason I brought it up."

"And what's that?" I snarked.

"That Rita was fearless. She was a bit reckless too." He leaned around me to get a better line of view of Rita. "We need her back. Whatever made you question yourself, it's not important. It doesn't fucking matter, because *that* woman...That's who you are and who the Dirty Dogs need you to be."

I sat back. Fuck, he had a point.

Rolling her lips together, Rita flicked her gaze at Matías then back at the road. "And if you're what made me question myself?" It was quiet, like she wasn't sure if she wanted him to hear it or not.

He gazed at her, his dark eyes unblinking. He wasn't even breathing.

"Then that's my sin to live with and you should know I would spend the rest of my life atoning for the ways I've wronged you."

Was this guy for fucking real?

Rita came to a stop on a deserted street and faced him, her expression literally melting.

"You're the strongest woman I know. Don't let a *pendejo* like me tear you down." He leaned forward.

Like two magnets pulling against each other, Rita leaned in too.

Until I stuck my head between them. "Let's keep driving, hmm? We have people to meet and sitting in the middle of the street isn't the best plan for us."

Rita sucked in a quick breath and pressed the gas, jolting us forward. Matías looked out his window, apparently lost in his own thoughts now. Whatever. I needed to get through this meeting so I could get Rita alone.

The new guys' headquarters was a solid thirty minute drive. An uncomfortable one.

We drove around the block and scoped the place out before parking on the street. Our guys took up various positions. They were as discreet as big bikers could be. They'd be noticeable though. The new club rode roadsters not motorcycles.

Turning the car off, Rita dropped her hands into her lap. "All right. I lead. You're my backup. But if you have questions, ask them. Just don't talk over me." She put her hand on the door and paused. "Don't try to undermine my authority." Her words were for Matías.

"Never."

Unable to sit in this Twilight Zone anymore, I hopped out.

We made it to the front of the restaurant and I had my gun in my hand. No matter if this was a peaceful call or not, Rita was not walking in there without any kind of protection. Matías pulled his weapon too.

Inside, there were only two tables and an old hostess who looked like she was half-Asian, half-Hispanic.

"We're here to see Matthews," Rita said as she stepped up between Matías and me.

The woman eyed her with a severe frown before calling back to the kitchen in some type of Asian language.

As we waited, the people at the tables eyed our guns, but we weren't in a tourist district, so they didn't freak out. Instead, they pretended not to see us.

The swinging doors to the kitchen popped open and Matthews strolled through. He wasn't even trying to hide his patronage with his US flag shirt. *Americans.*

"This is a surprise." He held his hand out to Rita.

She looked down her nose at the offer. I didn't think she was going to take it, but she slid her hand in his.

Raising it to his lips, Matthews started to smirk. Then Matías aimed at his head.

"You can shake her hand, but keep your lips to yourself."

Matthews dropped it and held his own hands up. "Got it. She's off limits." He glanced around and motioned for us to follow him. "We'll take this somewhere more private."

He led us through a different door. This one went to a staircase and we went up to the second floor. Oriental paintings and murals decorated the wall as traditional music played from old, static filled speakers.

Opening the first door at the top, he guided us into an office. An empty one. I wasn't a strategist, but I would have had a few buddies attend for backup. Matthews didn't grow up here, didn't understand the ways of the crime organizations.

A sun faded American flag hung up behind the desk and there were several pictures of men in service. So they were a unit when they served? Not surprising they'd want to stick together after they got out. What was surprising was that they wanted to turn to crime in South America.

Rita took her seat opposite Matthews and Matías took the extra chair. I stood directly behind Rita.

Matías could come and go, but my place was at her back. *Always.*

"So what do I owe the pleasure of this business?" Matthews threaded his fingers on the desk. His red hair fell in his eyes and he gave Rita a small grin. He wasn't completely at ease from the way his hands clenched and relaxed, but he wasn't high strung either.

"Let's cut the shit. Since you came to town, you've been nothing but a thorn in our side."

Matthews tutted. "That's not fair. We tried to be neighborly. From where I'm standing, the Dirty Dogs are the ones causing problems. Threatening us when we tried to make friendly contact." His gaze flitted to me briefly. "Killing our man when we were delivering our respect and condolences for your father. And then kicking out my men from one of the clubs."

Rita inclined her head as she crossed her legs. The motion was subtle, but it still drew his eye. I figured she wanted him under her spell, but I still wanted to pluck his eyes out.

On this, Matías and I were on the same page.

"I admit, we had a bad apple, which we dealt with and delivered his head directly to you. Surely, you can't hold the actions of one man against our entire club." She gave him a sultry smile. "And be honest. Do you expect rival clubs to mingle together when there's trouble brewing under the surface? That's asking for trouble."

She paused as Matthews mimicked her by inclining his head.

"But that's not the issue I'm here about today. It seems your club has killed one of our own, unwarranted."

Matthews' brows kissed in confusion. "We haven't killed any Dirty Dogs."

Funny how he didn't say *anyone*.

"Once your man died, you didn't declare war on the Dirty Dogs?" Rita's tone made it out like she wouldn't believe shit that came out of his mouth.

"I didn't say that." He smirked as he leaned back. "But I didn't get me and my boys where we are today by rushing off with my ass on fire. I prefer to observe and see where the weakest link is." Like a smug fuck, he laced his hands over his stomach and started twisting back and forth in his seat. "And it seems the Dirty Dogs aren't so stable with your father gone. From what I hear, it sounds like you have a bit of a leadership issue on your hands."

All of my senses snapped alert and Rita lifted herself to her full, rigid height. Even Matías twitched in surprise.

"And where did you hear that?" Her words trembled.

Fuck, Rita. Don't let your voice show your hand.

He shrugged. "Doesn't matter. What does is that your house isn't as locked up tight as you might think." He glanced at Matías and twisted his mouth to the side. "Although, I do think you have the upper hand just because of your connections. Matías, right?"

Matías nodded, staring him down with psycho eyes he'd inherited from his father. I'd never seen a man with such dead control over his eyes like that.

But with Matías, it wasn't a constant. The other night right before Rita walked out on us proved that.

"Interesting that you gave up your legacy to your half-brothers and to request to be a Dirty Dog."

Shit....

He had fresh information that no one should have except the people who were at the clubhouse this morning.

Matías didn't say anything, but his lips pulled down into a deeper frown.

"I ultimately do want peace for me and my brothers, so I'll throw you a bone. Believe it or not, I think you'd be the best option for the club. Don't trust anyone." His gaze moved between the three of us. "Except the ones in this room."

"Peace," Matías mulled over the word. "Then why send your men to shoot up Rita's house?"

Matthews blinked, careful to keep full eye contact with

Matías. It was a good show, but I wasn't sure I bought it. "That wasn't us."

Matías' eyes darkened as he sat forward while Rita tipped her head to the side.

We weren't going to get a straight answer out of Matthews. Not without reason to torture it out of him, and unfortunately, we didn't. That would have to wait and Matías would have to be patient.

"I think that's enough for today," I said as I touched Rita's shoulder. "Let's get the fuck out of here."

"I want your word that you had nothing to do with Tiago's death." Rita scooted to the edge of her seat. She was bringing the conversation full circle.

"You have my word." He didn't ask who Tiago was, but he mostly likely knew with the level of intel he had.

"If I find out you're lying, you and your brothers won't exist anymore."

"You think you and a broken club can get rid of us that easy?" He laughed under his breath.

"No." She returned with a smile. "But I have a lot more friends than you do. I've been making connections since I was born that have nothing to do with the club. Including his brothers," she jerked her thumb toward Matías, "and their new wife."

His humor faded. "Regardless of what you think, I'm not trying to start a war. And I believe you. Just remember what I said."

Rita stood and we excused ourselves without shaking his hand.

"We can find our own way out." She tossed over her shoulder. Matías took the lead and I followed up behind her.

The restaurant was empty as we left. Outside, our SUV

was exactly where we left it. Glancing down the street, two of our men were visible. Good. No one would have been able to tamper with it.

"That was either a success or a dud, I'm not sure which," I said to Rita as I opened the door for her, and she climbed in the driver's seat.

I'd just shut the door when Matías tackled me to the ground. I started twisting, ready to protect myself, then I heard it.

A bullet whizzed by us. Matías had just saved my life.

Holy fuck. *Matías just saved my life.*

21

MATÍAS

I grunted as I landed on Esteban. He tried to throw me off but stopped before we hit the ground.

That was good considering my fucking arm had been grazed.

Another gunshot sounded and I turned my head, fully prepared to roll us under the SUV.

I only knew two of the five men Rita had guarding us today. And Juan, who was the other street sentinel, fired back at the man who tried to take Esteban out.

That man was already on his bike, rounding the corner.

"What happened?" Matthews came running out of his restaurant with two of his men behind him.

Pushing off of Esteban, I held my gun loosely in my hand. It was a miracle it hadn't gone flying. When no other shots popped off, I stood. Rita tried to open her door, but I held it closed and shook my head.

The SUV was bullet proof and she needed to stay inside it if only for my peace of mind.

"Seems like someone doesn't like my friend, Esteban," I said lightly while Esteban brushed himself off.

He was shaken. I almost felt sorry for him.

The kid had probably never had to watch his back with his own club.

That was the story of my life, so this betrayal didn't cut so deep.

Shaking his head, Matthews peered up and down the street, as if he'd see the shooter. He was already long gone, and the other men who were our guards rode over.

No one said anything. Matthews and his men were still the enemy. But maybe now they were the enemy of my enemy.

"You all right?" Matthews eyed me like he was torn between offering me aid and not helping a potential rival.

"Fine. We're going to head out. If you change your mind on telling us who your contact is, give us a call." I pointed at Esteban. "Give him your number."

Without a fight, Esteban rattled off his phone number. Then we were in the car driving.

Rita's knuckles were white on the steering wheel and she kept sucking in tiny, stilted breaths. Since getting in the car she hadn't looked at either Esteban or me. I didn't even think she'd blinked.

"Do you want to pull over? I can drive us." I rolled my head on the headrest to face Rita.

"Fuck no. I need something to do to take my mind off of Rob trying to shoot Esteban. Rob. I fucking picked him to be part of our security." She cursed under her breath. "If you hadn't knocked Esteban down..." She shook her head and the car jolted forward.

"Hey, hey." I shh'd. "Don't think like that."

The more we drove, the more it became clear we weren't going to the compound. "Where are we going?"

"To your place." She uncurled and curled her fingers back around the steering wheel.

"If you're trying to lie low, the tail of Dirty Dogs isn't going to let you keep this secret." I nodded to the side where the four motorcycles now surrounded the SUV.

"I don't give a shit about that. But your place was locked down. Right? It's safe? I need to be somewhere where I don't have to worry about a death threat for just a fucking minute."

Pulling out my phone, I called Andre.

"Yes?" He answered on the second ring.

"What's the status of my house? Do you have a detail of men still guarding it?" I asked, keeping a close eye on Rita. Esteban was silent in the back.

"Parker had one of his connections upgrade the security so it's been on lockdown. It's monitored with our properties why? I thought you didn't want anything to do with that place."

I hadn't. But if that was where Rita wanted to go, then that was where I'd go.

"I changed my mind. Can you send a few of your trusted men over to guard us? We're going to stay there for a night at least."

There was silence for a few moments. "Sure. They'll be there in fifteen." He gave instructions on how to turn off the security system and rearm it. Then he hung up.

I could have told him what happened. He would expect it. But at that moment, my loyalty wasn't to him. It was to Rita and the Dirty Dogs. If she was okay with me filling him in, then I would.

We pulled up to my place. A mini mansion in its own right, though nothing like the massive structure that my father's had been.

The engine slowly stopped as the air inside the car became stuffier from no air conditioning.

We should get out, but I just stared. It had been a long damn time since I came home. The place would be immaculate. It always was. The housekeepers made sure it always seemed more of a museum than a home.

It was a reminder of everything that had gone wrong in my life.

Shaking my head, I popped my door open. "Let's go."

The Dirty Dogs sat on their bikes behind us, their helmets already off. "What's going on?" Juan asked, his voice solemn.

"We need a place to get our shit together that's one-hundred-percent secured. Can you guard the property? The wall is the property line and some of my brothers' men will be here in a few minutes. You can stay or go, up to you."

Juan took off his sunglasses and stared me dead in the eye. "We'll stay. You're Dirty Dogs and we'll protect you over your brothers' men." He cursed. "Fucking Rob. He was a lifer. What the fuck?" he said to himself.

The other men mumbled their agreement.

"Let me know if you need anything. I'll have to place an order for anything that's not dry goods or water." Hopefully Andre had the fridge cleaned out.

Juan nodded and climbed off his bike. He huddled with the others as they worked out a plan to walk the perimeter.

Rita and Esteban were just climbing out of the SUV. Both seemed shell shocked. Rita, I got. Esteban surprised me. Then again, it didn't.

"Come on." I led the way to the front door. Entering the code, after the beep and sound of the door unlocking, I pushed it open.

I stepped through first, because shit, I didn't trust that no one would be here. The alarm system blared loud and shrill. It took two tries to get it off and rearmed.

When I turned around, Esteban stared at me with a blank face and Rita glanced around, taking in every detail with unhidden curiosity. I followed her gaze, trying to see it as she did.

It was what my father expected of his son. Sleek, high-end opulence to show my status and wealth. Cold in decor and artwork.

Beautiful but lacking any kind of personality. I'd just grown used to it.

I laughed under my breath. I hadn't even needed to grow used to it. It was all I'd ever known until my teenage years, and then it was normal.

"This is just like the mansion," she said quietly, eerily. I wasn't sure if she was bothered by it, or if she was concerned that I was.

Then she suddenly walked over to me. "Are you okay?"

So it was me she was worried about. I tried not to get emotional as I twisted my arm. Rivulets of blood had already dried on my skin. Esteban cursed.

"Where's the first aid kit? Do you have one?" He kicked off his shoes and I grinned. It was like he turned a complete one-eighty.

"Under the sink, bathroom down that hall, last door on the right." Twisting my arm even deeper, I examined the graze. It wasn't bad. More of a decent gash. It wouldn't even need stitches. Just some disinfectant and a bandage.

"Let's go sit down." Rita grabbed my hand on my good arm and led me through the house. For someone who'd never been here before, she seemed to know her way around.

She found the living room and maneuvered me to sit on

the couch. The shades were drawn with only cracks of light coming from the edges. The place was also hot and stuffy.

"Hand me that remote." I motioned to the remote on the wall. She grabbed it from the holder and handed it to me. Hitting a couple buttons, the system kicked on and air started moving through the room.

Esteban came back with the kit.

Taking it from his hands, Rita opened it on the couch next to me. Her thick, dark hair fell, covering her face from view as she rifled through it, picking out what she wanted.

"Let's take your shirt off." Her voice was thick with emotion as she tugged on the hem of my shirt.

I gently grabbed her hands. "It's okay," I whispered.

"It's not." She violently shook her head. "You got shot again–"

"Grazed. Hardly a shot."

"You could have died. Really died. Esteban could have died. I swear, if one more person I care about leaves me, in *any* way, I will paint this town as red as the bottoms of my shoes."

A smile threatened to break free. She loved me. Still.

"I'm here," I assured her. "You can tend to it, but then we won't worry about this anymore, yes?"

"No," she griped. This time when she reached for the hem of my shirt, I leaned forward and let her strip me. The graze twinged from the movement, but it wasn't anything to worry about.

Rita froze, staring at the bullet wound that had long since healed. Then she reached forward, her fingers whispering over my skin as she closed her eyes. Then she took in a shuddering breath and dropped her hand.

My heart stuck in my throat. *Ah, Rita, I'm so sorry for all the pain I didn't know I caused you.*

Kneeling beside me, Rita used the supplies and efficiently cleaned and bandaged it up.

"You've been around death before. Why are you so upset?" The Dirty Dogs was a gang. A prolific one that hadn't shied away from violence. Not that I was complaining, it felt good to be cared about, but this was something different.

I glanced at Esteban to gauge his reaction. He stood about five feet away, staring at us with a thunderous expression and his arms crossed.

She busied herself putting the leftover supplies back in the kit and closing it up. I didn't think she was going to answer me. Instead, she kept motioning her head and mouthing words like she was arguing with herself.

Then, she stopped. Kneeling, head bowed. The only movement was her chest rising and falling.

I was mesmerized. I always had been by Rita, but this reaction on my behalf, it was intoxicating.

Her breathing became quicker, the gasps became audible. Fuck, she was having a panic attack.

"Rit–" I reached out a hand to touch her but she dove toward me, her hands clutching my shoulders and her mouth fusing to mine.

She swallowed her name up as she deepened the kiss. Shoving her tongue artfully around mine. A forceful, yet sensual, kiss made to drive me wild. She'd never kissed me like this.

I was her air. Her reason to breathe. That was how I felt.

Groaning, I pulled her against me. The bandage stretched as my arms flexed. I ignored it. If it peeled off in places, we'd fix it. That was one thing I had plenty of. Bandages.

I only had one Rita.

"Please," she gasped as she shot up for air before kissing me again. "Don't." A lip bite. "Leave me." This time she sucked on the side of my neck as her hand worked my pants. "Ever again."

"Never," I vowed. I meant it. Hell would have to pull me away.

She gripped my cock and gave me one strong stroke. My eyes briefly rolled back in my head. "What are you doing?" I panted.

When I opened my eyes, Esteban was no longer standing across from me. He'd taken a seat next to me. His brows were still low and his mouth was still set, but he wasn't trying to rip Rita away from me. He seemed content to watch her.

"Rewarding you," she breathed. "You could have let Esteban die. Hell, maybe you should have."

Esteban grunted and she continued to stroke the fuck out of me. Then she leaned over and spit on the tip, using her hand to spread it over my cock.

For the first time in over a year, maybe even two, she was really mine again. She wasn't just touching me out of grief or guilt.

Fuck, was she? No, this was gratitude. I'd take grateful all day long.

Not wanting to take her out of the moment, I tightened my hands into fists, pressing them into my sides. I would do nothing to risk breaking the spell of how perfect she was with my dick in her mouth.

"But you saved him. He could have died because of that *cabrón*," she spat, then licked me from base to tip. "Why?" Rita demanded before kissing the head of my cock in a nasty tease. She locked eyes with me as she laved the tip with her tongue, a line of spit hung from her mouth to my dick as she raised her head up.

"What?" I had trouble concentrating on what she was saying because the pleasure felt too good. Years of only my hand and then a quick and dirty fuck in a backroom killed my stamina.

"Why did you save him?" she asked again with just as much authority.

"Because," I gasped as she swiped her thumb over the head. Her spit glistened on my cock.

"Because..."

"He matters to you. So he matters to me."

Esteban cursed as Rita lowered herself to suck my cock between her plush, red lips. Finally, I let myself touch her again. I gathered her hair up on top of her head so I could watch her suck me off. Flexing my hips, I fucked her face. Each time her lips pressed against my groin, I grunted.

"So good. You're so good at this. Such a good girl." Words fell from my lips between groans. She worked me over until I started to swell. "I'm close. So fucking close."

Pulling back, she wiped her mouth with her fingers as she stripped. "You're not coming unless you're inside me."

My cock pulsed, threatening to do just that, even without her still touching me. Pre-cum beaded at the tip.

A gloriously naked Rita straddled my lap as she gripped my shoulders. "Esteban. Can you put him where he needs to be?" she asked so sweetly.

"Only because you asked nicely." He spit on his hand and gripped my cock, giving it a firm stroke.

"What the fu..." I groaned, gripping Rita's hips.

"I don't want you. Don't get scared. But I'd do anything for Rita. Any fucking thing. And if she wants me to line you up," he angled my cock as Rita sat on the tip, "then that's what I'll do and I'll make it good for her and you."

He moved his hand and she sank down on top of me.

"God." I could barely hold my eyes open for the pleasure of her wet warmth surrounding me.

Rolling her hips, she rose up and sunk down. Rita set a decadent rhythm and before long, I was close again.

"No, no, no," I muttered. She froze.

"What's wrong?"

"I'm fucking close," I complained, digging my fingers in her hips to slow her down when she started to move again.

"Then we'll have to make sure Rita goes right along with you." Esteban started strumming her clit with expert fingers as he turned her face to his. The erotic sight of his tongue lightly tangling with hers started the white hot tingle at the base of my spine.

Once again, I swelled and as I felt the first stream of hot cum erupt, Rita started bouncing on top of me. One of her hands cupped my neck, the other fisted Esteban's short hair.

He swallowed every one of her moans as she pulsed around me, milking every single drop of pleasure from my body. I groaned, long and low, rolling forward to suck and kiss her tits. I couldn't. The pleasure was so good that concentrating on anything but my orgasm was useless.

Wrapping my arms tight around her, I hugged the shit out of her and bucked my hips two more times. I stilled, my heart banging against the walls of my chest as I drifted along in sated ecstasy.

My harsh breathing was the first thing I noticed.

Then Rita's heartbeat.

Lastly, Esteban's chest leaned into me. I couldn't see what he was doing but somehow, he was pressed into me to touch Rita.

How did we get here?

Better question, where did we go from here?

22

RITA

As soon as my eyes opened, a new fire had been lit inside me.

I stretched my arms over my head with a groan, then I rolled out of Matías' bed to find my clothes. Matías and Esteban were already gone.

My clothes were probably still in the living room where I'd dropped them. After having the strongest orgasm of my life, only barely overshadowing the one Esteban had given me the day before, I'd been so drained I'd passed out right there on Matías.

One of them, Matías probably, carried me to his bedroom. I woke up sometime in the middle of the night with both men pressed up against me. Feeling the safest since *Papá* died, hell, since the brothers fought to take over the Institution, I'd closed my eyes and drifted back off into a dreamless, heavy sleep.

I could go to the living room and get my clothes, but I cringed at putting on a dirty dress that I'd sweated to death in. Instead I rummaged through Matías' dresser drawers.

Was this Matías' room? It was decorated exactly like the

rest of the house in dark, sterile furniture. There were no personal items, no pictures. Nothing to say this was his private space.

When we dated in the past, I had never been allowed to visit his house. It had been too dangerous. So now, seeing this glimpse of who he was, it was like crack.

Each drawer was full of clothes. They were arranged so neatly by article and color. Who the fuck did this? He must have housekeepers. The Matías I knew wasn't anal about useless shit.

I barked out a laugh. Andre probably had the cleaning service do it. He seemed like a man who color coded his briefs. I'd have to ask Amorette.

Plucking out a T-shirt, I slipped it on and padded through the house. My steps echoed back to me. Andre must have a crew come in regularly. Stopping by an art piece, I swiped my finger along the top of the frame. Dust free.

That was as thoughtful as it was eerie. It was like Andre and the others kept this place as a shrine to the brother they treated like shit.

I liked them, and I loved Amorette, but I couldn't make myself forget how Matías had always yearned to be part of their band of brothers. He'd never told me that, but I'd been at functions over the years and saw how he stared at them. Shaking my head, I kept moving.

This new energy was so refreshing compared to the morbid and sad shit that had been plaguing me for weeks. I wanted to embrace the hell out of it.

Both men were in the kitchen. Matías held a steaming cup of coffee to his lips as he blew on it while Esteban had his own mug on the counter in front of him.

Somewhere, Esteban had lost his shirt, and every single

one of his well-defined abs were on display. I ached to run my hands down his stomach.

They turned to me, and as soon as their gazes focused on my body, all the wanton desire from the previous night resurfaced. I shifted on my feet at the reminder of both their hands on my body. It had been a transcendent experience I couldn't wait to repeat.

So much bad shit had happened. My head had been reeling. Yet, somehow, last night it all came to a head. I didn't even know how it happened.

But it had been so fucking therapeutic.

The only plausible reason for my lapse in thinking was that Matías saved Esteban. For me. Because I didn't want him to die even though Esteban had been a shithead to Matías.

Matías still pushed him out of the line of fire, getting injured himself. That was the biggest gesture Matías could ever make to get back in my good graces.

"You look very determined today," Matías said by way of a greeting. A few soft curls fell over his forehead. He'd always had buzzed hair before.

Forgetting about the desire, I walked to the island and pressed my palms flat against the granite countertops.

I stared both men in the eyes. "We need to figure out who the rat is."

In all of Dirty Dog history, nothing like this had ever happened before. The thought that someone was actively leaking information to an enemy burned like poison in the back of my throat.

How fucking dare they do this to our gang. To *Papá's* memory.

He loved everyone of his men, even the assholes. For them to betray us like this...

I curled my fingers against the counter.

Esteban glanced at Matías before bringing his attention back to me. "I don't think not finding the rat was even an option."

Matías chuckled, and for a second I was thrown. When did these men become so friendly?

Leaning toward me, Matías' smile died. "What do you want to do about it Rita?" His voice was low and seemed to have a line directly to my core.

I sucked in a long breath, gathering my thoughts as I closed my eyes. Thinking was easier when he or Esteban weren't distracting me with their attention.

"A rat in the Dirty Dogs means that someone doesn't like who our potential leaders are." I reasoned it out.

"That's not true." Matías shook his head. "It could be Ricco. It could be Joel. Just because someone's giving information to the enemy does not mean it's not one of the leaders in power. Let's say for example, Joel wants to take Dirty Dogs for himself. He could be using this new club to take you off of the playing board."

Fuck, he was right.

"Okay, for Matthews to know that you requested to be a Dirty Dog, the rat has to be someone who was at the compound yesterday morning." I tried again.

Matías shook his head again. "Not necessarily. It took us at least thirty minutes to drive to the Chinese restaurant. Anyone could've called their friends, who could've called Matthews."

"Dammit, man. You're bursting all of Rita's bubbles." Esteban pushed away from the island to lean against the back counter.

"Sorry," Matías said. "Rita needs to be prepared for any situation."

"You're right." I hated how his corrections cut at my ego, yet I needed the reality checks. "Let's start with who was at the compound yesterday morning. We had Ricco, Joel, and about three-quarters of the Dirty Dogs. The chances are high that the rat is one of those men, but we won't rule anyone out. How the fuck are we supposed to find out who the rat is?" I rubbed my forehead, racking my brain for a solution.

How did you find a rat?

"You set a trap." Matías set his cup down and tapped his fingers on the counter.

He glanced at his coffee, and then he slid it across to me before turning to make a new cup for himself.

Esteban and I exchanged glances before we both got lost in watching Matías move around his kitchen with such ease.

I'd never seen Matías do anything so comfortably in all the years I'd known him. Part of me was happy to see him like this. The other part, the bitter part, was sad that I never got to see the real him. He apparently never felt comfortable enough with me and that fucking hurt.

Nope, I needed to get rid of those toxic thoughts.

"A trap," I restated to myself.

"Has Ricco or Joel tried to contact you?" Esteban reached out and touched my hand.

I flipped my hand and laced our fingers together. He gave my fingers a squeeze.

The coffee in front of me smelled so good, yet I just couldn't bring myself to sip it. Not while all of these thoughts were raging inside my head.

"I haven't checked my phone."

Matías came back with his new cup, but he glanced at my untouched one on the counter. "Do you want the fresh coffee?" he asked.

"No. I'm going to drink it in a minute, I just–I need to get my thoughts together."

I went to grab my phone from the living room. The screen lit up with two dozen missed calls and texts. Not only from Ricco and Joel, but so many other members in the Dirty Dogs.

Shit, I needed to go through the messages, but we need to plan more.

"Here." Esteban held out his hand. "I'll go through them."

I slid my phone over to him.

"Rita," Matías called my name. "I think the best thing you can do right now is go back to the compound. You have to tell them what happened and watch their cues. The very best tells are in the body language." He dropped his gaze to the counter as if thinking. "I'm well liked in the Dirty Dogs, and I know Esteban is too, but I don't trust anyone enough to put your life in their hands by not seeing their reactions for ourselves."

"Nothing here," Esteban chimed in. "Only people asking about what happened and wanting to know why you didn't come back. Joel is threatening to ride out on the new club," he added, his voice filled with irritation as he pushed the phone toward me.

"We can't let that happen." What had gotten into Joel? He'd been a level man. He helped keep some of the younger guys in line. Where did this sudden thirst for violence come from?

Could he be the one who was informing Matthews?

A scream bubbled up the back of my throat. I hated how I was now suspicious of everyone who had been there for me my entire life.

"It doesn't look like any of the men you picked to join us

yesterday called it in." Matías' words penetrated my deep thoughts.

Calm descended, clearing away the buzz that had settled inside me. I knew exactly what we had to do. Matías was right. We needed to fill the Dirty Dogs in on Rob's betrayal and watch every single person and their reaction.

"Matías, do you think your brothers' men would come with us? Not inside the compound, but just be close by? In case anything happens."

He nodded. "Absolutely."

"Then let's head to the compound," I sighed. "Esteban, will you send a text message in the group thread and let them know there's an emergency meeting in..." I tapped on my phone screen to check the time. "Twenty minutes."

I went to Matías' master bathroom to get ready. Today wasn't a day where I could put on my armor, but I pulled my hair back in a sleek ponytail. What the hell was I going to wear? Doing the walk of shame back to the compound just gave off the wrong vibe.

There was a knock on the door.

"Come in!"

Matías stepped in holding a hanger and dress in his hand.

"What's that?" I turned around.

He ran his fingers down the front of a black dress. It would have been business appropriate if it wasn't for the shape and stretchy material. It was as form-fitting as anything in my closet.

A soft smile curled his lips as he gazed from the dress to me. "Just because you never came here before didn't mean I didn't want you to. I saw you went through my drawers, but you must not have stepped into the closet. There's a small section with clothes, the designers you like, your favorite cuts, all in your size."

I stopped breathing. Then I pressed my fingertips to my lips as tears welled in my eyes. That was all I'd ever wanted. To be part of his life.

It wasn't that he bought me clothes, it was that he paid attention to what I liked. He went out of his way to do this for me, even if he couldn't give it to me then.

Where saving Esteban had been a grand gesture, the clothes were a small one. Combined, I didn't feel like loving him was a mistake anymore.

"Do you not like it?" His brows furrowed as he glanced at the dress.

"No, I love it," I choked out.

I laughed as he thrust it toward me, still unsure. Wrapping my hand around the back of his neck, I pulled him down for a kiss. His lips were firm and warm against mine. The moment was bittersweet as he lingered.

Then I pulled back. "I'll get dressed and meet you in the living room."

Ducking out of the bathroom, he left me alone. Probably to get ready in one of his other bathrooms. From the size of this place, I imagined he had at least five to spare.

Quicker than I've ever gotten ready, I put on the dress, brushed my teeth, and left the bedroom. I didn't look anything like my usual badass self, but I was serious, stern, and had zero fucks to give.

Perfect.

Esteban whistled as I came down the stairs. Both men stood side-by-side, wearing matching tees and jeans.

It was so strange.

Esteban was handsome. He had always been handsome and embraced who he was. Matías, on the other hand, was trying out this new style. Did he want to fit in with the Dirty Dogs or was this what he really liked?

It didn't matter, he was hot as sin too.

When we got at the compound, rows of bikes were lined up out front like they were getting ready to ride off to war.

"Looks like we made it just in time," Esteban muttered.

Matías grunted. "You're not wrong."

Several of the men rushed over with Ricco leading the pack.

"Rita! What the fuck happened yesterday? You didn't come back and you never called to check in." His tone was chastising, as if I were a small child. "I thought something bad happened to you." Ricco turned to the men who guarded us yesterday.

"Don't look at them."

His gaze snapped back to me. I'd never spoken to him in such a stone-cold tone.

"Inside." I started marching into the compound. "I'm calling a meeting."

There weren't any of the usual chairs. No one had had time to bring them out and arrange them. That was fine. They could all stand in the middle while I was on the platform.

Matías and Esteban each took an arm to lift me up. Then I turned around and faced my men. And they *were* mine. Every last fucking Dirty Dog. Mine to take care of, or mine to pull retribution from.

It only took a few seconds to realize some people were missing. Wait, there were quite a few people missing. "Ricco. Where is Due?"

Esteban jumped on the platform. He searched the crowd with me. "Due's missing," he muttered. "So is Emil, and Treg, and Hap." He rattled off another half a dozen names.

Joel and Ricco spun left and right.

"This is a mandatory meeting," I called out.

"Where are the others? Where's Rob?" Joel asked, glancing at the four men who guarded us yesterday where they lined up in front of the platform.

I gave him a severe frown. I wanted him to know I didn't trust him. I also wanted him to know that this was the fuckup of the entire gang.

"Well," I raised my voice so the entire room could hear me. All conversation quieted. "It seems like we have a rat in the club."

23

MATÍAS

"No fucking way!" Joel's face turned red.

"Not in our gang!"

"The hell you fucking say!"

Several of the men in the crowd yelled obscenities and Ricco cursed. They didn't believe there could be a rat inside Dirty Dogs.

"Quiet!" Rita shouted.

Men continued to shout their disbelief. Esteban's face grew thunderous as he took a step closer to the edge of the platform. Whatever he was looking for in the crowd, he wasn't finding it.

I stuck two fingers in my mouth and gave a sharp whistle. That caught their attention.

Rita glanced down. "Thank you," she mouthed.

"Why do you think there's a rat?" Ricco raised his voice.

Rita quirked an eyebrow. "Yesterday, after we finished our meeting with Matthews, one of our very own men tried to kill Esteban."

Esteban's shoulders bunched as he stared at something at the back of the room.

I craned my head, but I still couldn't see what it was.

"Who?" Joel demanded.

"Rob." As soon as the name left her lips, there was a commotion somewhere behind me.

Esteban pointed. "There! Grab him!"

I pushed through the crowd, shoving men left and right, trying to get to the back. There he was. I remembered this guy from my time with the Dirty Dogs–Kurt. He shoved away from a man trying to contain him and sprinted toward the door.

Putting on a burst of speed. I launched myself at him, tackling him much like I tackled Esteban yesterday, except I let the full weight of my body slam him into the ground. He grunted, and so did I.

The cut on my arm stung as if it tore open.

"Matías!" Rita called. "Take Kurt to the shed." Manny, one of the VPs, came up and helped me off the ground. He shoved his foot on Kurt's back, holding him to the ground until I was all the way back on my feet. Then we picked him up together and I slammed my fist across his cheek.

"That's for making me chase you." I caught him under the chin with my next hit."And that's for being involved in whatever plan that almost got Rita hurt."

"The meeting with Matthews went as great as I could've expected," Rita said from the platform as the men quieted down. "He wasn't hostile. He didn't try to harm us, and we came to an agreement, however, he had information that he shouldn't have..."

That was the last I heard before the door shut.

"So what happens now?" Manny glanced at me over the top of Kurt's head. Kurt was out of it, letting his head hang and his feet drag as we carted him toward the shed. If he'd been awake, he'd be fighting for his life.

The people who entered the shed never left. Not intact.

Like the rest of the Dirty Dogs, I've never had a problem with Manny. Yet in light of everything that had happened, I wasn't sure I wanted to trust him either. Still, you had to give a little information to see how people reacted.

"Let me ask you this, Manny. Have you heard anything? About anyone being angry at Rita for stepping up or Esteban for having her back?"

Manny was older than me by five years. He had a deep scar along his cheek, and his skin was weathered. He'd also been in more fights than half the gang, and when he met my gaze, fury burned in the depths of his eyes.

"What makes you think there's anybody who's upset about Rita?"

"That's not what I asked, Manny. I asked if you'd heard anything." I narrowed my eyes on him.

Manny blew out a harsh breath as he kicked the door to the back courtyard open. The shed was an outbuilding that Javier had always used to do his dirty work. He said he didn't like the mess in the compound. That was the one thing he and my father always had in common, not that there weren't enough crimes that happened inside the mansion, but blood was avoided if possible.

Kurt started to rouse between us. I was tempted to punch him a third time, but we needed answers inside the shed. Manny and I worked together to bind Kurt's wrists and hang him from the hook in the ceiling. I used shears from the table along the wall to cut his shirt off. He needed to have skin exposed for anything Rita would want to do to him.

Once he was secured, Manny turned to face me, swiping a hand through his thinning hair.

"The club is a mess right now. Rita hasn't seen it. She's not been around very much, but since Javier's death, the men are scared shitless. They don't know who's going to be able to take charge of the club and keep everybody in line. Hell, or be intimidating enough to keep everybody else away. These new kids on the block are the worst possible thing to happen at the time of Javier's death, it just made everybody that much crazier."

I crossed my arms. "What are you talking about? Rita's a solid choice. I don't think Joel is terrible, either. But the Dirty Dogs could do better, Man."

He chuckled softly. We all liked Joel but he was no Javier.

Squinting at me, Manny got a glint in his eyes. "You on the other hand..Javier didn't make it a secret that he always wanted you to take his place."

"Don't start that shit," I warned.

He raised his hands. "I'm just saying."

"Well, don't."

Kurt raised his head, looking between me and Manny, then dropped it back with a groan.

"Don't let yourself get too comfortable." Manny kicked his shin.

"I don't know what you're talking about." When Kurt looked up again his eyes were red as if tears were on their way.

"Yeah, right." Manny said. "Then why were you running away from the crowd when Rita was talking about a rat?"

"Look, I'm not the rat. If I were, do you think I would have come to this meeting? I would've known yesterday an attempt was made on Esteban's life. You want to find the rat? Look at the men who aren't here."

I had to give it to Kurt. He did have a point.

The door opened and Rita stepped through, followed by

Esteban, then Joel, and Ricco. I wanted to hold out my hand to pull her into my side, but I wouldn't do that to her. Not here. I had screwed up enough and I wouldn't do anything else to make her look weak in front of her gang.

"How did it go in there?" I asked.

Pulling her shoulders back, she glared daggers at Kurt. "It went about as well as expected. About half the men were enraged that someone tried to kill Esteban. The other half believe Rob was working on his own."

The weight of her gaze sliced into me.

"I think you and I both know there are too many coincidences." I stepped back to stand next to Esteban. He glanced at me. I wouldn't call his expression friendly, but it was missing the hate he'd been carrying. I'd take it.

He nodded in solidarity and I returned it.

Ricco huffed, but Joel stepped forward.

"What about these two?" I stared at Ricco and Joel as Rita glanced at them. "Can they be trusted?" I took a half step toward her.

"What do you mean, can I be trusted?" Ricco boomed. He pointed a beefy finger at me. "I have supported you from the very beginning. Do you think that I would do something to jeopardize the Dirty Dogs?"

"The one thing I know right now, Ricco, is that Rita isn't safe and we're not going to trust anyone until she is," Esteban said as he puffed up his chest. The way he squared off with Ricco and Joel, he craved to shield Rita with his body. It was written all over his face, but he remained behind her.

Rita still hadn't answered, and when I dropped my gaze back to her, she still watched Joel and Ricco.

"They can stay," was all she said.

Joel and Ricco weren't happy with that answer, but they didn't argue.

Then she walked close to Kurt. His breathing turned ragged as he held her gaze.

"Strange seeing you here in this situation." She tapped her finger on her bottom lip. Her gaze slid over to the tables that lined the wall. The inside was like any other shed with all the tools hanging up or set out that one might find in any gardener's arsenal. "You were one of *Papá's* biggest thorns in his side. So, I'm not surprised after all."

"I'm not a rat, Rita." He tried to convince her as he tugged on his arms. The chain holding him up rattled.

Rita walked over to the table and picked up a set of pliers. Slapping them against her palm rhythmically, she returned to Kurt. "You're not the rat?" she asked.

"Hell no," he said, puffing out his cheeks.

"Convince me."

I raised my brows. I hadn't realized Javier had let her in on the interrogations. I'd been in a few myself, for men that never left breathing, but Rita had never joined us.

Yet, she was solid and steady. She didn't even seem to twitch at the thought of hurting him. Although, she did always have a mean streak.

His eyes widened and he glanced around from person to person. Whatever was going through his head, he was panicking.

Rita slapped the pliers on her palm one more time then reached out and clamped it on his nipple.

"Ah!" he screamed as she twisted so hard his skin seemed to tear. I winced. My father had been ruthless and sadistic, but I never saw him go for the nipples.

She stopped twisting but still held his nipple clamped in the pliers. "Why did you run?"

He made gasping noises but words never formed.

"Your balls are going to be next. Those will burst like sad little grapes. I'd answer if I were you."

Joel held his stomach, a little green in the face as Ricco stared at the wall. Esteban watched Rita with a fucking hard on.

All right, the kid was growing on me. It helped that he wasn't trying to drive me out of town anymore. Or toss me over a cliff.

I grinned. Esteban caught me looking at him and he raised his brows in question. I shrugged.

It had been long enough that I could joke about my death now, if only to myself.

"Esteban," Rita said. "Take down his pants."

Kurt twisted to the right and left, throwing his knees up as if that would save him. Esteban gripped the band of his jeans when Kurt screamed.

And screamed. His pain pushed his voice higher as tears leaked from his eyes.

"Okay! Okay!" He panted once Esteban stepped back, understanding it for the near miss it was. If he was stripped, Rita would have latched onto his balls and not let go. I'd seen her do it more times than I could count in the clubs and that was without her tools.

Releasing his bloody nipple, she stepped back. "Go on."

"I was out the other night, before Javier's funeral. Tiago was with us. Rob too." His breathing became more erratic like he was more afraid to tell her the truth, but didn't want his balls crushed.

"If I have to ask again, I'm going strip you and you won't get an opportunity to speak."

Swallowing, he continued. "Tiago and Rob were best

friends. I don't know what happened after I left, but you know that, right? That they were friends?"

"Everyone in the Dirty Dogs is friends," Esteban deadpanned.

"Yes, but we still have cliques like school kids!" Kurt almost shouted. "Tiago, he was talking about how this was an opportunity to make the Dirty Dogs feared again. He said...He said–"

"Spit it out." Rita opened the pliers and stepped closer.

"He said that since the Institution fell, we'd lost our spines. Then this new club rolls in and tries to take over our best businesses, the ones we didn't want to leave–" Kurt cut himself off like he realized what a mistake that was.

Rita hummed, her voice dropping low with emotion. "Interesting. I hadn't realized that so many people have issues with the way Dirty Dogs is going." She glanced over her shoulder. Joel and Ricco refused to meet her gaze.

They knew. But were they part of it?

"Tell me more," she purred, leaning into him.

He pulled his head back as far as he could with the way he was strung up. "It's not everyone. It's not even me! I just like to keep my head down! I like being included. That's it."

"What did Tiago and Rob say?"

"That..." Kurt gulped, glancing at everyone in the room but Rita. "That the only way to move into the future was to clear the past. They wanted to get rid of you because you are part of the old Dirty Dogs."

"Because Javier is my father," she concluded.

He nodded in jerky motions.

"That doesn't explain why you ran."

His face scrunched up as sweat rolled down his face. His perspiration and fear perfumed the tight humid space.

"There were only a few men there. All of them are either

dead or missing today. I knew it would look bad. I didn't want anyone to accuse me."

"How would we have known?" Esteban moved beside Rita. "How the hell would we have known about that conversation, if you hadn't told us? We wouldn't have known you were there."

The blood drained from Kurt's face. "There was one other person there."

"Who?"

"One of the men from the new club."

That motherfucker, Matthews. He knew about a coup and he didn't say a goddamned thing other than not to trust anyone.

I was going to pay him a visit this time. By myself.

24

ESTEBAN

R ita held the door open to her room for Matías and me to step in. Then she shut the door, twisted the lock, and flopped down on the bed. She groaned behind her hands that spanned her face.

Matías pressed his knees into the edge of the bed and smoothed an errant strand of hair off of her forehead.

"You were magnificent in there, Rita," he said softly.

The familiar jealous ache that seemed to tear through my body each time I saw them together was missing. It was really fucking hard to hate someone when they saved your life. Especially when you were a dick to them first.

Only, an anxious weight sat on my chest that had nothing to do with either of them.

I grabbed the chair by her desk and spun it around, straddling it as I faced them.

"That was awful."

Matías chuckled under his breath. "It was bloody and beautiful. You had a purpose, you stopped when you met that purpose, ending his misery, and you walked away. That's what's important."

She pulled her hands back and stared at him, most likely trying to gauge his sincerity. I didn't doubt it. All I'd ever heard about Matías when I'd joined Dirty Dogs was that he lived with a fucked up psychopath, he witnessed horrors we couldn't begin to fathom, how strong he was to not be crazy after all those years inside that hellhole.

I could name a hundred other statements Javier had said in his favor.

Rita glanced at me. "Did you know?"

"Hell, no. That's what's making me question that little asshole." I believed he met with Tiago and Rob. That rang true. I believed that one of those new *pendejos* was there.

What I had a hard time with was a sect of Dirty Dogs that wanted to fuck everything up and go back to our roots.

I scrubbed a hand down my face. "Shit, I know some of the guys hate that we left the skins and drug business." Leo had chirped about it like an annoying bird hovering in my ear. "But I haven't heard anything on a large scale that divided the club." I tightened my grip on the back of the chair. "I haven't heard anyone make plans like that."

"We don't know who the rat is, and now we know the issues in our gang run deep. Deeper than I ever thought possible." She pouted and it was hard for me to hide my smile.

Life was shit right now, and it would be for the foreseeable future. But Rita was damn funny when she pouted. Sexy as hell too. That soft, full, bottom lip sticking out was begging to be nibbled on.

"This is good," I said, trying to convince myself, and Matías nodded his agreement. "We know who wasn't here today." I ground my teeth. Due better have a real good fucking reason for not being here.

At no time had he ever expressed any desire to overthrow Javier or kill Rita. He hadn't even made comments about leaving our old ways behind.

"I know that!" she snapped, huffing her irritation and expanding those gorgeous tits of hers.

"We also know a few names of the people who Kurt was scared of," I continued.

"Yeah? What are we going to do about that? His information doesn't make any sense. Who killed Tiago if they were all in on it together?"

I clamped my lips shut.

"We'll find out." Matías pressed a kiss to her forehead. "Which leads me to my next request." Caging her to the bed, he dipped until his nose brushed hers.

She started breathing quicker. He didn't smile or even blink. Damn it, she was getting turned on. A tiny spark of jealousy flared in the pit of my stomach.

I wanted her to react to me like that.

"Hmm?" she hummed.

"I'm going back to catch Matthews. Without you."

The spell broke as her brows pinched and she pushed herself up on her elbows. Matías jumped back to avoid a smashed nose. "The hell you are! We stick together."

Matías' expression iced over. "I keep you alive." His tone brooked no arguments. "Matthews knows more than what he told you. I plan to get it from him."

"That's where Esteban was almost shot!" Now she sat on the edge of the bed and she looked like she was two seconds away from locking Matías in the bathroom. Her eyes were wide and her bottom lip trembled.

Shit, she was scared. For me or for him? I rubbed my chest.

"There won't be a detail and no one will know I'm going

there. Believe it or not, I know how to be discreet," he said wryly as he started to turn.

"It's too fucking dangerous!" Rita jumped to her feet and caught his arm.

For him. She was afraid he'd leave her again. Or get taken from her. Exhaling, I curled my fingers tight against my palm.

"I'll go with him."

They whipped toward me with matching shock on their faces. I smirked. "Don't look so surprised I'd offer."

"You were almost shot there," Rita repeated as she took slow steps toward me, dropping Matías' arm.

Some of the tightness in my chest released. She was worried about me too.

"It will be safer if I go by myself," Matías argued.

"No, it won't." I raised a brow. "You need someone to watch your back."

"Rita would be alone." A frown tugged on his lips.

"Then we all go," Rita tossed out like that settled it.

"No," Matías and I both said. I didn't want her anywhere near that place. It wasn't ours, we didn't have it secured, and just fucking no.

Matías glanced at the floor for a second, then glanced back at Rita.

"I'll take Esteban with me. We won't be gone for more than two hours. You'll stay locked in this room. If nothing else, I believe you'll be safe here. If we don't check in or we're not back, my brothers' men will come get you and you can ride to the Chinese restaurant to get us."

Rita rotated her hands as she processed his words. Finally, she said, "There are so many holes in that plan."

He dipped his head. "We don't have a choice. If there are

men planning your death, I'm not going to wait on them to act to figure out who they are."

Rita had to see that neither of us were going to risk her life. Not if we could stop it before it happened. Gang princess or not. Leader or not. She mattered too much to me.

I glanced at Matías. Fuck.

She mattered too much to *us.*

"I hate you right now."

"No, you don't," he said in a cocky tone of voice I'd never heard from him before.

I set her chair back, then cupped her hips from behind. At the same time, Matías boxed her in from the front.

"We'll be back as soon as we can," I murmured in her ear.

Matías cupped her throat with one hand and her breast with his other, swiping his thumb across her nipple.

Her breath caught.

In for a pound, I tugged her dress up, slipping my hand to the vee of her thighs, cupping her sweet, hot pussy. I groaned as she pulsed against my fingers.

"You're so fucking turned on," I muttered, dropping my forehead to her shoulder.

"You're both sexy and your hands are on me. A nun would be dripping right now," she breathed, lacking any bite. Matías grinned then pressed a kiss to her cheek.

We both knew she probably meant for it to be sassy, but she was too turned on to deliver it properly. I loved stealing her sass like that.

"Be good, and when we get back, we'll finish what we started." He glanced at me and I nodded.

Stepping back like we planned that shit, we moved toward the door.

Rita stiffened, but didn't follow. "You guys are dangerous. I expect you to check in as soon as you get there, when you're done, and when you leave."

I had my hand on the lock, but before twisting it, I narrowed my eyes on her. "You're not going to argue?"

She sniffed and sat on her bed, raising her legs until her toes balanced on the edge and spreading them to show off the wet spot on her panties.

I groaned and Matías tensed.

"I want the orgasms you promised me. Multiple. So hurry the fuck up, or I'll take care of my needs myself." Her eyes blazed as she started to pull the middle of her panties to the side.

Did Matías really need me?

Shit, I needed to get out of here or I wouldn't be going anywhere.

Out in the hallway, I panted. Rita was such a fucking tease. Now I had to walk around the compound with Matías and a fucking erection.

Matías pounded his fist once on the closed door. "Lock it up!"

The locks engaged and then we started for the stairs. No one was in the hallway. Good. I didn't have to threaten bodily harm on my brothers.

We were almost to the front entrance when Joel called my name. He was coming from the back, eyeing Matías.

"Can I have a quick word?"

"Sure." I shrugged. There wasn't a reason for me to beat his ass, so I'd wait until he gave me one. But knowing he and Ricco knew there was discontent brewing and didn't tell me, an *officer*, broke the code of the Dirty Dogs.

Why keep it hidden?

"Alone."

I glanced at Matías then stared Joel down. "Why alone?"

Joel gave him a withering smile. "What? Are you two a package deal now?"

Matías and I exchanged looks before I turned back to Joel. "Say what you have to say, and then I have to check something outside."

Pressing his lips together, Joel lost his friendliness. "I wanted to catch up on what we found out from Kurt. And figure out a plan on what to do about our missing people, one of whom is an officer."

"That's not me you need to plan with. You need to talk to Rita." Done with this conversation, I motioned for Matías to start walking, but Joel touched my shoulder.

"She's not fit to lead the Dirty Dogs. I know you're fucking her, hell maybe you both are, but that doesn't make her a leader. Stop putting ideas in her head that she can do this."

That got both of our attention.

"Why isn't she fit?" I asked, a warning note threaded through my words.

"Come on, Esteban." Joel's brows kissed his forehead. "We don't have women in Dirty Dogs. It's all men...And Rita. She's been kept on this pedestal her entire life by Javier."

"As she should be," Matías cut in. "Would you rather Javier had treated her like a pawn and used her for his own gain, or whored her out? Maybe he should have ignored her and treated her like a useless trinket." He shook his head. "We know exactly how that played out. Remember? Valentina killed our father for that reason."

Joel puffed out his cheeks. "That's not what I meant and you know it."

"Why do you want to lead the club?" I asked.

He straightened his back and lifted his chin. "Someone has to."

"Right..." Matías drew out.

Whatever, I tapped Matías' shoulder and we started walking.

"I wasn't done talking to you!" Joel shouted.

"Funny, you sounded like you were done. Call Rita to make any plans you want to make. Then we'll have the vote soon."

I tossed Matías the keys and climbed into the passenger seat. The compound was mostly deserted and all the bikes that had been outside were gone.

Matías got in and slammed his door. He sat there for a few minutes, not putting the key in the ignition.

"Are we going to get this show on the road, or are we wasting more time for shits and giggles?" I was only half-joking. Being away from Rita after that weird interaction with Joel rubbed me the wrong way.

He started the car and pulled out of the compound.

"I don't get it," he said quietly, more to himself than me.

"I'll play. What don't you get?"

"A lot of things. The one at the top of the pile is why you offered to go with me." He peeked at me. "Shouldn't you want me dead and out of the way?"

I shifted in my seat. "I never wanted you dead," I said, then sighed. "I was jealous as hell of you. I want what's best for Rita and you weren't it. You disappear at the drop of a dime."

"And now you think I won't?" There was only curiosity there.

Leveling him with a hard stare, I shook my head. "I don't

know that." The words were slow and his jaw worked. "What I do know is that you've done all the right things since you've been back. It would have been easy for you to try and take control of Dirty Dogs. Or even fuck her and leave her–which I saw the night of Javier's funeral."

The skin under his eye twitched but that was the only reaction.

"You still could. A week of good deeds doesn't mean shit, but..." I dropped my head back against the headrest. Rolling to face him, I studied him. Several years older than me, a world away in terms of life experience, and so much loneliness clinging to him, it was like a chill surrounded him. "You saved my life. I'm willing to give you the benefit of the doubt."

He barked out a short laugh. "You're overlooking everything your gut is telling you because I saved your life?"

I grinned. "Yeah, pretty much." We both chuckled. Then I sobered up. "Don't fuck with her again. Not like you did before. If you do, I'll flay every inch of your skin, and save the nipples for Rita."

We cracked up again.

"That was something, wasn't it?" He smiled at the windshield.

"Damn straight it was. Rita loves going for a man's sensitive bits. That's how Javier trained her."

"Yeah."

The rest of the ride was spent discussing nonsense. Nothing related to the Dirty Dogs drama or the new club. It was like an olive branch.

It felt dangerous to put my faith in a man who had a high track record of breaking Rita's heart. But for her, I wanted him to be different this time. To not make fucked up decisions for the right reasons.

For me, I wanted to believe he was different this time. Because damn, when he tackled me, I realized that the people who had your back weren't always the people you thought they were.

And the man who should have had my back was the very one who tried to put a bullet in my heart.

25

MATÍAS

I did the slow loop around the block, searching for anything or anyone who looked out of place. This wasn't the tourist district, so it was missing a lot of the bumbling crowds, but there were a few people walking down the street.

"Park at the end." Esteban jerked his head toward the next block.

"Really?" I asked. I was already heading there.

"What?" he asked as if he didn't have a clue that he was being obtuse.

"Nothing." I flipped the car and parked on the corner behind a banged up white van. The windows were blacked out with scratches like all pedos vehicles were.

"That's a nasty ass looking van," Esteban commented as he climbed out.

"Yep." I walked close and tried to peek in the windows. I couldn't see a damned thing. Even where there were scratches, it was too dark inside.

"Let's go. We have to get back to Rita." He brushed by me.

Not wanting to be here any longer than I had to, I pulled my gun and followed him. Usually, I wouldn't carry on the street, but this area was mainly run by corrupt police looking for a payoff, and I wanted to have access to my weapon if I needed it.

The bell on the door rang and the same hostess came through the back. She slowed her steps when she saw us.

"Matthews is not here." If she were a cat, her hackles would be up.

I motioned her forward with my finger. It was in between lunch and dinner and the dining area was empty. No reason to pretend this was a friendly visit.

She gulped but shuffled forward. When she was a few steps away, I caught her shirt in my fist and pressed my gun to the side of her throat.

"This angle may not kill you. It could. Or it could just take out your voice box. But the close range also plays a part. Now tell me, is Matthews here?"

"Y-yes." Her eyes blinked back tears.

"Yell for him."

Closing her eyes, she screamed, "*Señor* Matthews!"

It was only a few tense minutes before the stairs creaked. "Ting, the phone works better than breaking your–" He froze when he was down far enough to see us.

I smiled.

"Let her go."

"Gladly. She served her purpose." I released her, careful not to shove her too hard. But I did not put away my weapon. "I came for a friendly visit."

Matthews' freckles stood out against his pale skin as he glowered at me. "Call me crazy, but this doesn't seem friendly."

"You've never had friends like us before," Esteban said. I

glanced over and his dimples were on full display from his tight lipped smile.

"Apparently," he returned, grim. "Let's take this upstairs."

The hostess was already gone. I took the stairs first and Esteban brought up the rear. At the top, Matthews pounded on the wall. "Dingo! Trace!"

Two men popped out of the room at the end of the hall, both sweaty and in workout clothes.

"Yeah, boss?" one asked.

"I need backup."

Esteban kept grinning, but I'd lost my desire to smile. Now that I had an audience with Matthews, it was time for business.

Both men snapped alert when they saw us and immediately prowled toward us.

"In here," Matthews said. He was waiting with the office door open.

Again, I went in first and Esteban second. Matthews' two guys stood on either side of the closed office door with their arms crossed. Shocking that they hadn't taken the time to get a weapon. Unless they were hiding it in the ass of their shorts. Unlikely.

The three of us sat down, Esteban taking the chair Rita had sat in. Leaning back, I let my gun hand dangle from the end of the chair arm. I still had a good grip on the weapon, but this way, they wouldn't feel like I was aiming it at their chests.

"So, what brings you back with so much *friendliness*." Matthews bared his teeth.

"It seems you left out some key details when we were here."

Matthews snorted. "Of course, I did. I'm not from here, but I'm not stupid."

"Hey, I get it," Esteban spread his knees and got comfortable. "We're not allies or anything like that. Why would you tell us anything at all?"

"I think I gave you plenty." From the heavy set of his brows, he believed he had.

"You did," I agreed. Flicking my gaze to the men at the door, I checked their expressions. They were stone-faced. Either they had a hell of a poker face, or Matthews had filled them in on what he shared. "The question is, why did you share just enough to get us killed?"

Matthews started twisting from side to side in his chair. "Your buddy would have tried to kill you whether I gave you that information or not. In fact, it worked in your favor, because, not only did you uncover a person who tried to kill you, you survived."

"The funny thing is, he could have been your rat." I watched for a cue.

Not even the most minuscule twitch of his face or hands that were in full view.

"He's not," I deduced.

Matthews slowly relaxed as if he felt the danger had passed. "He's not."

"If he was, you would have said something. Maybe or maybe not." Twisting my mouth to the side, I pretended to think this through. "But you or someone in your–Do you have a club name yet?"

A real smile broke out on his face. "No, not yet. We thought about Freedom Fighters and all kinds of cheesy names, but none of them feel right. So we're just the club until we think of something better."

"I wished I could help you, but I'm shit with names. Javier came up with Dirty Dogs," Esteban said lightly and Matthews relaxed further.

"Not a big deal. It will come to us when it's time."

"Which one of your guys has been hanging out with the Dirty Dogs?" I asked.

Matthews froze. "What makes you think that we're hanging out?"

"That's the funny thing. You see, Rita's cleaning house, and we discovered that someone from your club has been hanging out with some of our problem children."

"Our?" Matthews asked, likely as a distraction.

"What can I say? I put in my application so I already consider myself part of the club."

His nose twitched. He didn't seem to appreciate my sarcasm.

"You became part of the club when you started sticking your dick in Rita," Matthews returned dryly.

What the fuck?

Esteban shook in silent laughter.

"Don't look at him like that. We already knew. The first time I met Esteban, I told him I'd done my homework on every single person's name I could find." His gaze shot to me. "Which includes you."

"Who has been meeting with the club?" I asked again. I didn't give a shit about what he did or didn't know about the club. I wanted his contact. I wanted any information he had on a plan to hurt Rita.

"I have." One of the men by the door said. He was a burly motherfucker. A full head of hair and scruffy beard. Not anything I thought a US military man would look like.

"And you are?"

"Dingo." His face and voice were void of any inflection. He was a robot.

"Real name?" I squinted. I didn't care about Matthrews' research, but I'd happily do my own.

He grinned. "No."

"Tell me who the rat is?"

"I can tell you who he's not," Matthews interjected, bringing the conversation back to him.

"And who would those people be?" I already knew his answer, but I played along.

"Neither of you."

"That's not good enough."

"It will have to be. You've been around a long time. You wouldn't give up your best intel for nothing." He raised his brows as if he was willing to keep talking.

"You want to negotiate?" *Fuck that.*

"Of course." Now he rocked back and forth in his chair.

"Rita would be the one to negotiate with, but I can tell you right now, she probably won't give you what you want," Esteban said.

"*If* Rita takes over the club."

"Why wouldn't she?" Esteban sat forward.

Matthews shrugged and exchanged glances with his men. "That's not ours to say."

I reached over and pressed a hand into Esteban's chest to stop him. His charm dropped away in a blink of an eye as his face darkened in anger and his eyes drilled holes in Matthews.

"If there's a plan to hurt Rita and you know about it, I–"

"What do you want?" I made sure Esteban was going to stay quiet before I removed my hand.

"I want a home for my brothers. We want to operate our businesses without any trouble."

"That will never happen. Even if the Dirty Dogs allowed you to take over the businesses they dropped, my brothers wouldn't allow it. Between the two, you'd never get the businesses going, and you wouldn't leave town alive." I paused to let the weight of my words settle between us. "What else do you want?"

Matthews cursed. Glancing out the window, he worked his jaw back and forth.

The man really thought he'd be able to work it all out. It was clear now, he wasn't a player. He wasn't even on the board, not really.

Our issues were inside our own house.

"We're done here. You don't have anything I want, and I'm not willing to part with my secrets for shit." Matthews stood up.

Canting my head, I tried to figure him out. He seemed like a smart man. He'd done so much research, but had thought it would be a real possibility to pick up skins and drugs. "Why come here?"

"What do you mean?"

"Of all the places you could have gone, why did you move to our territory?"

"The Dirty Dogs and the Institution co-exist here just fine."

I shook my head. "Not really. The territories don't overlap, and there was never peace between the two. If you knew who my father had been, you'd understand that. The Dirty Dogs had only existed because he allowed it for his pleasure and his amusement."

For some reason that irked Matthews. "Yet your father isn't here."

That caught me off guard. "You know the Institution no longer exists, correct?"

He scoffed. "Of course, I do."

"Then you know how Vicente Castillo lost his power?"

He eyed me, like he wasn't sure where I was going. "The

details around his death are murky at best. I couldn't find a definitive answer."

"My father was killed by his only daughter. Valentina." May she rot in Hell. "You know how she died?"

His eyes widened for a fraction of a second. Whoever he had used to get his information had left some gaping holes.

"I didn't realize there was a sister."

Laughing, I slapped my knee like I was having a damn good time. Then I killed it. "There was. She was the bane of my existence and the second person I ever truly hated. The first was my father. She died at the hands of that lovely little woman my brothers call their wife."

His mouth popped open and Esteban lost it. "I had the same reaction the first time I heard. But I already knew she was a little badass."

"My point is, the Institution didn't fall because of a rivalry. The Institution fell from the inside. No one but his children could have ever touched him. And all that power now belongs to my brothers."

"That you don't want, even if it was rightfully yours," Matthews pointed out.

Esteban's gaze burned a hole in the side of my head as if he too was interested in this answer.

"No, I don't want it. It was ours, not mine, and they're much better suited for running Carnage Industries."

Matthews stretched his arms across the desk. "Yet here you are, trying to be at the top of the Dirty Dogs. You want power, you just don't want to admit it."

I raised a brow and didn't deign to answer him.

"I heard that there's an office being cleared for you as we speak at Carnage Industries. Your brothers want you to work for them. Are you sure you're so loyal to the Dirty Dogs?"

The burning in the side of my head intensified.

"Don't question my loyalty and I won't take your heart and deliver it to Rita." I stood. "I'm done here, Esteban. It was a wasted trip."

Esteban remained sitting as he narrowed his eyes on Matthews. "You know, I can figure out who the rat is. But if you have information about Rita and you don't share it, I will make it my personal mission in life to erase every single one of you from existence." He flicked his gaze to the men at the door.

"You won't be alone." I clapped Esteban on the shoulder.

He glanced at me, a question in his gaze. He wanted to know if what Matthews said was true. He trusted me so little that he was concerned I'd leave and work with my brothers.

I loved those four assholes, and I wouldn't betray them for the world, but my place wasn't with them.

My place was with Rita, and the more time I was back, I was starting to think my place was with Esteban too.

Esteban dipped his head, then turned back to the men at the door. "Do you have anything to tell us before we walk out that door?"

Dingo glanced at Matthews who gave a minute shake of his head. "Nope. I got nothing."

Standing, Matthews pushed his chair in and rounded the desk. "I don't want a war. I really don't. But if I have to fight one...we have plenty of experience to make sure we come out on top." It was a warning.

I wanted to deliver my own.

"When your man died, he was shot by a *pendejo* who we beheaded as our own form of justice and delivered to you as proof." It didn't matter that the man acted on his own without Dirty Dogs' permission. "He could very well be the rat."

The skin under Matthews left eye twitched. Interesting.

I continued, "Your vendetta isn't with the Dirty Dogs. Not really. It's with the *cabróns* who are trying to flip their shit. If something happens to any of us three, that's different. For us, it will be personal, and I will hold you responsible."

"Just you three, not the Dirty Dogs?"

"I will fight for the Dirty Dogs. But if Esteban or Rita are harmed and you could have prevented it, you'll die. That's a promise."

Esteban and I let ourselves out.

As we headed down the street, Esteban shifted closer. "That was a bust."

"Yes and no. I assumed he wouldn't tell us anything. I mainly wanted to deliver my own threat."

"He doesn't seem to care about that." He scratched his temple as we reached the SUV.

"It was a lot of posturing, wasn't it?"

"Hell yeah, it was. And repetitive too."

"Good. I want him to remember my words. Something bad is coming. I feel it. Maybe this repeated reminder that we're bigger than they are will loosen their tongues and they'll find us later."

Esteban rolled his eyes. "Like that will happen."

"You never know, kid."

"I'm not a fucking kid," he griped.

I grinned as I drove us back to Rita. We should even have thirty minutes to spare.

26

RITA

Esteban: We're on our way back. With all ten fingers and toes.

I snorted and stopped pacing my kitchen.

"They're done and on their way." I sighed in relief as I turned to Amorette sitting at the table.

Joel and Ricco had both tried calling me, and when that hadn't worked, they banged on the door. They both knew better than to break down my door or pick the lock. They both had the skill. Everyone in the Dirty Dogs did.

But the lack of peace was enough to have me calling Amorette to come save me. And she came with Grey and Parker in tow, who were so gracious as to sit outside in their bullet-proof SUV and watch the street.

Me: Fingers and toes, but what about your pretty faces? And come to my house. I couldn't stay at the club with everyone pounding on my door. Amorette and two of her guys are here with me.

Esteban: Got it. You think my face is pretty?

I rolled my eyes as some of the fear that had gripped my chest lightened, giving way to tingles deep in my stomach.

That was what he got stuck on. Now that they were mostly out of danger, I felt like a schoolgirl with a crush, not the twenty-seven year old gang princess, soon to be Dirty Dog leader.

Me: You're every girl's wet dream. I've seen plenty of them with you over the years.

"That's great. I'll text the guys. We'll head out as soon as they get here." She picked up her phone and tapped away.

Esteban's dots started bouncing but his response didn't come immediately like before. Shit, maybe he was offended I brought that up like some kind of faux pas.

But come on, we were a gang. I'd had as many hookups in our clubs as the rest of them. I just tended to stay away from Dirty Dogs. Why shit where I eat?

Matías had only been so easy to want because he had been accepted by *Papá* but not a Dirty Dog.

I should be chatting with Amorette, being a good host and friend. But all of my focus was on the text chain. I was so fucking relieved there wasn't a repeat of our last meeting.

Esteban: I would have been yours from day 1

My breath lodged in my throat. Esteban had joined right when Matías started coming around. He'd been too young for me then.

I couldn't think of a response and set my phone down. Sitting my ass in my chair, I closed my eyes and ran through every single scenario of what could have happened at the restaurant.

There could have been a friendly chat, a good meal with fake smiles, or another gun fight in the street.

Shit. My eyes popped back open.

Esteban hadn't clarified if they had any holes in their body that hadn't been there before.

Amorette rose and gave me a hug. "I'm heading out. I can tell you're going to be busy as soon as they get here."

I gripped her arms and squeezed. "Thank you. You're the best friend a girl like me could ask for." I meant it.

"You mean crazy?"

I smirked. "I was going for badass."

Laughing softly, she made her way to the front door. It closed behind her. Wait, I needed them to stay until the guys got back.

I reached for my phone but there was a knock on the door.

"It's us," Matías called, his voice muffled.

Rushing to the front of the house, I swung my door open.

There they stood, Matías' head almost hitting the door-frame, his black curls hanging over his forehead and a glint in his eyes. Esteban was beside him, slightly shorter, broader, and grinning with his dimples popped out. Only his smile seemed forced.

Both were gloriously unharmed.

"Thank God! I'm never going to be left behind–" I was going to finish with "again", but Matías placed a large hand on my stomach and moved me back so they could step in.

Esteban's phone rang and he sighed as he answered it.

"I've been trying to call you–" Joel griped.

"Sorry, emergency meeting. You're not invited. We'll find you afterward." Esteban hit the end button as he slammed the front door and twisted the lock. When he turned around, his face scrunched up like he was beyond fed up with Joel.

Matías caught my hips as Esteban walked around me.

"What–"

He ducked and caught my lips in a kiss. I moaned into

his mouth as his tongue swept into mine. He tasted of bitter coffee and cinnamon. An addictive cup of coffee on a lazy Sunday morning.

Esteban shifted my hair off the back of my neck and he pressed a soft kiss to my nape. His fingers lingered, sending chillbumps racing down my arms.

"We promised you a reward if you stayed here like a good girl, but you didn't, did you?" Esteban said darkly. "Should we punish you instead?"

My brain short circuited. *Hell yes.*

"Mm, maybe the reward is her punishment? Do you think she can handle us both?" Matías asked Esteban.

I wanted that. Bad. This last week, it had been all I'd thought about when I allowed myself to unwind. The feel of four hands and two cocks. The two men I couldn't get out of my head no matter how hard I fucking tried.

I hadn't ever expected it to actually happen though.

They didn't like each other. They barely tolerated each other. Even if it was more one-sided on Esteban's part.

"You're going to fuck me? Together?" I breathed, rolling my head back as Matías cupped my breast, pinching my hard nipple.

He dropped his head to leave wet kisses on the other side of my neck. Both men lavished me with sweet attention. It was heady, and powerful, and drugging.

Matías chuckled. "Have you met Amorette and my brothers?"

His words brought me back to the surface of reality where the haze of desire lifted. Just a bit. "What the fuck do they have to do with this?"

He frowned when he realized I'd lost some of my buzz. He bent to capture the back of my thighs. Then he picked me up and I wrapped my legs around his waist.

"They all share with no problem. Lean back."

I did. Esteban stripped me from behind and unsnapped my bra in record time.

"Are you saying for sex?" He wasn't making sense. I mean, it did, but it didn't.

One side of his mouth kicked up in a crooked grin. "Well, they do share for sex."

I shook my head. "You two want to fuck me?"

Which I had no problems with. But as much as I didn't want to ask questions and potentially stop this, I needed to know where they stood. What to expect. My bruised heart couldn't take another pounding and survive.

"But what about after? Is this a one time thing?"

Esteban cupped both of my breasts, squeezing them and pushing them up and together as he pressed against my shoulders. His hot breath moved my hair and tingles erupted deep in my stomach. "That depends on you."

"How?" I gasped as he pinched both nipples to the point of pain.

"How can you do that after she tore Kurt's nipple off?" Matías grimaced. "I have ghost pain."

There was stark amusement in Esteban's voice. "I don't know if you noticed, but watching Rita get bloody turns me on."

It had, I'd noticed how his hard cock had pressed against the seam of his jeans. It just amped up my desire to leave Kurt broken. Not that that asshole didn't deserve it anyway.

"How does this depend on me?" I clarified, wanting to get back to the good parts.

"I love you, baby. You must know that," Esteban pressed his cheek against the top of my head as he continued to work my breasts.

Did I know that? Did I love him back?

All the times Esteban had my back crossed my mind. The times he made me laugh, the way he worshiped my body, how he looked at me as if I was the only woman in the world. He'd always looked at me like that, from the very beginning. I realized that now.

Just his presence flooded me with warmth.

"I know."

"I love you too, *mi corazón*." Matías stared deep into my eyes.

Matías had always been the one bright love of my life, that grand relationship that would make or break me, and up until this point, had done nothing but break me.

Still, I loved him.

But, I loved Esteban too.

Maybe we weren't meant to have one great love, but two, or many. There were no limits on love.

"You're ours. We've decided." Matías smirked as his eyes twinkled.

That both set my ovaries on fire and lit the indignation deep in my soul. "If I'm yours, then you're mine."

"Undoubtedly." Matías didn't even blink.

He walked back to my bedroom and set me on the edge of my bed. Somewhere, I'd lost Esteban's touch and he was now sprawled naked against my pillows, lazily stroking his cock.

"Come ride me. Show Matías how well you fuck me." He wasn't smiling, his eyes were dark, and his tongue snuck out to lick his bottom lip.

Kneeling in my panties, I took in the beautiful sight before me. "I'm not ready to."

Matías stuck his thumbs in the sides of my panties and I raised up so he could peel them down. I helped him get them off all while keeping my gaze locked with Esteban's. His dark brown eyes were almost black.

Then Matías walked to the other side of the bed as he stripped out of his clothes. His thick, veined cock bobbed against his stomach when he shucked his pants.

He crawled into the spot next to Esteban, adjusting himself against the pillows and tucking his arms behind his head.

My face blistered at the scene of Esteban and Matías laid out before me like a fucking feast. Esteban with his asshole charm, and barely there smirk that said he knew exactly what this was doing to me. Matías watched me with dark eyes and so much heat that a bead of sweat rolled provocatively down the curve of my spine. He wasn't smiling. His expression was both tense and smoldering.

This was everything I didn't know I wanted and I refused to end too fast.

"You both want this?" At this point, I didn't care, but I still asked because it seemed like the right thing to do. Fuck right.

I was grabbing onto this dream with both hands and like hell would I let them tear it away from me now.

Crawling up the bed, I positioned myself directly between them, sliding my hands up their bunched abs. The way their muscles twitched under my touch was such an aphrodisiac.

They locked gazes and some kind of message or emotion passed between them.

"We're willing to try," Esteban answered, looking back at me. There was only sincerity in his eyes. "We both want you enough not to make you choose." His words twisted at the end as if he thought at some point I might.

"We want you to be happy, and we want you to live a long

fucking life. You'll have the best chance to do that with both of us at your back." Matías finally fisted his cock, setting it straight up. "Start with him, *mi corazón*."

My eyelids fluttered shut and I pressed my hand to his wild-beating heart. Matías had never used any kind of pet name for me before. I'd never heard him address anyone with a term of endearment. It felt good. More than good.

The sense of belonging that both of them created inside me when Esteban called me *baby* or Matías *his heart*, was breathtaking. I wanted to hold onto it forever.

I gave Esteban every drop of my attention as I crawled closer. His eyes flickered as if he wanted to look at Matías but he didn't. His jaw slackened as I took over stroking him. With my ass in the air, I sucked him into my mouth and made love to his beautiful cock.

The entire time, I kept my eyes locked on him. I wanted him to know this was all for him.

Esteban's eyes crinkled in the corners as he bit his lip. Then he threaded his fingers through my hair.

I popped up for just a second.

"Fuck my face," I gasped, sucking in air. Wetness pooled between my legs at how tightly he was holding onto his control. He was about to break, and I was the reason. I held so much power between us that I could make him break. "Come on." I gave him a hard stroke, then squeezed the base of his cock. He grunted. "You know you're aching to."

He tightened his grip in my hair, forcing my face down once, then back up. I gagged from the way he hit the back of my throat. Saliva spilled from my mouth, wetting him and making the glide that much easier.

"Fuck, do that again," Matías mumbled as he got behind me. His fingers dipped between my legs. "She's so fucking

wet. Christ, Rita, *mi corazón*. You really want this. Both of us."
He sounded strangled.

"Damn right, she does," Esteban growled, then pushed
me down again. This time, he didn't pull me back up, but
stayed pressed deep in my throat.

I couldn't breathe.

"Breathe through your nose," he said softly. "That's it."
Then he pulled me up.

The head of Matías' cock lined up, and the next time
Esteban pushed me down, Matías plunged inside. I tried to
cry out, but I was too full of Esteban.

"Ah, fuck. Your throat is contracting around me." He
dropped his head back and his mouth fell open. He slowly
lifted my head up, and I kept my lips as tight around him as
I could.

Matías pulled back. "You feel so good. You feel like *mine*."

Together, they worked me, Matías fucking me with the
same rhythm that Esteban fucked my face. I felt stuffed,
overexposed, and over stimulated. My entire body was
alight and wave after wave of heat washed over me, leaving
me a sweat-slickened mess.

The deep way Matías bottomed out every time was
almost uncomfortable.

"I'm getting close," Esteban gasped, forcing my head up
and down. He was moving so quick, I could only let him
fuck my mouth.

Matías panted as he picked up speed and reached
around to strum my clit. It didn't take much, it barely took
half a second, before I started jerking and crying out from
the intense, brutal orgasm sweeping through me. My voice
was garbled as Esteban continued to piston his hips.

My vision darkened around the edges, and my arms
gave out.

Cursing behind me, Matías wrapped an arm around my waist as the first stream of salty cum jetted against the back of my throat.

Esteban shouted, and Matías grunted, both bucking hard against my limp twitching body.

It took forever to come down and to be able to breathe again. But eventually, I roused, tucked so neatly between them. Esteban propped his head on his hand as he traced the bridge of my nose and eyebrow, studying my features.

Behind me, Matías molded so firmly against my back and ass, I was sure he wanted to fuse himself against me. His arms were wrapped tight around my waist and chest, and his face was buried in my hair.

"You two wrecked me," I croaked. "I'm fucking destroyed."

Esteban smiled and it transformed his face into an expression so blinding, I closed my eyes.

"Good. It means you'll never want to go looking for dick anywhere else."

I snorted. Like I could even walk after that. The fierce way Matías had taken me left my legs a shaky mess. I doubted I could take myself to the bathroom.

"This was..." Matías said against my hair. "This felt real. Like before, but better."

Before...Before he left, before he tossed me aside out of fucked up good intentions. I waited for the pain to kick me in the chest, but no sneaky feelings of betrayal popped up.

It seemed like time...and orgasms had healed my wounds. I wasn't so naive to think this was permanent, but for now, I happily accepted it.

I laced my fingers with his.

We must have laid there for hours. The sun started to set and the room was thrown into darkness.

A pounding started on the front door. "What the hell?" I tried to roll out of bed but Esteban stopped me.

"Let Matías get it. He's the elder. It's his responsibility to protect us." He grinned.

Rolling his eyes, Matías pulled on his pants and walked out of the room. "If it's Ricco or Joel, I swear to Christ..."

Esteban snuggled into my side, leaving wet kisses along my neck until I giggled. I fucking giggled.

"Rita!" Matías yelled in a strange tone.

I bolted to a sitting position as Esteban jumped out of bed. "We better get out there, that sounds like a situation." All humor was gone from his voice.

Grabbing a fresh shirt and shorts from my dresser, I got dressed. In the living room, Matías stood so still, staring down at a picture in his hand. His face was set like stone as anger emanated from him.

He wasn't alone. A skinny kid of thirteen, maybe fourteen, stood by the closed door. His gaze shot to us, then wildly searched the room like he expected an ambush. Wringing his hands, he was two seconds from bolting.

"What's going on?" I asked, sliding up to Matías' side.

"This kid lives in the neighborhood. He saw the attempted driveby the other day and grabbed a picture." He might as well have been speaking gibberish as I examined the photo.

A dark SUV was on my street. The tinted windows were up, and Matias was at the end of my walk, his gun aimed their way. This had to be after he shot at them.

What made the picture so interesting was that the windshield wasn't tinted. At least not the bottom two-thirds.

The man in the passenger seat was lifting up a mask.

And I recognized him.

My fucking heart was going to explode from my chest.

How fucking dare he. This whole time I was certain it was the new club, even if they didn't want to admit it.

Maybe it was, but a Dirty Dog in the vehicle meant...

Fuck, I needed to lock it down while the kid was here. Blowing out a hard breath, I forced a smile on my face.

"What's your name?" I asked, moving away from Matías. I didn't need to see that shit in Matías' hand anymore.

"Crisanto," he muttered, watching his feet.

"Hey." I stepped forward and touched his shoulder. "Why did you bring it here?"

His gaze shot to mine. "You're a nice lady. You're nice to my *mamá*. I saw what happened and I had my phone out anyway." He shrugged.

"Why now?" Matías asked, shoving the photo in his back pocket. "Why not bring this the day it happened."

The kid mashed his lips together. "At first, I was..." He shook his head. "I was scared. By the time I got the courage, you were gone. I printed it, but I haven't seen you since."

Well, shit. I had been gone a lot.

There was zero emotion on Esteban's face, yet his muscles were bunched so tight that when he pulled his wallet out, I thought the seams on his shirt would burst. "Here kid," he said, gruffly, handing him a faded auto shop card. "If you ever run into trouble, you call me. I'll come no matter what. Got it?"

Crisanto clenched his fists and jaw as he tucked his chin. Esteban shook the card, and when he raised his hand to take it, his lips trembled.

"Thanks," he mumbled.

Matías opened the door, peeked out, then stepped back to let Crisanto out. "Don't be a stranger. You did more than you realized, and we're in your debt."

He jerked his head up once and then slid past Matías.

We crowded the door and watched him walk home. His family lived three doors down across the street and I never knew they had a son.

I was an ass.

"What are we going to do now?" Esteban asked.

"We're going to the compound, we're going to take the gang for Rita. Then we're going to clean house." Matías rolled to a sitting position as he stretched his arms over his head.

"And after that?" Esteban grinned over my head.

Locking my rage and betrayal in a tidy little box, I smiled. There would be plenty of time to let those babies out to play.

"Then the guys get the girl, don't you know that?" I placed a hand on each of their chests.

Despite the fury that I could feel trembling in their bodies, they busted up laughing and I smirked.

I was serious, even if it felt like a happy ending for us was still miles away.

27

MATÍAS

E steban and I waited in the living room as Rita got
ready. Her house was exactly as it was when I'd
been here before. Nothing had changed. Except
for us.

She was both stronger and softer than she used to be.
More jaded.

I wasn't a slave to my father anymore. I was grabbing
hold of what I wanted with both hands, consequences and
fear be damned.

Then there was Esteban. This kid was more complex
than I gave him credit for. I'd never pegged him as anything
other than a pretty face, but he'd already punched two holes
in her living room wall.

Rita came out and raised one brow as she held some
make up brushes in her hand. "You done?" Was all she'd
said.

"Hell fucking no, not until I get my hands on that
cabrón," was all he'd said before he'd fallen on the couch.

He was someone I never saw coming, but somehow he

fit. Where Rita and I were strained together, he made us stronger.

Glancing at my phone screen, I worked to relax my clenched jaw. "It's after nine."

Esteban made a noise like he wasn't sure what to do with that. Fuck, I think I was just making conversation.

Regardless of the tension of the coming fight, there was a calm in the air. We'd discussed exactly what we needed to do. And how we needed to do it.

"Let's go." Rita stepped out of her bathroom, and I swallowed hard.

She wore one of her signature skintight dresses, hugging her from her tits down to her knees. But it was made from stretchy material so it could be pulled up to her waist if she needed to run or ride...Or be fucked.

She'd always raved about how versatile they were.

I opened the door, glanced out in the hallway to make sure there were no threats, then stepped back for her to precede me.

Leading had never been my dream. I wasn't sure it had even been Rita's, but as I walked behind her, next to Esteban, two things stuck out.

She oozed confidence in a way I never had. Rita knew exactly what she wanted and as soon as she made up her mind, she let no time rest before she went after it.

The second? Her ass was so damn fine, I could never complain about the view.

I snickered and Esteban glanced at me, but I ignored it.

From blocks away we heard music thumping and the distant roar of bikes. Of course there was a fucking party right now.

At the bottom of the stairs, several Dirty Dogs lounged in a group of chairs. There was a small speaker by the wall playing low music and a few of the gang's girls were there, draping themselves over the guys.

Joel and Ricco were among them.

When they noticed Rita, they both jumped up like they'd been waiting for her.

"Rita–" Joel marched toward us.

"It's been hours!" Ricco tried to push right into her space.

"Why do you want to lead Dirty Dogs?" Rita sidestepped Ricco, staring at Joel.

He pulled up short, then twisted around to look at the guys as if to say *is she serious?*

"Why do *you* want it? Because you think you were born into it?" He shot back. He wasn't much taller than Rita. With her heels on, they were the same height. Though he tried to pull himself up and lean into her as if he needed to feel like the bigger man.

She didn't cower. Instead, her fingers twitched and I had to bite back my smile. I knew *mi corazón*, and she was itching to grab him by the balls.

"Because I love this gang. It's my entire life, my legacy, and I care about every man inside it. Now tell me why you want to lead it." Her voice took on a deeper, husky quality. Not sexual by any means. I was highly acquainted with those sounds and this was like none of them.

It was downright cocky in the best way.

He sputtered. "You think I don't love this club? I've been with Javier since almost the beginning, little girl."

"That's great and all, but that's not a reason why you want to lead the Dirty Dogs," she answered drolly.

"Rita," Ricco said as he stepped forward, trying to diffuse what could be an explosive situation.

She turned her head toward him. "I'll deal with you in a minute."

He snapped his mouth shut as his face mottled purple in anger. I stepped forward and pressed a hand into his chest. "No."

When his eyes lifted, there was so much fury, it was shocking on Ricco. But even still, his form of anger was nothing like my father's. Or mine. "Let her do this. Your club depends on it."

"Let me ask you this?" Rita pressed up on her toes so she had the slightest advantage over Joel. Most of the men were starting to crowd us now. The ones who had the girls draped over their laps shrugged them off so they could get close too. "When *Papá* made the call to pull out of drugs and skins, did you like it?"

Joel cut his gaze to the side, likely categorizing who was here.

"What do you think?" he gritted out.

"I know what I think. I want to know what your answer is." She snapped her fingers out to the side. "Donnie, turn the speaker off."

The music stopped.

"*Papá* made the decision to take Dirty Dogs out of the skins and drugs game. What did you think, Joel? Did you support his decision?"

"No," he pushed out.

"No?" she repeated.

As she stared him down, Esteban and I cataloged the expression on every single face. Ricco's first. He was shocked as he whipped to face Joel.

"No. That's been our bread and butter since we built this club. Why would we cut ourselves off at the knees?"

"We don't need those businesses. We still smuggle. We now run the chop shop, which is making almost as much as a week's profit of drugs with one car. Because the price tags are big. So why is that cutting ourselves off?"

"Because now we're fucking pussies."

"Hmm. Right." She walked around Joel, making her rounds in front of the small group of men. "Who here feels the same way?"

Only two men raised their hands. Promising.

I caught Esteban's eye. He nodded. We both knew exactly who they were and who they hung out with.

"Ricco?" She spun to a stop and faced Ricco. "Did you support these changes?"

"Yeah," he grunted, his gaze darting between Rita and Joel. "You know I did."

"Actually, I didn't. Javier made the decision and I didn't think anything else of it. Partly, because I was the one who raised the ideas to him. Partly, because I'd been oblivious to the people I called family." She laughed. "I had no fucking idea that so many men I knew and loved were scum."

Joel and the other two guys stiffened.

"Let me tell you how this is going to go." Rita resumed her walking, eyeing down each man. The girls had started to edge back toward the wall, as if they could sense the rising tension. "The Dirty Dogs will not *ever* run those businesses again. Am I clear?"

"Like fuck we will. There's going to be a vote–" Joel pivoted so he could keep her in his line of sight.

She raised her hand and wiggled her finger back and forth in a tutting motion. "That's where you're wrong. There is not going to be a vote. I'm calling it. After all the shit and espionage leading to several of the deaths in this club, I'm taking over."

Joel bellowed, raising his hands as if he was going to choke Rita.

I jumped forward, pulling my gun, but before either Esteban or I could get a shot off, Rita kicked out her heel, stabbing Joel right above the knee.

He cursed as she yanked her shoe out of his leg. She bent down and adjusted the shoe over her heel. Glancing at Esteban, she said, "Make a note to get straps added to my special heels. We'll get them made for the girls."

I grinned and Esteban laughed. Such a random thing to say in the middle of *this*.

Joel was bent over with blood gushing through his fingers. She placed the ball of her shoe on his shoulder and pushed him back. He rolled onto his ass as he cursed.

Smiling, she faced the men.

"Like I said, there's not going to be a vote. We will not be going back to the old ways. We've progressed. Now, there are plenty of things we could vote on, but not who's going to lead, and not about picking businesses back up that hurt women and children." Her smile dropped and her expression was chilling. "Clear?"

No one answered.

"Is that clear?" Esteban boomed.

A couple men chorused agreement but most men remained quiet with their jaws open.

"Now, here's your one out. You don't like where we're at? You get a one time pass to leave. You don't have to stay in the Dirty Dogs, but you can't stay *here*. You want out? Fine. Leave. But you better leave this country. Because if I find out you've restarted businesses, I won't be the only one on your asses."

Rita pointed out the two men who had raised their hands. "Are you staying or going?"

"Staying."

"Good. Glad to have you still be Dirty Dogs." She walked

over to Ricco, touching his shoulder as if in consolation of the harsh way she'd snapped at him. "I know you're on my side, as much as you can be while thinking there's a better leader for the gang. Fine. You don't have to like me at the top to respect me. Because I will do what's right for all of us. But I need you to do something for me."

"What's that?" he asked gruffly. He seemed so confused.

"Lock up Joel and those two men. Joel, because he's been conspiring against the Dirty Dogs, and we need to make sure those two aren't involved before they're allowed to be let go."

"What the fuck?" One of the men started running as Joel started yelling expletives, but his voice was a rasp.

She reached her hand back and I placed the picture in her hand. Without missing a beat she slapped it against Joel's chest. "Here's your proof. This piece of shit tried to execute me in my own house. Maybe he would have if Matías hadn't been there."

There was a moment of silence as Joel's eyes widened. The photo fluttered to the ground and landed face up.

As soon as it settled, chaos reigned as shouts went up and several men raced forward and started punching and kicking Joel. He didn't even try to defend himself.

Shaking his head, Ricco moved forward, lifting a bloody Joel off the ground. Ricco grunted but Joel didn't seem to be putting up a fight.

The runner was caught as the other man held his hands up.

"I'm going to go easily because I have nothing to hide." He made sure to make eye contact with all three of us. "I may have liked the way we were, but that does not mean I wanted any of my brothers to die."

"Fair enough." Rita motioned for them to be taken away.

Once the three men were gone, the remaining Dirty Dogs came up and spoke to Rita, letting her know they had her support but expected a full detailed report once she knew exactly what had been going on.

"I'll deliver it. There will be no secrets like this in the Dirty Dogs anymore. But I have a job for the rest of you. If you're up for it."

They didn't even need to think about it. Every single one was in.

Rita glanced over at us with a smile painted on those gorgeous lips.

"Make the calls, boys."

28

ESTEBAN

We reached the outside of one of our clubs. The rain had just let up and the orange glow of street lights glistened off of the broken pavement and concrete of the buildings. A fair amount of graffiti also littered the walls. Ours and some punk kids.

We liked their art, so we'd left it.

Javier hadn't been torn up over ego things like that. If he liked it, it stayed.

Rita rode on the passenger side this time, and Matías drove. He parked on the side of the street just far enough back to be out of the way of the people coming and going.

It was our dirtiest club. While it was technically open to the public, it was mainly a hotspot for illegal activity. This had also been our number one playground for peddling recreational club drugs.

"Did they respond?" She glanced over her shoulder.

I glanced at my phone, the screen blank. "No." The word was torn from my throat. "But they'll be here."

Due had been my best friend from day one. We'd come up through Dirty Dogs together, fucked girls together, and shot the shit together. We had even done most of our jobs as a pair.

If there was one thing I knew about him, it was that he didn't back down. He would come if only because he couldn't force himself to stay away from a challenge.

I just really fucking hoped I was wrong.

She reached back and squeezed my hand. "Let's get inside then."

The three of us talked about the possibility of what happened if he was out to tear Dirty Dogs apart. I needed to look in his eyes and ask him if he lied to me.

If he did want to go back to our old ways, or Rita dead, and he hid that from me? Already my chest squeezed at the betrayal. It would mean everything with him was a fucking lie.

We hopped out of the SUV as other Dirty Dogs who had been at the compound pulled up around us. The Dirty Dogs who were hanging out by the club paused to watch us walk up.

As instructed, they alerted the men we were coming. A group text had gone out, minus the men who had dropped off.

I sent those out separately, letting them know they had one chance to clear their names.

Loud rock music spilled onto the street as the door was held open. Black light painted all the walls inside and everyone wearing white was now lit up in blinding neon blue.

The people parted and the ones who weren't part of the gang were knocked out of the way. There was a fight coming and everyone knew it. It stank in the air.

Women in white, slashed, crop shirts and cut-off jean shorts holding trays of liquor, stopped on the side of the room. We used to own these girls, but now, they were paid a more than generous wage.

Sex was still on the table if they wanted it, but they kept the payment.

They seemed especially interested. One of the men must have told them what was happening.

Rita headed straight toward the couches in the back, falling right into the one Javier always favored. Matías walked around the back, and I took his lead. If we all sat, it would have been too easy for someone to get the drop on her.

I wanted to trust my brothers, but until we had this all out and sorted, no one had her back but Matías and me.

The music kept playing as the Dirty Dogs arranged themselves around the room. Most wanted to be close enough to hear, but not close enough to get involved. Due and our other brothers who were with him were still liked. At least until we could get their side.

We'd also pulled everyone in. This club specifically was big enough to house us all. It was also the most off the beaten path.

Then we waited.

And waited.

"Do you think they won't show up?" Matías asked out of the side of his mouth.

"They'll come." I was sure of it. Due would just make us wait. For the sole reason that he was an asshole and this was his way of sticking it to us when he knew he had a fight on his hands.

Another thirty minutes went by, then an hour.

Dancing had long since started back up and drinks were getting served. Some of the guys weren't drinking at all, too wired for the coming fight. But some were slamming them back.

A yelp came from the front, then people pushed toward us.

Rita stood. "They're here," she said just loud enough for us to hear.

Matías and I moved around the couch to stand on either side of her. If things went sideways, I didn't want to waste precious seconds jumping over furniture to get to her.

When the crowd parted, there was Due leading the pack. That fucking answered any question I had about his loyalty. With him were seven other men. All Dirty Dogs, and all fucking traitors.

I sneered.

But Due didn't look my way. His face was twisted up in hate as he glared at Rita, nasty piece of shit betrayer.

My fingers twitched to reach for my gun, but I didn't pull it out.

Not yet.

Rita wanted to avoid shootings in the clubs. We ran neutral territories and she didn't want us to fuck with that. Once the rule was broken it was only a suggestion and way too fucking easy for thugs to ignore.

Adjusting her feet shoulder width apart, Rita crossed her arms and waited for Due and his asshat betrayers to come closer.

The music cut completely and Dirty Dogs ushered anyone out who wasn't associated with the gang.

"Due," Rita greeted coldly.

"Rita," he mocked as the men behind him dropped coolers down at their feet.

Fuck. My heart pounded into overdrive. I hadn't even

noticed them carrying them at first. They were dark gray, blending in under the black lights.

"Are you going to confess your sins or do I have to spill your secrets for you?" Rita took a step forward. Just a small one.

Due smirked like a fucking tool. "Confess my sins?" Then he laughed, glancing back at Hap, then twisting to Trig. All of them seemed to be having the time of their lives. "What about your sins?"

"We're not here to discuss my sins. Why did you kill Tiago?"

A murmur rumbled through the crowd. As some men looked on at Due with disgust.

"He was a weakness." Due let his hands hang down by his sides as if he wasn't a threat. A bald-faced lie.

"He was a Dirty Dog."

"He was an idiot who wanted to kill you. Is that a man you wished was still living?"

Rita sucked in a sharp breath. "So you're telling me that you killed a fellow Dirty Dog in my honor?" She raised a brow.

"No. That had nothing to do with it, but it was a nice side benefit for you. Do you wish I would have let him live to complete his fucked up mission?"

"I wish you would have turned him in and let the gang deal with him."

Due spat on the ground. "What gang?"

"The Dirty Dogs. The very one you've been part of for years."

"You're not even part of it."

"Really?" Rita's voice was deadly. Due was two minutes away from getting his balls ripped off. From the way he leaned back, he knew it.

Shaking his head and shoulders like he was getting rid of dirt, he glanced around the room. "Dirty Dogs! We were one of the most terrifying gangs in this country, second only to the Institution." He slid his gaze to Rita. "And what happened? The fucking Carnage Brothers happened. And their little cunt. They tore it apart from the inside out and now they're only operating a third of what they used to. Their most lucrative businesses? Gone. What do they spend their time and money on now? Training little bitches."

Rita started forward, but Matías and I reached out, grabbing her arms.

She glanced back and I shook my head. *Let him get out what he wanted to say.*

"You want to follow her?" He tossed out his arm to encompass Rita. "She's the worst of us. She got in bed with the enemy. Literally." He cut his gaze at Matías. "Then she went into business with them. Where does her loyalty lie? It's not with us! It's with her cunt and her own interests. Fuck the Dirty Dogs. Right? Rita?" He swung back around.

Who was this fucking guy? This was not my friend.

"Who the fuck are you?" I stormed forward.

"Esteban." Rita stopped me in my tracks.

One side of Due's lip curled, wrinkling his nose. "I'm the man I always was."

"No you're fucking not!" I yelled, tensing up my shoulders. "You never said one goddamned thing about not liking the way the club was going. Or any of this shit!"

"You know why?" Due raised his voice so everyone could hear him. "Because you're their lapdog, Esteban. You have your nose so far stuck up Rita's ass, that you would never see her the way we see her."

The men at his back mumbled their agreement.

"You worshiped Javier. It would have been a wasted

effort to try and change your mind. Our entire friendship wasn't a lie. I didn't always feel like this. But when the Institution fell and Javier started making changes, bad ones, you were the perfect cover because you were so fucking loyal to the wrong people. No one doubted me."

I swung.

It was the only thing I could do. This asshole had used me.

"Don't shoot!" Rita screamed.

It didn't stop me from taking Due to the ground. I grabbed his shirt and slammed his head into the floor, then again. He groaned as I pulled back and snapped my fist across his face.

Arms looped through mine and dragged me up. "You fucking prick! *Cabrón!* You nasty-ass, little, bitch!"

Black edged my vision as I stared down at him, and I was able to stomp my boot in his stomach before I was fully pulled back.

Good. He fucking deserved it.

Due pushed himself up on his knees, then he wiped his mouth with the back of his hand. The hate that stared back at me as he watched men pull me back was alien. I didn't know him. I didn't know who the fuck he was, and I never did. He'd got one over on me and I was too fucking stupid to realize it.

Huffing air out, I was deposited back next to Rita.

She cupped the sides of my neck and stared up at me. "Are you okay?" she whispered.

I glanced at Due again, as if he were a magnet pulling me back to him over and over again.

I forced myself to look down at Rita. "I'm good." The words came out low and gravely.

"Why don't I believe you?" she snipped. For a second, the

darkness cleared up, but it only lasted for a second. "I have to share what he did. The Dirty Dogs need to know. Are you good?"

I was fucking this up for her. Cracking my neck, I stepped back. "Yeah, I'm good."

Raising up, she pressed her lips to mine, then when she dropped back, her gaze shuttered. She was ready to tear his ass up, and I couldn't wait to see it.

"Sorry about that. You know how it is when you're betrayed by one of your own," Rita said to the crowd of men. Some laughed. Most were silent. Watchful.

Several had their guns out, but somehow, Rita had stopped them from firing.

Due climbed back to his feet and sick satisfaction swelled inside me at the already swelling bruise on his face. It looked much better on him than Matías' had when I busted his face up.

"I've always been for the Dirty Dogs. Working with Amorette and the brothers has only given us an alliance. More protection. I won't apologize for that." She walked closer to Due and Matías followed behind her.

Fuck, I couldn't let him be the only one. I took three long steps too.

"But Due and his friends? They schemed to take the club back to those businesses, never mind it would start a war with Carnage Industries. Did you think of that?"

Due raised his chin. "We're not strangers to war."

"Sure, when we were on the winning side." She shook her head and gazed at the crowd again. "I won't say the Bastards would win easily, or win against us completely if it came down to it, but we wouldn't escape it alive. At least half, if not more Dirty Dogs would lose their lives. For what? To peddle flesh and drugs? Those are the absolute worst businesses to be in."

Rita spun on her heels, taking in our guys and even the women who were still here.

"That's not who we are anymore. You don't like it? You can leave. I won't hold you here, but Dirty Dogs is not that club anymore and you damn sure won't run those businesses in our territory." She pointed to Hap. "You want to bring back that business?"

He nodded. "Fuck yeah."

"Fine. Then bring Gloria to the club. We'll put her to work just like the other girls."

His eye bugged. "Our wives and daughters are off-limits. Always have been."

"That's why those businesses are evil. Do you even hear yourself? Women aren't commodities. We never were."

The women along the walls whooped.

"You're forgetting one thing, Rita," Due said casually as he scratched his jaw.

"What's that?"

"We're not going to just let you have the gang. I wouldn't be a Dirty Dog if I did." He snapped his fingers at the men behind him. They reached for the coolers as he continued speaking. "I'm making my claim for it."

"You and seven men?"

"You're forgetting Joel." Due smirked. "But no, there's more of us than that."

Then the coolers were tipped. Five or six heads were dumped out. One rolled right to Rita's feet.

Alarm and fury fought for supremacy. I recognized that head.

And it opened a shit storm we didn't want to fight.

Matthews' sightless eyes stared up at Rita.

29

RITA

Sound disappeared as the sweaty head rolled right to my feet, face up.

I swallowed the bile as a few drops of dark blood hit my shoe.

Matthews. It was Matthews' head. I kicked it away so it wasn't resting on my feet and glanced at the others.

Due had declared a war. I didn't know how many men were in Matthews' club, but six couldn't be all of them.

Somehow, I managed to tear my eyes away from the floor and meet Due's gaze. An arrogant smirk stretched across his face as he wiped his chin.

"What did you do?" I whispered.

"What was that?" He cupped his ear and leaned forward.

"How many men did you leave?" My voice was stronger now. I had to be stronger. I needed to prepare for whatever hell was about to rain down on the Dirty Dogs, whether it was from the new group or from within our own fucking gang.

"That's the beauty of my leadership. I didn't leave a fucking soul breathing." He cast his gaze around the room.

I wanted to look, to see how the gang responded to him, but I couldn't. A surge of adrenaline filled me so fast, my fingers trembled.

"No." I shook my head and moved toward him. "No! That's not leadership. That's a psychopath! You wiped out a club before giving them a chance to become allies? Before giving them a chance to leave? You know what that does?"

I met the eyes of every man I could see. Some were sickened. Some avoided looking at the floor all together as they faced the wall. Then some watched Due with feverish approval.

My heart stopped.

"Places us at the top," he said lightly. Was this the Due I'd known for years? He didn't seem like it. He was cocky, exuberant, and unhinged. Not in a good way.

Oh God, this was going to kill Esteban.

"No. It makes you a target." I lowered my voice. Esteban and Matías both rested hands on my shoulders as they stepped up behind me. I stood straighter with their support. Taller knowing they had my back. "If you can't play nice in the sandbox, you'll get buried in it. Maybe not by these men." I swept out my hand, encompassing the floor. "But by everyone else still in it."

"That's funny." The light in Due's eyes grew brighter. "Because right now, the only target I see is you."

"You're outnumbered. You'll never leave here alive." He only had seven other men. I had the rest of the gang at my back.

"That's where you're wrong." His smirk widened, creasing his face in a macabre image. "We have *many* more than seven."

He whistled and all around us, Dirty Dogs attacked Dirty Dogs.

Fuck! Fuck, that was what I was afraid of.

Due had to go. If he was dead, we'd end this. The rest would stop fighting. I believed that in the depths of my soul.

I pulled the small handgun tucked safely in the back pocket of my dress, and jumped forward.

Esteban beat me there as he caught Due by his throat and slammed him into the ground. I aimed. But I couldn't get a good angle with Esteban trying to punch through his stomach.

Two men caught my arms and I screamed, kicking back. They avoided my hits as they dragged me away.

Hap and Trig had my arms. "You fucking traitors! Let me go!"

Esteban glanced over his shoulder. Then he abandoned Due and raced toward me.

I wildly searched for Matías.

There he was. Surrounded by three old Dirty Dogs. They had been some of *Papá's* best friends. When I got my hands on them, they would regret the day they ever decided to turn against us.

Esteban reached us and smashed his fist into Hap's face. He stumbled back, taking me with him. Trig tugged on my arm, and I winced at the way they were pulling my body in separate ways.

"Let her go," Esteban growled as the cool edge of a blade slid against my neck. Trig wrapped his arm around my chest as he notched the knife tighter against the underside of my chin. I tried to swallow, but the knife bit deeper.

Across the room, Matías bellowed.

I couldn't see him. Was he hurt? Or worse?

Clamping my eyes closed, I thought of how he held me. My arms were pinned to my sides, but if I could just angle my hand backward...

"Nuhuh, bitch." Hap snatched the gun out of my hand and tossed it to Due who was now behind Esteban.

"Est–" I tried to warn him, but the knife was too tight. I was going to slice my throat open if I talked. Widening my eyes, I glanced behind him.

He understood, spinning to face Due, raising his own weapon and aiming it at Due's face. Three men raised theirs and pointed them at Esteban.

"You're going to regret this!" Matías screamed as he came closer. I could just see him out of the corner of my eye, as guy after guy tried to step in his path. He threw punches, tossing them aside, but there were two men for every man he dispatched.

"Maybe," Due agreed. "But not before your brothers are dead."

Matías froze and RJ, one of my least favorite Dirty Dogs, got a hit in across his cheek.

"That's right, Matías. There's an attack on your brothers' place as we speak." Due slanted his gaze my way. "Did I say I cleared out the new club? I meant I cleared out the *problems* and left a handful alive who wanted to separate from Matthews' insufferable rules. They agreed to assist if I promised them a slice of the pie. With both you and the brothers out of the way, there's no one else for them to worry about."

Amorette. The *baby.*

Matías' phone blared like an alarm. He reached for his pocket, and when he pulled his phone out, his face drained of blood. His gaze collided with mine and I wanted to fucking cry.

It was true. They were under attack.

And I had a fucking knife to my throat.

Esteban tried to move closer but one of the guys fired a shot at his feet and he stopped.

"None of that. We're friends. I don't want to hurt you. I'd rather you join my side." Due turned to Esteban. For the first time since Due walked in, he looked like the man I knew. A serious expression carved into his face as he watched Esteban.

I glanced back at Matías. Matías' body vibrated and his face twisted up into something ugly.

My heart sank, knowing what he had to do. It was fine. We'd get out of this. He had to save his brothers.

As tears filled my eyes, I nodded as much as I could. Trig had loosened his grip a fraction of an inch. Just enough for me to let Matías off the hook.

"It's okay," I mouthed.

He shook his head. He wanted to go to them. It was written all over him.

That was how it always was with Matías. His brothers came first. Now his niece would come first. There was never a time that I didn't understand that.

Nothing had changed. The only thing I wanted was for him to *come back* to me. To *keep* coming back to me.

"Eat shit," Esteban snapped, raising his gun to aim directly at Due's head.

Sighing as if this was exactly what he expected, Due nodded. "I figured as much. But you won't shoot me, because as soon as you do, Rita is dead." He glanced back at Matías. "You're still here? I thought you would be gone already, just like you always do when your brothers need you."

Matías shivered and shrugged his shoulders like he was shaking off whatever indecision hung over him.

Around us, Dirty Dogs continued to fight against each

other. I had no idea who was on whose side. Only that we were ripping each other apart from the inside out.

"I know where my place is."

My gaze snapped back to Matías. His face was calm and he implored me with his eyes. To what? To believe him? To understand? I did!

I understood too fucking well.

"And it's here with the love of my life." Too quick to process, he fired his gun. The bullet whizzed by my ear, hitting Trig in the face. The knife slipped across my throat as I leaned back, trying to minimize the impact.

Fuck, it stung, but it was barely a scratch. I wiped my throat and came away with only a few drops of blood. *Just a scratch,* I chanted over and over to myself.

Matías gave us the distraction we needed.

As I fell on my ass, Esteban dropped and kicked Due's feet out from under him. The three men holding their weapons on Esteban were now engaged in their own fights with other Dirty Dogs, their guns forgotten.

Matías lifted me from the floor with one arm, holding me to him.

"You should go." My voice shook as I curled my fingers against his chest.

"Fuck that," he spewed, firing his gun, taking out every man he deemed a threat. His aim was impeccable and the Dirty Dogs started giving us a wide berth.

"Waste of space. Waste of a goddamn Dirty Dog," Esteban screamed as he grunted.

I peered over my shoulder to see Esteban was beating the literal shit out of Due. Slamming his fist into his nose until blood sprayed. Dropping elbows on his neck, and raining hell over his chest. Due gasped and jerked with each hit until his motions slowed.

Esteban kept attacking and screaming at him. He did this long after Matías stopped shooting. The fights around us stopped and a crowd formed around us.

Matías tipped my chin up, checking my neck, swearing as he moved his thumb gently just under where the knife nicked me.

"Esteban," I called. I tried to step out of Matías' arms, but he didn't let me go and Esteban didn't stop. Matías dropped his hand from my neck and hugged me to him as he murmured unintelligible words against my hair.

"Esteban!" I yelled.

My voice must have pierced his fury because he dropped his hands, his shoulders drooping forward as he panted.

"You were my best friend, you fucking cunt." He delivered one more punch to Due's face. He didn't move or twitch. He wasn't even breathing. At some point, Esteban beat the life out of him.

"We don't have time for this." I pushed at Matías' chest.

My heart fluttered, knowing Matías chose me. He wasn't leaving my side. It soothed the last jagged crack in my heart, but I couldn't fully appreciate it. Not knowing that my friend was under attack.

Around us, the fight was over. Some of the girls had their hair torn down and their make-up smeared. One girl held two pieces of a broken tray.

"Girls!" I pointed at them and motioned for them to come forward quickly. "Work with Jonny and Rio. We need to sort through the men who are against us." Rio and Jonny stepped forward, baring their teeth. The fight was over, but they were ready for more. With how some men edged toward the doors, they might get it.

"Lock the doors! No one in or out until Jonny and Rio allow it."

The girls huddled together, whispering as they looked to Jonny and Rio. They heard things. And with the way many of these men liked to pillowtalk, they had a good chance of making sure nothing slipped through the cracks.

"You got it." Rio's gravelly voice skated across my skin as he and Jonny started working through the crowd. A couple of the girls walked after them.

"Rio! Jonny!" I had one last order before we left.

They turned. Swallowing hard, I held their stare. "If they aren't on our side, they don't walk out of this building."

The words burned on my tongue. It felt like I was tearing down *Papá's* legacy, but these men, they'd had enough chances. They were a poison that would just keep chipping away at the club if we didn't eradicate it now.

They jerked their heads and I rushed to Esteban.

"Esteban." I cupped his cheeks, wiping away the tears that tracked down his face. "Oh, baby. I'm so sorry. I'm so fucking sorry, but we have to go. Amorette and the brothers are under attack. We have to go help them."

His gaze skated past me but he relaxed when he glanced over my shoulder. He thought Matías would have left too.

"Okay," he rasped as he raised his hand to check my throat. When he was satisfied, he pushed up from the floor. "We need to load back up in the office. Then we can go."

We rushed to the office, reloading clips, grabbing extra weapons. I selected a holster and added a few more guns. I usually only had what I could hide in my dress, but fuck that.

My best friend was in trouble.

Esteban drove this time, flying down the road and racing around cars. We saw the fight before we got there. Bikes lined the street and gunfire popped off.

Esteban swerved over to the side of the road, slamming

on the breaks before we could see their place. "We'll go on foot from here." He threw his door open.

We exited the car and I left my heels. Clanking across the pavement would signal our sneak attack from a mile away. I just hoped I didn't tear up my feet too badly.

Next to Matías, I reached out and squeezed his hand. He glanced from me to Esteban and nodded to himself.

At first, I thought he was going to speak, but as we moved closer to Amorette and the brothers, it hit me.

Us, being here for Matías, soothed something for him too.

As much as I wanted him to stay, he never could before. I didn't think he knew how. No one had ever stayed for *him*.

30

MATÍAS

Roman, that asshole.

I'd had drinks with him before I started to distance myself from the Dirty Dogs. He was crouched behind a bush, trying to shoot at the windows, probably just hoping to catch someone.

Without an ounce of regret, I shot him, execution style.

We moved around the perimeter, picking off a small group.

They didn't look like they made it inside. Anton was running along the roof, and some of my brothers' men were right there with us, clearing them out. Until the threat was almost gone.

As far as we could tell, there was one lone man standing.

Tad. He was a fuckup. A big one. Javier always complained about how much money Tad lost the Dirty Dogs. But Javier was fond of Tad's mother, so he never kicked him out.

The Dirty Dogs had always been strange like that. They cared about people. Valued family. It was a weird attraction that I'd wanted to figure out. At the time, it had been like nothing I'd ever experienced before.

I raised my gun, but Rita placed her hand on my arm. I glanced at her, and she shook her head.

"We need him." Then she turned and shot the fucker in the back of the knee. He screamed, falling to his ass, but not letting go of his weapon.

"Shit," I muttered, adjusting myself. And just because I still had rage sitting in my stomach, I shot his hand, and he finally dropped his gun.

"Call them. Let them know we're here." Rita walked up to Tad, aiming her gun at his face. "Well, Tad. Looks like we have a bit of an issue, don't we?"

"Rita," he gasped, flopping between trying to cup his hand and tuck his knee to his chest. Failing on both accounts as he wailed.

Esteban tucked his gun in his waistband and yanked Tad off the ground. "You're the last one standing. Guess what that means?"

"That he gets to be our plaything." Parker opened the door before I even had a chance to pull out my phone. His eyes glittered as he crossed his arms and leaned against the frame.

His signature smirk was nowhere in sight. My baby brother was pissed.

"He's lucky Cossette is sleeping, or he'd be in a world of pain."

Grey appeared behind him, moving him out of the way with the back of his hand. "What are you talking about? He's in for a world of pain anyway. Just not upstairs. We have a room specifically designed for that."

Then Amorette stormed out, wearing one of their T-shirts. She could have been naked underneath since it covered her like a dress. Appearing like a kid wearing her dad's shirt also took away from her anger.

"Sorry, this one is mine." Amorette ducked under their arms as they tried to catch her.

"Amorette," Rita breathed as she caught Amorette up in a tight hug.

"Rita!" Amorette exclaimed, squeezing her arms tight around Rita's neck. Without her heels, Rita didn't tower over Amorette how she usually did. "What's wrong? Why are you shaking?"

"It's a long story," Rita said with a shaky laugh. "I'd love to tell you all about it, but I have to get names out of Tad."

"Tad." Amorette glared at Tad in Esteban's grip. He still moaned as his bad leg was raised off the ground and his bloodied hand was clutched against his chest. "I'll help you. Lafe is with Cossette and Andre is in there now too. Nothing will wake her up."

"Rita, don't do this."

"Shut up," she hissed, pulling halfway out of Amorette's embrace. "Your time for sympathy ended the second you teamed up with Due."

"Come on, Esteban." Parker waved a hand. "Let's get him into our special room."

Esteban grunted and carted Tad like he didn't weigh anything. That was one strong little fucker. Not that he was small, but damn, he was almost a decade younger than me. It still took some getting used to.

Amorette and Rita walked inside, arm in arm, their heads bent close together as they whispered furiously to one another.

"Well?" Grey asked as I followed after them.

"Well what?"

"Let's have a drink and you can fill me in." Grey tapped on his phone. "I let the guys know the threat was gone, but they're going to do one last sweep.

"Why weren't you all outside taking care of the attack?" I scratched the back of my head.

It was always a mind fuck leaving an intense scene and dropping into a room so clean and crisp, like I stepped into a parallel universe. My adrenaline was automatically leveling as if my system realized that clean dishes and counters meant the threat was over.

And it was.

As long as Tad gave the girls everything he had. And if he was apprised of who was involved.

"Our house is pretty much attack proof. The windows are bulletproof and the doors are reinforced. Cossette's nursery is a glorified safe room." Grey grabbed a bottle off the shelf and got down a handful of glasses.

"Poor girl doesn't get to have any windows." Lafe walked in carrying a baby monitor in his hand.

I'd spent a decent amount of time with them since I'd come back and it was still just as shocking to see my hard as shit, deranged brothers so happy in domestic bliss. Even if there was a twist, like making their nursery into a safe room.

"She doesn't need windows." Andre came around the corner sighing, like he'd had this conversation with them thousands of times. "Windows when she's sleeping means someone can break in. Windows when she's awake means that she can break out. Neither option works for me."

"She's less than a year old," I reminded Andre. "She's not breaking anywhere."

"That's what you think." Parker joined us and Esteban was right behind him.

Grey grabbed two more glasses and started to fill them as Parker and Esteban found a spot on the island, Esteban moving next to me. The glasses were slid out with two fingers of bourbon.

The label caught my eye. "Does that say what I think it says?"

Grinning, Grey twisted the bottle around. "Yeah. Bastard Brothers. It's a gold label liquor. Just a fun side business because Amorette is adamant that we have enough above board businesses to cover our more *illegal* activities."

Andre glanced at me, before shifting his gaze to Esteban. "Want to tell us why we had a Dirty Dogs attack? And why Esteban isn't in the basement with the other guy?"

Esteban tensed, his fingers turning white on his glass.

"Relax." I nudged him with my elbow. "Andre is joking."

Steel slid through Andre's gaze. "I'm not joking."

I blew out a breath. "Fine, then take my word for it. Esteban doesn't have anything to do with it." I downed the liquor, enjoying the sweet burn. Immediately, warmth spread out through my stomach and I started telling them the story.

Leaving out the more intimate parts, of course.

Esteban remained quiet, happy to let me fill my brothers in. As I got to the part about tonight, and the heads rolling across the floor, Parker whistled as Lafe winced.

"That's ruthless." Parker sounded impressed.

"That's reckless," I returned, the words whipping through the kitchen. Grey filled my glass up again and this time I sipped it.

"Did you do the research I asked on the group?" I'd called and given Andre everything I had on them. Hopefully they wouldn't have anyone left to take revenge in their name.

While Rita was right, we should have given them a chance, I didn't want to take the chance that anything like this could happen again. If even one of those *pendejos* were still alive, they had to go.

"They were a unit of soldiers who served in the Iraq war. A couple of them got dishonorably discharged. Some got out when their next term was up. And two retired in the last few months. All single. No kids. They seemed to enjoy the war side of life a little too much. It seemed like they all had trouble assimilating back into civilian life," Andre rattled off like he memorized a report.

"That was twenty years ago. They've just been hanging out since then?" I took the last sip. When Grey went to fill up the glass again, I waved my hand and pushed it back. That was enough for me. We may still need to deal with the club tonight.

Esteban hadn't even touched his, instead eyeing all five of us with too much interest.

"And several of the men spent time in and out of jail or prison for various charges. Nothing related to any kind of trafficking. Surprising, since those are the businesses they wanted to start up."

"It's easy money." Parker rolled his eyes. "That's why."

Lafe curled his lip, his eyes glued to the monitor. He was such a good daddy. All of them were to the point that it was sickening.

"Hmm." I checked on Esteban again. "You okay?"

"Of course, he's okay. Why are you checking on him like he's your kid?" Parker always ran his mouth.

"It's not like we're scary." Grey gave him a closed lip smile.

"Right," Esteban laughed, but it was good-natured and not filled with fear.

"He's fine." Parker waved his hand. "I remember how he handled himself and Rita."

I ground my teeth. That must have been after I was gone. For the thousandth time, I kicked myself for leaving. At the time, it had seemed like the right idea. Now? I wished I'd never left.

Checking the time, Grey tapped Andre on the shoulder. "Pull up the footage of the girls. They've been down there too long."

Andre did, setting his phone on the counter.

The sound wasn't on, but the camera was high definition. Amorette and Rita both circled Tad. His head hung low like he was exhausted. Knife marks lined his arms and the ends of his fingers were bloody stubs.

He must have said something because Rita reached over and wrote something down on a notepad.

Amorette must not have liked what he said because she reached over and stabbed him in the thigh. His head shot back and cords of muscle stood out in his neck.

"I love when she goes psycho like that." Grey had a manic grin on his face.

Esteban and I shared a look and laughed. Rita had always been a little bloodthirsty. What were the chances that she'd rubbed off on Amorette?

"What's this now?" Parker pointed between Esteban and me, his eyes narrowed.

"What's what?" I played dumb just to fuck with him.

"The last we spoke, you wanted to fuck his shit up for touching Rita and he hated you just as much. Because you also touched Rita," he added on as if we needed the explanation.

"Always a shit-stirrer," Lafe mumbled, clearly listening in on the conversation even while watching over his baby girl.

"I don't fucking believe it," Andre said. He glanced between us with his mouth open. "You followed in our foot-steps." A grin broke out over his face.

Esteban popped a dimple with his closed lip smile. He thought this was funny as fuck.

I just sighed. "Yeah, maybe I did."

31

RITA

I held the folded piece of paper tight in my hands as we drove back to the compound.

I'd received calls from Jonny, Rio, and Ricco on the status of where everything stood.

Joel was still locked up. One of the two men had been cleared, the other was sharing the shed with Joel.

Rio and Jonny's call had been the hardest. They'd had to put down twenty-three men after we left the club. They hadn't shared names, and I could only hope they were the names that we'd extracted from Tad.

My heart physically hurt as if someone had decided to take a knife to it over and over again, just for giggles. There wasn't a spot on it that didn't feel touched in some way by all this shit. So much death. So much heartache. And for what? Because we were trying to be *less* villainous people?

I wasn't like Amorette. I didn't mind getting my hands dirty. On the right occasion, I enjoyed a petty side dish simply because I liked the rush it gave me afterward.

But there was nothing wrong with protecting innocent

women and children, damn it. On that, I agreed with Amorette wholeheartedly.

The sun was peeking over the top of the compound as we pulled up. Soft peach and gold lighting up the sky. Rows of bikes were also parked exactly like before. Except now, there weren't near as many.

Because of death. Because of betrayal.

Matías parked us right in the center. As if they realized we were coming, the guys had left a path right up the middle.

"You ready to get this over with?" Matías glanced at me.

Esteban cupped both of my shoulders from behind, giving me a gentle squeeze.

"You got this, baby."

"You're right. We do." I touched Esteban's hand, gave Matías a small smile, then got out of the SUV. "We're going to have to do something about my car, Esteban," I said under my breath as we waited for Andre to join us.

He and a few of his men had accompanied him.

"Why?" He glanced at me with a divet between his brows.

"Because it's only a two seater. There are three of us."

He shook his head and chuckled. "I don't know what's gotten into you lately, but you're saying the most random things."

I shrugged. We could always take one of our SUVs, but I was desperately thinking of anything other than facing the others.

"You ready?" Andre adjusted the cuffs of his suit as he walked up. He'd followed behind us in his own protected SUV. Leave it to him to dress up to come to a biker compound.

No, but also more ready than I'd ever been in my life. "Let's go."

Matías took one side and Esteban took the other as we led the way into the compound.

There was no music to disrupt the somber mood. Three-quarters of the Dirty Dogs congregated in the open space. Some had pulled out chairs. Some were standing defensively with their arms crossed, and some were sitting on the floor, leaning against the wall.

Everyone seemed shattered.

More even than when *Papá* had died.

"Rita." Ricco came up, scrubbing his face. He eyed Andre with a heavy dose of suspicion, but he didn't comment on his attendance. "What are we doing with Joel and Dag?"

"That's what Andre is here for. He's turning Joel and Dag over to his contacts."

Ricco blinked and some of the men closest to us leaned in to hear what I was saying. No need. I'd project the message for them.

"Dirty Dogs!" I had everyone's attention as they stood and moved closer. Esteban and Matías pushed closer to my back. "Let's never repeat last night again."

Some barked out a laugh as others smiled. Most understood it for what it was. Dark humor because that was the only way to deal with this shit hand.

"I won't force you to listen to my speech twice. But I'll ask. Is there anyone here who feels the Dirty Dogs is not your home anymore?" No one raised their hand. "Is there anyone who won't follow my lead?" Still silence. I took a deep breath. This should have been eradicated last night, but I had to ask. "Is there anyone here who will not follow *my* rules?"

"What are your rules, Rita?" Someone in the back called out. I didn't recognize the voice and I couldn't see the person. It didn't matter. I'd answer it. They deserved to know.

"My rules are that if you have a problem, take it up with me. Don't cause dissent. Don't kill your brothers, and don't start wars on behalf of the gang and for the gang without our entire buy-in. It's that simple."

"Good enough for me," he called back.

"Why is he here?" Jonny nodded at Andre. There wasn't an accusation there, but it was close. "I'll follow you without a doubt, but I won't be part of Carnage Industries. We'd be footboys at best."

"We now have an alliance with Carnage Industries. It was unofficial before, and last night we made it official." Some alarming expressions moved over their faces. "The only thing this means is that if we're under attack, they'll provide support, and vice versa. We already do that."

Most of the guys relaxed. Except for Jonny. "Why is he here now?"

"He's taking Joel and Dag to his contacts."

"Contacts?"

"US government officials. It will make working in the US easier for us after he hands over our traitors."

Ricco nodded as if he was impressed. It wasn't common knowledge Andre had these kinds of connections. Or why. Not that it was hidden either.

"Bring them out," I addressed Ricco.

He called to a couple of the younger members and they ran off toward the shed.

In a few minutes, they came back, dragging Joel and Dag between them. Both were unconscious and battered to hell. Black and purple bruises mottled their skin.

In a way, I was glad to be done with it. No more confrontations, no more arguments.

"Load them up," Andre ordered his men. In an efficient manner, they were carted out.

It was all so anti-climatic, I busted up laughing.

Andre cut his gaze at me. "You okay?"

"Great." I grinned. This whole nightmare was over. I knew it deep in my bones that the threat was gone.

"All right." He glanced at Matías. "Call me later. I need to get in touch with my old contact."

"Cash?" Matías asked.

Andre smiled. "Not that crazy asshole."

Lingered for a minute, Andre eyed the Dirty Dogs. He looked as if he might say something, then shook it off and waltzed out like this was just another Tuesday at Carnage Industries. I snorted.

Once the doors shut behind him, I faced the men again. Holding up the piece of paper, I sucked in a deep breath.

"I have the list of every name who was implicated in Joel's fucked up scheme." I surveyed the room, searching for any names on the list. There were none, and I released a shaky breath. Passing it over to Ricco, he unfolded it.

"We have a lot of repairs to do. Our gang has been hit from the inside and I have no desire for it to ever happen again. From now on, we'll have weekly meetings. You have grievances, you air them there. If this ever happens again, what happened to these men will be a child's play. Is that clear?"

One of the younger men stepped forward. He was barely twenty-one and full of hot air. He eyed Matías with slight hostility. "How do we know that he's not going to try and lead us for his brothers?"

So much suspicion where there hadn't been any before. I blamed Due and Joel for that.

I rolled my eyes. Did these guys think I was such a doormat that I'd allow it?

Matías raised one brow. "I have no interest in leading. I've made that clear by walking away from the Institution—now Carnage Industries. I am at Rita's disposal only." He caught my hand, raising it to his lips. His gaze burned into me as he pressed a soft kiss on my knuckles, then stepped behind me, clasping his hands behind his back.

Heat curled in my stomach and I almost raised my hand to fan myself.

Clearing my throat, I turned back. "His loyalty is not to be questioned. He's proven it many times over. In fact..." Normally, we gave new members thirty days before voting them in. But I didn't want this looming over any of our heads. "All in favor of Matías being a Dirty Dog?"

Everyone's hand raised and several whooped.

"All against?" Crickets.

I tipped my head toward Matías with a smile on my lips. "Looks like you're officially a Dirty Dog."

He grinned, scooping me up into his arms and swinging me around.

He set me down, and smoothed the hair back from my face. "It's going to be okay."

"I know." I nodded.

Esteban stepped up behind me, cupping my hips. "This is just the beginning."

Oh yeah, it definitely was. I knew the first major change I was going to make too.

EPILOGUE

ESTEBAN

"**Y**ou're sure those bastards are fine with this?" I asked, walking alongside Rita as we headed into the school.

She'd tried to get me in a school uniform. Not the student's version, but dress pants, dress shirt, and a sweater vest with the school emblem on the breast.

Abso-fucking-lutely not.

I crossed my arms and stood my ground while Matías laughed in the background. He'd traded his jeans and Tee for a suit today, but he was used to this shit. He'd practically grown up in one.

I hated how the shirts choked me and I was teaching a shop class anyway. Every single piece of clothing would be stained with grease at the end of the day.

She'd relented with a dark glint in her eyes.

I squinted at her. The little witch didn't actually care what I wore, she just wanted to fuck with me.

"Are you ever going to stop calling them that?" she sighed.

Nope. "Why? Do you think they're offended?"

Cutting a quick look at me before nodding to the guard opening the gate, she said, "No. But it's rude to call our business partners bastards."

"They are bastards. They call each other bastards all the time. It's a term of endearment at this point."

Rita waved at a group of girls on the playground. They'd installed it last month, but it was more of a deadly obstacle course than an actual playground. Her and Amorette were adamant that everything available to the girls served as some kind of lesson.

"From each other. Not you."

I laughed. Last night, I'd played pool with all of them, Matías included, at one of our clubs. Next week we were going to catch Grey's fight. "I'm practically one of the guys at this point."

Pink suffused her cheeks. Not embarrassment or desire, but the way her face softened when she was happy. "I know."

Matías had changed over the last few months since he was voted in and we cleaned up all that shit with Joel. It was everything Rita wanted for him.

I hated to admit it, but he wasn't as bad as I thought he was. He was just a little more sensitive than he let on. A little more self-sacrificing than was healthy. But since we started this little trio, he seemed to lose some of that.

We'd keep plucking away at him until he was just as selfish with his own wants as he was with ours. In fact, I had a little surprise for him later.

"Ms. Aguilar!" Molly, the scrapper I'd met the first time here, grinned as she ran up. She didn't hug Rita like she usually did, but she was bouncing with so much energy, she was practically vibrating. "I'm ready! I did all the homework Mr. Esteban gave us last time." Her gaze slid to me as her face stained red.

Now, that was from a crush.

I grinned and winked at her.

She tried to bite her lip to stop her smile from spreading wider but she couldn't contain it.

Rita chuckled. She thought it was cute, even if she got annoyed that I charmed them so much. I was a fun guy. I couldn't smile and toss winks out to everyone but little girls. That would make me an asshole.

"You'll pass the quiz?" Rita gave her a stern, yet affectionate look.

Twice a month, Matías and I had been teaching workshops. Today, I was teaching the girls how to hotwire a car, and they had to pass a quiz at the door before they could enter.

Matías was teaching the oldest girls how to tell the good wines from the poor and how to order like old money. Something that was natural to his fancy-ass upbringing, but boring as hell to the girls.

I was the favorite and I couldn't pass up a chance at rubbing it in his face.

The bastards had even started running workshops.

Parker taught art history, bringing in stolen art from his heists for giggles. Grey taught offensive fighting. Lafe, as much as he hated the drug business, taught them how to tell legit drugs from knockoffs. He didn't approve, but at the same time, he knew it was invaluable information. Not so much to prevent the girls from being drugged, but to help them drug others. His class paired nicely with the poisons class.

Then Andre ran a class on building a spy network.

The girls loved that.

In fact, the classes were such a hit, we had a special set of workshops next month. A week-long group of intensive zooms from some contacts of the bastards.

A hacker, an ex-FBI agent–I was dying to know how he was hooked up with this group, a chef, and for lack of a better term, a serial killer. The kicker was, Rita said the serial killer was a woman.

I might sit in on that course and see what she had to teach.

And the one from the chef. Rita said he was also covering crime scene cleanup.

The day flew by, and the girls ate up the class like a treat. Molly was the best and most naturally inclined, but I never doubted she would be. She was Rita's favorite for a reason.

Rita texted me, letting me know she'd gone home early and her and Matías would see me there.

I took my bike, and headed straight to Matías' Goliath of a house. Our house now according to him.

We'd also started training some of our men for security work so they could provide as efficient of a detail as the bastards' guys.

I acknowledged the two men who were visible from the front door, and punched my code in. Toeing off my shoes, I called, "Honey, I'm home!"

"In here!" Rita called.

Making my way to Matías' office, I pulled off my T-shirt. If I played my cards right, flexed my abs just right, then I could talk Rita into an early dessert. For me.

I came around the corner and froze.

Matías was on his knees, a hand on Rita's ankle as he licked up her calf.

Rita had her special shoes on, but only the toes were

placed on Matías' shoulder. I swallowed as I let my gaze move up the rest of her body. A skintight skirt with a high slit up the thigh of the leg she rested on Matías. A tight button down blouse, with several buttons undone to show her cleavage.

Her wild curls had been slightly tamed with half pulled back into a bun. A few tendrils framed her face and black, sharp-rimmed glasses rested on the end of her nose.

"You're late." She pursed her blood-red lips.

Holy fuck, was she hot, dressed like the wettest dream of every man.

"We had to get started without you." She slapped the ruler I hadn't even noticed in her hand across her palm.

"Sorry," I muttered because I couldn't muster anything louder than that. The room intensified in heat as I stepped inside and shut the door behind me.

"On your knees." She pointed her ruler to the spot next to Matías.

"Yes, Ms. Aguilar." I found my grin even though my face was burning. Shit, I was just the right height too. On my knees, I could bury my nose right in her pussy.

In just my jeans, I got down on my knees next to Matías. Her good boys waiting to do whatever she asked of us.

He didn't glance at me, keeping his gaze on Rita. Of all of us, he loved role play the best. It was such a kink for him. I didn't even think he realized he liked it before I introduced it with a spare police outfit from one of our guys Rita had worked with Andre to get onto the force.

He was my size and I wanted to have some fun. When he found out, he'd scoffed and told me to keep it.

She shimmied her skirt up and slid onto the desk right in front of us. "Take your cocks out. I want to see them."

Matías didn't waste any time as he freed himself, squeezing the base.

I took a slower approach, holding eye contact as I pulled down my zipper, reached inside my briefs, and pulled my cock out. She spread her legs, showing a dripping pussy.

Matías caught his breath as I groaned. No panties today. I loved these days.

With small circles, she started to pleasure herself, making sure to dip her fingers in her pussy before finding her clit again.

Precum leaked from the tip of my cock.

"No stroking," she barked, and I stopped.

"Yes, Ms. Aguilar," I murmured, still grinning, although it felt darker now.

"Matías, for being such a good boy, you get rewarded." She crooked her finger at him and he walked on his knees until his face was a breath away. "Show me how good of a boy you are."

He wasted no fucking time devouring her. Rita tossed her head back and threaded her fingers through his hair, moaning. She arched her back and the buttons threatened to pop at her tits.

"Fuck," I cursed, giving myself a tiny tug. Like she had some kind of radar, her head snapped down and she glared at me.

"Stop, Matías." He sat back, resting his hands on his thighs, and she closed her legs. "Esteban wants to be punished."

Rita stood from the desk and walked closer to me. Then her hand fisted my hair and she yanked my head back. "You want that, don't you?"

"No, Ms. Aguilar. I just want to come." The grin faded from my lips as I stared up at her. She was so fucking beautiful. More now that she was mine than before when I watched her from afar.

It wasn't a trick of the mind either. She had been distant, sad, or downright angry.

Now that Matías and I broke our backs to make her happy, there was a glow about her that drew the eye.

She pushed my shoulders until I fell back on the floor with an oomph. My head narrowly missed the table behind me. Dropping the ruler still in her hand, Rita climbed over me, grabbed my cock, lined me up, and sank down *hard*.

"Matías, secure his hands and feet."

He moved to obey.

I twisted to see him by my head, pulling cuffs from the legs. Rita pinched my jaw and yanked my face back to hers, gripping me so tightly as she rose up slowly, then slammed back down. I groaned, thrusting my hips up, but she rose completely off of me until my wet cock slapped my stomach.

"Hm..None of that. This is a punishment." Then a devilish smirk took over her lips. It was so tauntingly sexy, I tried to rise up and kiss it off her face. "Matías. Line him up for me?"

Then a warm hand gripped me and I sucked in a sharp breath. Matías stroked once, then twice before sliding my head along Rita's slit. Rocking my hips, I bit my lip. This was fucking hot as hell.

Then Rita notched herself on the head and slammed back down.

My back bowed. Matías fucking shocked me, and he chuckled behind Rita like he knew exactly what I was thinking.

My wrists and ankles were secured and Rita was randomly fucking my brains out. Not enough to make me come but she was damn close. Every time I started to throb she'd get off completely and Matías would bend her forward to eat her while they waited for my breathing to even out.

Her little gasps against my skin and nails digging into my shoulder while I couldn't do anything about it was pure torture.

Sweat poured from my head. It felt like it was a hundred degrees in here.

"Have you learned your lesson?" She glared down her nose at me as perspiration shone on her face as well. Some of her hair was even starting to stick to her face.

"No, hell no. Teach me some more," I gasped as she cupped my balls.

"Brave," Matías muttered as he got something from his desk drawer. A cap flipped open and the sound of liquid squeezing out followed.

Lube.

Excitement shot straight to my balls.

Rita lowered herself back down as she pulled her blouse out of her skirt and unbuttoned it. Then she tossed it to the side.

Matías knelt behind her, cupping her tits before pulling them out of their cups. Then he massaged one and used his other hand to push her forward until her nipples brushed my chest.

She clenched around me and I shivered. I was so fucking close to coming. I'd last one stroke from Matías, damn it.

Pressing her lips to mine, she breathed me in as Matías sorted himself out. I knew the exact moment he started to push inside her. I could feel it through the thin barrier of skin separating us. The backs of his fingers dug into me from where he gripped Rita's hips.

He took her slow, working himself into her with a patience that was ripping me apart. Both Rita and I were gasping and grunting, making small cries. She was so full of us, and I was right *there*.

He bottomed out and she relaxed on top of me. Out of nowhere, he shifted his knees between my thighs, then pinned them down with his shins as close to my groin as he could get with Rita on top of me.

But as Matías pulled himself out almost all the way, I pulsed as I felt the first spurt of cum.

"No, no, not yet," I griped.

"He's coming," Rita cried out as her nails dug into my shoulders and she pushed her hips down as hard as she could.

"Fuck, you assholes!" I bellowed, as I tried to move my hips and couldn't. I couldn't buck, or thrust, or even lift my ass off the ground.

Matías laughed as he started fucking Rita's ass with so much force, she was a sobbing mess of pleasure. I emptied everything I had inside of Rita as she orgasmed, and that asshole didn't stop.

He kept going. Kept fucking her with a single-minded devotion, sawing against me, moving Rita up and down my still hard cock.

"Fuck," I groaned as one more ribbon of cum escaped my raw as hell cock while I shivered.

Rita went limp from pleasure on top of me as Matías lost his rhythm, thrusting harder before he slammed into her one last time on a fucking sigh.

A fucking sigh.

While I had lost my mind in the most erotic torture ever.

RITA

I called a meeting for my leadership. We'd restructured things around here. Not that *Papá's* way didn't work, but things needed to change.

Moving to how Carnage Industries operated, we now had divisions. Leadership for each business that made sure profits rolled in. Then we had the gang. It operated separately. We still partied, we still went on rides, caused trouble. But we made sure there was plenty of separation between our families and the businesses.

That was one difference between us and Amorette's businesses.

They had employees, and we had a family.

Ricco and Manny were my official seconds in command. Esteban and Matías were my unofficial seconds, but we were more of a unit, and the Dirty Dogs accepted that.

Jonny and Rio were third, and then there was everyone else.

Their purposes were to squash fights, pick up slack if there was any, and organize our response to threats *if there were any*. However, since we put ourselves back together again, there had been no whispers of any kind of trouble.

It seemed like the Dirty Dogs and Carnage Industries had created such an alliance that everyone was too afraid to test it.

Good. I liked life on the low key side.

There hadn't been any signs of the new club either. It seemed like Due had told the truth. Except for the few who died on the brother's property, he actually wiped the rest of the club. Although they had been new, so I wasn't sure that was the feat he would have wanted it to be.

For those Dirty Dogs who had a little too much pent up

aggression, Grey opened the roster and they started fighting every third Saturday at his hotel. Sometimes against each other, sometimes against outside fighters.

"Morning, boys." My heels clacked against the concrete as I made my way to the table. Today, we'd be discussing a new order, but it wouldn't be a vote. Not really. Yanking the Dirty Dogs into the future was what I did best.

If they wanted to fight about it? They could challenge Esteban and Matías in the ring. Which was a win-win for me. They hadn't lost a fight yet and I'd never been hotter in my life than watching them beat the shit out of my adversaries. Although, it was all done in good-natured fun and once the fight was over, so was their anger.

"I have a change coming. I wanted you to be aware first."

"And what's that?" Ricco asked hesitantly. After a month of seeing I wasn't going to run the Dirty Dogs into the ground and that I was actually good at this shit, he became his old self again. Except, he recognized when I was up to something that wouldn't go over well.

"We're welcoming women into the Dirty Dogs. I have a few in mind, and Amorette and I have already talked about a venture between us and Carnage Industries that will be crazy lucrative. A shared unit that bridges our...affiliations."

Ricco blanched as Manny stared at the table. "I'm surprised it took this long."

I laughed, and the sound was bright, even to my ears.

"That's right. The Dirty Dogs is now a co-ed gang. Not that it wasn't before," with me here, "but we're broadening our horizons."

MATĪAS

"You're serious?" I peeked at the front gates of the compound.

There was a shiny new bike sitting out front. I knew how to ride. But it had been over a decade and I only learned because my father had arranged lessons on how to drive everything. Cars, boats, planes, choppers. If it had an engine, I learned it.

"You can't be a Dirty Dog and not have a fucking bike." Esteban walked around it, wiping the chrome with a cloth.

"I have a very nice SUV."

He gave me a droll look. "That's what an old man drives. You have to fit in or we're kicking you out. It was in the fine print of the acceptance."

The click-clack of heels signaled Rita coming and I turned to find her.

A dream, just like she always was, carrying a black leather jacket. "You can't ride without protection." She tossed it to me.

I caught it and held it up. It was smooth, buttery leather, and a Dirty Dog patch taking up the entire back.

Shit. My throat closed up. It was just now starting to cool off enough to need a jacket, even if I'd burn up in leather.

But riding, Rita was right, I would need protection.

"Fine," I said, but I wasn't angry. I was...Fuck, I was touched. After I had it on, I circled my arm around Rita's neck and pulled her in for a kiss. "I love you." I let out a breath through my nose. I wished this had been the first time I told her. Or anytime after the first. But I also wouldn't change a goddamned thing.

"I love you too." She held my sides and peered up at me through her lashes.

Esteban walked over. "And I love you both," he snickered. He did that. Told me he loved me when he told Rita. I hadn't said it back, and he seemed to be getting more and more aggressive in trying to pull it out of me.

I never realized before, but underneath his silly charm was a cinnamon roll.

Rita tipped up her face and pursed her lips. He didn't let the opportunity pass by and dropped a kiss to her mouth.

"There's a surprise outside the gates waiting for you." He motioned to where the bike was.

Was this a trap? It felt like one.

"I'm not joking. Go check it out."

Releasing Rita, I walked toward the bike. Both were right on my heels.

As soon as I passed through, I froze.

There were my brothers. All four of them were on their own bikes. Waiting.

Parker raised an eyebrow, Grey smirked, Lafe shook his head in exasperation before gazing back at Amorette who stood there with Cossette on her hip. Lastly, Andre was swinging his leg over his bike with impatience.

Something told me these were all loaners from the Dirty Dogs.

"We have a job and it's going to take all of us," Andre said as Amorette walked our way.

"You're going with them," Rita whispered as she pressed into my side. "Amorette and Cossette are staying here with me. You'll get a little over twenty-four hours with your brothers. Consider it a brotherly bonding trip. And just think, there will be no wars or enemies to fight."

"There will be fighting," Grey cut in.

Rita scoffed. "Fine. But this is a fun family trip. Enjoy."

Esteban clapped me on the back and the girls headed inside. "You need me to give you a tutorial?"

"Fuck off," I growled.

He laughed, tossed the cloth on his shoulder and headed in.

My brothers had brought a whole contingent of men who had somehow stayed out of sight of the gates.

"To protect the girls while we're gone," Lafe answered my unspoken question.

"Dear brother, are you going to stand there looking pretty all day, or are we going on a joy ride?"

"Why are you all on bikes?" *That was what I decided to ask?*

Parker laughed. "Because Rita asked us to. She said you wanted to hang out, so we organized a trip. We're just mixing a little work with pleasure."

"Right." I threw my leg over my bike, grinning like an idiot. "Let's go."

And then Andre led the way as Parker and Lafe were next, side by side, and me and Grey last.

Except we didn't hit the highway. He took us on a scenic tour before bringing us back toward the compound. He pulled off on a street right before we were back where we started.

A garage opened, and we all rode in.

The outside of the building was a mess like all the others in this area but the inside was as high tech as anything the brothers owned.

We turned off our bikes and I took off my helmet.

"What are we doing?"

Parker rolled his eyes and Lafe smiled.

"Amorette actually thinks all four of us would leave her to go on a brotherly bonding trip," Grey scoffed. "We'll bond just fine right here behind the compound and be close by in case they need us."

I laughed. Esteban was there, but this was just like them.

"Who's going on the business trip?"

"José and some of our other men." Andre climbed off his bike. "Come on. There's a full bar and we can show you everything we've done. You three can use this anytime you want a break from the compound."

If we needed a break, we'd go farther than a few buildings over, but this was nice to hang out with them. And the girls could feel like they had their independence.

Parker looped his arm around my neck as we walked inside.

"Now, tell us...How's everything going in your threesome?"

Fuck, I didn't know what normal brothers talked about, but surely it wasn't this.

The END of The Bastard Brothers of Carnage Series

AFTERWORD

Cue Tears It really feels like I said goodbye to these wonderful, frustrating, and absolutely lovable characters!

And I got to do it through Matías' happily ever after! I've said this other places, but you can thank my PA, friend, and editor, Elisabeth, for this book. Matías was originally supposed to die. Legit, never come back die.

She raged that I couldn't do that to him! So, for her, and for many of my Matías girlies, I brought him back in the epilogue.

You know, when I first plotted Outcast, I knew I wanted Matías with Rita and Esteban. I just felt their connection while writing the BB series. Let me tell you, I was SHOCKED at how well they all fit together, but I think what was more surprising was the level of feels I had through the first third of the book. These characters were breaking my heart!

I hope you enjoyed the ride as much as I did, and you never know! I do love my cameos so you may see them in future books and series.

From the bottom of my heart, thank you so much for reading. It means the world to me. <3

If you want to chat all things Outcast, come see me in my Facebook group <u>Blake's Book Babes</u>! There will be a spoiler post pinned AFTER the book officially releases in January.

If you're looking for your next read, check out Snatched if you haven't yet! This series is set in the same world and there are cameos! Who doesn't love a reverse beauty and the beast but with *toxicity* and a bit of stalkery vibes? You can check out the series <u>here.</u>

If you want to keep up with me, you can join my newsletter for sneak peeks, random life hacks and survival skills, as well as news updates!

Join the newsletter <u>here</u>.

And... If you're stalking game is strong, follow me here too!

<u>Facebook Author Page Bookbub TikTok Instagram Amazon</u>

Thanks for reading and I'll see you in the next book!

XOXO

Blake

OTHER TITLES
THE COLLECTION

Snatched

Edged

Crazed (Coming early 2025)

Bastard Brothers of Carnage Series

Addict

Convict

Killer

Psycho

Traitor

FRAGILE MINDS DUET
FRACTURED

Altered

Standalone RH Romance
Pin-up Girl

Co-Writes with my Co-wrifey
Standalone Series
Kiss of Fate
Taste of Karma

CARDINAL SINS SERIES

KILL SONG

WHO IS BLAKE?

Blake Blessing is a mom, wife, art enthusiast, and author.

She attended ten different schools growing up, so books became her constant friend. Escaping into books of all different genres made life fun and exciting. Blake was also raised on music and still blasts it through the house and car at every opportunity.

She has a weird sense of humor and a penchant for chocolate milk. It only makes sense she would one day go on to write her own stories.